TO
FIGHT
FOR

PHILLIP HUNTER has a degree in English
Literature from Middlesex University and
an MA in Screenwriting from the London
Institute. He was also part of the team that
sequenced the human genome.

By the same author

To Die For

To Kill For

Phillip Hunter has a degree in English Literature from Middlesex University, and an MA in Screenwriting from the London Institute. He was also part of the team that sequenced the human genome.

TO FIGHT FOR

PHILLIP HUNTER

First published in the UK in 2015 by Head of Zeus Ltd

This paperback edition first published in the UK in 2016
by Head of Zeus Ltd

9 7 5 3 1 2 4 6 8

A catalogue record for this book is available from the British Library.

Paperback ISBN 9781781853436
Ebook ISBN 9781781853443

Typeset by Adrian McLaughlin
Printed in the UK by Clays Ltd, St Ives Plc

Head of Zeus Ltd
Clerkenwell House
45–47 Clerkenwell Green
London EC1R 0HT

WWW.HEADOFZEUS.COM

To my mum, Betsy, and my sister, Louise, as always.

ONE

Outside, the war raged. Men were murdering each other or siding up to one of the powers or keeping their heads down, shotguns within reach, just in case it all spilled over.

Vic Dunham and Bobby Cole – the lords of London – were at each other's throats. There had been blood on the streets, shootings, arson attacks. Both sides were giving it their all, but Cole was getting out-punched and nobody thought he'd go the distance.

It seemed like most of London was in arms, one way or the other. It wasn't, though. The killing was only among us lot; the civvies had no idea what was going on. They sat on the tube and in their cars and in the pub, and they read their papers and bought their lottery tickets and lived and carried on. But they didn't know what it was all about. They never fucking knew.

I was in a bad way when they dragged me in. Browne was sober, for once, probably waiting to see if I was still breathing. They put me on the sofa downstairs and Browne went at it, fixing me up as best he could, putting me back together. It was like the old days when I'd be led from the ring, blinded by the blood in my eyes, nothing more than a walking chunk of meat. They'd take me back to the dressing rooms and lay me out on a slab, and Browne would come in and prod me, and look in my eyes.

'This can't go on, Joe,' he'd say.

And I'd nod, not really understanding what he was on about – not really caring.

And now he was near me, night and day, pushing the needles in, changing the dressings, cutting me open to see what was keeping me alive, telling me it couldn't go on. Nothing changes.

In the last few weeks I'd been battered and cut and shot. But that was okay. Those were flesh wounds and I'd recover, or not, or whatever. I thought I'd broken my hand when I'd smashed it on Paget's head, but it turned out it was just bruised and swollen, so that was okay too. I needed that hand. I needed it to destroy things, people.

The knife wound Paget gave me was worse. My arm split with a kind of sharp-dull ache. The blade had cut deep into the muscle tissue and there was nerve damage. My arm was partly dead, but I could still use it, and that was all that mattered. Browne said it might heal, it might not. Some fucking help.

Then there was the pain in my side, the broken rib. Browne reckoned Paget's bullet had hit at just the right angle to ricochet.

'That rib saved your bloody life,' he said. 'You should have it stuffed.'

But he was worried about it and kept prodding and cutting me open, looking for any more bone splinters.

'I'm not a bloody surgeon,' he'd say. 'You need to go to a hospital.'

'It doesn't matter,' I told him. 'Nothing matters,' I told him. I don't think he believed me – not any more, not after what I'd done.

Besides, Cole wouldn't have let me get to a hospital. He sent his own doctor, who came one morning, looked at the wound and gave Browne a cold stare.

No, flesh wounds didn't bother me. It was my head that was the real problem. Browne reckoned I had more swelling on the brain, or something like that. He kept looking in my eyes and asking me dumb questions like did I know who I was, did I know where I was. Mostly I knew the answers.

'Don't worry about it,' I'd say.

'Who the hell else is going to?' he'd say back.

I think he wanted to worry. I think it gave him something to do – something other than getting drunk, anyway.

So, I told him it didn't matter, and I told myself the same. But I knew that was a lie, even more than Browne did.

It did matter, in one way; I was losing Brenda. I was losing the only thing that kept me going, kept me fighting. Her face was going from me, even in those moments when she came to me it was fading, and when I was awake it was almost gone completely. The more I did what I had to do, the more beat up I got and, then, the more I lost of her. It was some sick sort of justice. Quit now and I might keep of her what I still had. Carry on and I might finish so fucked up I wouldn't even know what I'd been fighting for; her black hair and dark skin and huge, brown eyes slinking backwards into the shadows.

3

It had been getting worse, over the years. It used to be I couldn't stop seeing her. Now, with all those bangs, I had trouble remembering her when I was awake. But I'd see her still in waking dreams, in cold moments, in the dark and the night and the emptiness. I don't know why that was, why it was always in the darkest moments that she was brightest.

One time I dreamed about her and woke up coughing, clambering for breath. Browne stood above me, staring down, the light behind him glaring into my eyes. I shook with sweat and panic, and he gripped my head in his hands and I could see that he was shouting something at me, but I couldn't hear him.

'I'm okay,' I said, pushing his hands away, thinking I was on the canvas being counted out or that my corner had thrown the towel in and the crowd was jeering at me, crying for more blood.

I tried to stand up and pain collapsed me and Browne pushed a needle into my arm and when I opened my eyes again everything was dark, and I thought I'd had it, finally. I felt a surge of anger because I knew there were things I had to do, even if I couldn't remember what they were. But then, after the anger sank and drained away, I felt nothing; no fear, no regret, no sadness. Nothing. I just thought, It doesn't matter.

Then a light came on.

Browne came over and peered at me. He must've been waiting for me to come round. He was sober, too, so that told me how worried he was.

'How are you feeling?' he said.

4

'Okay.'

'The flashbacks, the blackouts… they'll get worse.'

'They've been getting worse for ten years.'

He nodded. His mouth was drawn tight, his lips thin, but he wasn't getting angry.

'I can't imagine what damage you've done to your head. I've seen fighters who've taken less than you end up dribbling wrecks. I'm amazed you can still function, to be honest. Well, most of the time you can function.'

He smiled a soft, sad smile and I had the feeling he was being with me as he must've been with a terminally ill patient back when he'd been practising.

'You're killing yourself,' he said quietly.

'I know.'

So, yes, I sometimes wondered if I was dead, murdered by my own rage. It was like I was standing in front of this body, laid out on a slab – my body, cold and grey – and even though I knew it was dead, I kept stabbing it, trying to kill it all over again, but no blood came out and I knew it was really dead, even though it moved.

But I had odd thoughts like that in those days. And it was getting harder to sort things out. I was running out of time.

Everything I did was too late. I'd wake from some half-sleep, drenched in sweat, not sure where I was, when I was, who I was – what I was. I'd be in the ring or on that fucking mount in the Falklands, and I'd see a shadow near me, and I'd reach out to her and she'd reach forward with red hands.

Then, of course, people wanted me dead. They hadn't come for me yet, but they would – or, anyway, they'd try.

A lot of people had tried. A lot of people weren't alive any more. Maybe I was one of them, a victim of my own hatred finally turned inward. Browne told me it was all I had, the hatred. He might've been right.

But it was something, at least, the rage. It was some fucking thing and it kept the blood pumping, kept me alive – just.

Outside, hell was let loose and it didn't matter a thing to me. Let them destroy each other, let them tear London apart, let them bleed, just as long as I got Glazer and gutted him and watched his blood spill over the ground, watched it pool at my feet.

TWO

It had been a lousy winter. Now it was a lousy spring: cold wind rattling the thin trees, rain coming at you sideways, sleet, snow, mud.

I hated mud. I'd had my fill of the stuff years back. When I saw it now it reminded me of the misery of slogging for days, dragged down by hundred pound bergens, the straps covered in gaffer tape but still cutting into our shoulders, unable to keep from slipping every few yards, trench-foot rotting us from the ground up. The mud clumped and clung to our boots when we tabbed mile after mile after mile, making heavy legs a few pounds heavier, as we moved towards the dug-in Argentineans who were probably as sick of the mud as we were, sicker even.

Maybe that was why I stayed in London, so I wouldn't have to walk in mud again. But Browne lived out a bit, in the suburbs, and there were playing fields to cross, and parks to cross, and verges to cross, and I was sick of it all, sick and old and going nowhere, living out of my time in a world I didn't understand, where gangs imported small girls and sold them, where I no longer knew how to rob an armoured van, where my business was now as muddy as the sodden ground after all these lousy months of rain.

When I was able, I'd go for a walk twice a day, once in the morning to pick up a *Times* for Browne, then in the evening to get a *Standard*.

The first time I went, I was still in a daze, my head murky with things half-thought, half-remembered. I knew I had to find Glazer and kill him before he got to me; kill him for what he'd done, but I didn't know how.

I probably shouldn't have gone out.

'You're not up to it, man,' Browne had said.

'I'll be okay,' I said.

'Joe, son, I hate to tell you this, but you'll never be okay again.'

I think he liked telling me that.

I said, 'I know.'

I went anyway, and trudged across the playing field, staring down at my feet as they sank an inch into the ground. I looked up at the bank of fog ahead. I'd seen fog like that before. Only, back then, it hadn't been fog. It had been smoke. I could taste it as it crept down my throat, filled my nostrils. It burned with the taste of cordite.

But this was only fog. I had to remember that, had to keep remembering that. Fog, mud. That was all.

The field was flat, greasy with mud and trampled grass. I saw the broken white lines marking out a football pitch. That was good. Visual signs helped. I knew where I was.

I remembered a playing field like this when I was a kid. It was in Edmonton near the North Circular. I'd go there by myself and run, just for something to do, just to get out of the house, away from the old man. Even then, it was always muddy. Football pitches must be about the only part of the country that haven't changed in a century. And the smell of them was always musty, dank – at least, in my mind it was.

I couldn't run fast as a kid, but I could run for a long time, which was all that mattered. I'd spend hours plodding around that football field, following the white line, going miles and going nowhere, just running for the sake of it, in circles.

I never really thought about those days. But it seemed to me now that I was still doing the same thing; going around in circles, never getting anywhere. My head was going round and round while men I knew and men I didn't know were circling me, and all the while I was going back and forth in time.

Yes, I was going round in circles, and the circles were getting smaller.

I thought about all that as I stood there, like an idiot, lost in an unknown, known landscape.

Then I saw them.

They stood at the far end of the playing field, where I'd been a few minutes before. They weren't doing anything much, just waiting there, talking, looking at anything but me. And that made my gut turn. Two men standing at the edge of a playing field, not doing anything. That was trouble.

If they wanted to take me out, they must've needed to get close to do it. In that case, they'd wait until I'd crossed the playing field and then follow me over. They'd want to kill me in a less exposed place.

I wasn't tooled up. That was dumb. I was dumb. The Makarov should've been glued to my hand.

I started to walk. I knew they'd be following me. I scanned the distance for cover. There was an old oak tree, thick around the trunk. I could use that to screen my movements for a while, maybe run when it was between us. But as soon as I was out of sight, they'd run too.

There was the fog, of course. There was always the fog, far off and always getting further. I walked towards it, and tasted the cordite again. My foot caught in the mud and the ground turned up at right angles and slammed into me.

I tried to stand, but the world was out of control, sliding around my head. I fell again.

When I finally managed to stand there was a weight in my arms. I looked down at the SLR I was cradling, the body clean except for some mud on the magazine. A hundred years before, my platoon sergeant would've bollocked me for that, but now he was covered in as much mud as the rest of us.

I felt the weight of my bergen, pulling me down into the wet ground. I felt the straps biting into my shoulders.

Around me, men of my platoon were fanned out, some of them wanting to get to the kill, most of them cold and tired and sick of it all. I might've been one of them or I might've been one of the mugs who wanted to get to the fight. I don't know. I can't remember that far back.

I heard the sound of heavy calibre automatic fire, like a hundred drummers beating the same drum. I heard the odd crack of far-off thunder that wasn't thunder at all. I heard the order to fix bayonets, and fumbled with my rifle. I saw the bulk of the mountain, looming, dark. I heard the thwump of a nearby mortar.

Then I saw the fog again, the white lines, the mud, my empty hands.

When my heart left my throat and the sweat turned cold, I looked behind me. There was no one there, and I thought, What's real?

I made it to the corner store. I don't know how. I can't remember.

I bought Browne's paper from the young bloke behind the counter. He looked at me like I was robbing the place.

I saw the car when I came out. It was on my side of the street, facing away from me. It pulled away from the kerb as I passed. I reckoned they'd come up slowly behind me, put a few rounds in my back and drive off. I waited for the sound of a door opening, a window rolling down, something like that. I was trying to think what I should do. I couldn't fight. I couldn't hide. And I couldn't outrun a bullet. So I just walked and listened and waited to die.

Nothing happened.

I kept on walking and the car moved with me. When I got back to the playing field, the car slowed and two doors opened.

THREE

Browne was waiting for me in the hallway. He had his jacket on, and his shoes. He'd tucked his shirt in.

He stood back, looked me up and down.

'What happened to you?' he said.

I saw that I was covered in mud. I didn't know how that had happened. I glanced up the street, saw the car park. I closed the door.

'I fell,' I said.

'Fell? How?'

'It doesn't matter.'

'Did you trip? Or lose your balance?'

'It doesn't matter.'

'Of course it matters.'

He was doing his old lady act again, fussing about everything.

'Why does it matter?'

'Well…'

He ran his hand through his messy grey hair, making it messier. He knew I was right; it didn't matter.

'It's getting worse, isn't it?'

'Pack it in.'

'Was it another flashback?' he said. 'I mean—'

12

'There are men outside.'

That stopped him.

'Men?'

'Yeah.'

He looked at me like I was going barmy right there and then.

'Men,' he said again. 'Outside.'

He must've had a bit of booze because it was taking him a long time to cotton on.

'In a car. Watching us.'

Now he was getting it. He glanced around the hall as if he was expecting them to come out of the wallpaper. His mouth opened and closed.

'Well,' he said, finally, 'what men?'

'I don't know.'

'Dunham's men? Police?'

'I don't know.'

There was something else he wanted to say. I waited, but he just stood there, staring at the mud on my clothes, a look of sadness creeping into his eyes. Then he took his jacket off and hung it up and padded back to the living room. He mumbled something, but I didn't catch it.

When I went in there, he was watching the TV. He'd made a glass of Scotch appear out of thin air. It was a neat trick. I slumped down on the sofa. He was watching a programme about ants in Borneo or something. Finally he turned to me.

'Are we in danger?' he said.

'If they'd wanted to get us, they would've done.'

He thought about that.

'What are they waiting for?' he said.

13

I'd wondered the same thing.

Browne didn't say anything for a while. We both sat and watched the ants. They were going round in circles, or so it seemed. The day was cold and dull. You could feel the coldness seeping through the window. You could feel the dullness in the air. Anyway, I could.

After a year of that, Browne turned to me.

'Tea?' he said.

That was his solution to everything.

'Okay.'

He went and I shut my eyes and lay back and tried to figure out what the fuck I was doing, tried to remember why I was doing it and where that mud had come from.

I might've passed out. I might've slept. I didn't know. It was getting harder to tell the difference. I saw her, next to me, smiling, her head angled to one side, in the way it used to be when she watched me and didn't think I knew – at least, I think it was her. I couldn't make out her face, and that scared me. More than anything else, that scared me. Maybe it was because I had no photographs of Brenda, nothing to hold in front of me when I had bad moments, nothing to look at and say, 'Yes, that was her.' There'd been photos, but they were gone now. I had a film of her, of course, but I wouldn't watch that.

So, her face faded more and more, getting murkier. It was like everything else these days – turning to mud and fog. I got glimpses of it sometimes, in parts; her smile, her bright eyes, her smooth, dark skin. And sometimes, if I was lucky, I'd remember something. And sometimes, if I was unlucky, I'd remember something.

There was this one time I liked to try and remember. She'd made us a picnic. It was a warm day, clear, bright, blue.

We'd gone to a small park somewhere. We sat on the grass and ate the lunch and drank the wine and did all the things couples did when they were together and alone and away from life. So, we lay together and stared up at forever, me on my back, Brenda sideways, her head on my chest, her hand on my stomach.

But when I tried to remember that day, Brenda's face blurred and clouded over, and it became something I could only see out of the edge of my eye when I looked away from it.

Sometimes I wasn't sure if that had been real or just a dream.

I opened my eyes. The light was dull, the TV was off and Browne was there, in his seat, the glass of Scotch tight in his hand. I looked around for the tea. I couldn't see any.

'You were dreaming,' he said. 'Of faraway things.'

Faraway things. Yeah.

He reached for the TV remote control and flicked the box on. I wondered how long he'd been sitting there, waiting for me to come round. I suppose he must've thought I wouldn't ever open my eyes again. Still, that hadn't stopped him drinking.

'You were saying her name,' he said.

'Her name?' I said, knowing I'd been speaking Brenda's name, screaming it, probably. 'Whose name?'

'You know whose. Your woman's. Brenda's.'

'Uh-huh.'

15

He took a gulp of his drink and pretended to be fascinated by some programme about earthquakes.

'Do you go back there, Joe?'

This was something he did now and then, this interrogation, like he was some kind of brain doctor, like he was going to sit there, drunk and disappointed by his own failures and work everything out for me: where I was going wrong, what I should do, that sort of thing.

'Go back?'

'When you have your flashbacks. Like today.'

'Today?'

He went to take another gulp of Scotch and found that the glass was empty. He frowned, then lifted the bottle and tipped it up. A dribble came out. He frowned some more and glared at me, as if it was my fault he'd finished his booze.

He said, 'Hm.'

He stood slowly and staggered out of the room. When he came back, he had a fresh bottle of booze. He made a big thing of cracking the seal in front of me.

He said, 'Hm,' again and fell back into his seat.

He filled his glass, put the bottle onto the floor, leaned back and lifted the glass. And stopped it short of his mouth, peering at me over the rim.

I could feel a lecture coming on. I didn't have the strength to do anything about it.

Before the lecture, though, he decided to drink his Scotch. He said, 'Ahh,' and put the glass on the floor by his foot.

'You know,' he said now, 'when you first came here a few weeks back, I thought you were a goner. You had that .32

round in your shoulder and there wasn't enough blood in you to fill a thimble.'

'I remember,' I said.

Well, mostly I remembered.

'Why did you come here? To me?'

'Nowhere else to go.'

'You could've gone to a hospital.'

'You know what I mean.'

'Yes. You mean there was nobody else you could trust to fix you, to help you.'

I hadn't thought of it like that, but he was right. There was nobody else.

'Yeah.'

'You can't carry on like this.'

'You told me that.'

He had told me, hadn't he? It sounded familiar, anyway. Now his face was red and shining.

'Christ, you make me bloody mad, man. You're killing yourself. And for what? Revenge, rage, fury, the only bloody things that seem to keep you alive. It's ironic, you're killing yourself to stay alive.'

'You're drunk,' I said.

His eyes flashed for a moment.

'Bastard,' he said.

Then, as quickly as it had come, his anger went and he sank into himself.

'Drunk,' he said to his Scotch. 'I should bloody well hope so.'

He looked up at me and his eyes were swimming and I realized he'd had a gallon more booze than I'd thought.

I was killing myself with fury, sure, and he was killing himself in sympathy.

'So I'm drunk,' he said to me. 'So what? And besides, what's it to you, anyway? And besides *that*, your observation is less than keen considering I try to be as drunk as possible for as long as possible as often as possible. It's quite an art, you know. Quite an art. I would suggest you try it but I think it would kill more of your brain cells than you can afford to lose. And besides... uh...'

He creased his forehead and scratched his ear. Then he lifted his shoulder and dropped it and reached over for his glass. He'd used that stuff on me before, about the art of boozing, all that. But he'd forgotten. It'd been a long time before.

Everything was back, nothing forward, except ruin and death. My life was there in the past, hanging on a nail in Brenda's flat, right where I'd left it. I should go look for it someday. Maybe that's what I was doing. Maybe that's all I'd ever done.

FOUR

We were in a pub, me and Brenda. The weather was warm, that thick warmth you get in the evening of a hot day when the air is soaked through with sweat and fumes and nobody can breathe too much, though they're all gasping.

This was the day after we'd been up the West End and looked in all those fancy shop windows. This was the day after I'd bought her the box of soaps and creams and stuff. It was a week before she died, before Paget sliced her face off. She knew she was in trouble. She knew she was using me. She was cut up inside. When Paget killed her, he was just finishing the job she'd already started. She never said anything to me about it all. I suppose I never asked the right questions.

We'd been in her flat before the pub, and she'd started drinking early, chain smoking. The cigarette smoke made my eyes sore, made my head hurt, but I didn't tell her that. She had something on her mind and I just let her get on with it. I knew later that she was scared. I knew later that her fear was the only reason she was with me; because she'd thought I could protect her. Well, there might've been other reasons, but that was why she'd come on to me the first time.

19

'Let's go to a pub,' she said through the smoke. 'I know one.'

At the time I thought she just wanted to get away from the small space of her flat. I suppose that 'I know one' should've tipped me off.

She was wearing a cotton dress. It was the one I'd bought for her. It had flowers on it. It stuck to her flat stomach, the middle of her back. She'd worn it before, too – that day we spent walking down Bond Street and Regent Street, looking at all the pricey gear the toffs bought, diamond rings, two-grand handbags, that kind of thing. That was the day she was happy, for a while. That was the day before the day before the next, when she had to make the film.

We got a cab from her place just off the Caledonian Road. She told the cabbie to take us to the Fox and Globe, on the Seven Sisters Road, up by Finsbury Park. As the cab rolled along, I watched the world scrape past, remembering places I'd known years before, decades before. I remembered how it was when I was young, wandering these streets with a blank mind, a blank life, a blank future. I never would've thought then that I'd be with someone like Brenda who had no blankness at all.

I knew the pub too. It seemed like a long way to go for a drink, but I guessed Brenda wanted to make sure she avoided people.

The Fox and Globe was a place I used to go sometimes when I fought nearby. But that had been a long time before and I figured it would've changed. It hadn't. It looked just as I remembered, not dirtier, not different. It was as if the place had been kept waiting for me to return. I think it still had the same beer stains on the carpet, the same dried-in blood on the wall, the same shrivelled barman behind the same battered bar behind the same weary punters. It was all circles. The further I went from the past, the nearer I came to it.

It was one of those sixties brick things, not popular with anyone except the locals, and even then not really popular, just a boozer nearby, the kind of place people went when they didn't have anything else to do, anywhere else to go. There was a jukebox and someone had put music on, soft, slow stuff. There was a pool table in the corner and a few kids sat around it and drank and hit the balls now and then, if they could be bothered. Mostly, though, they sat and gazed at the table and chatted about something or other: girls, probably, or what they were going to do when they finally had the guts to leave this place.

Me and Brenda took a seat in the corner and the old geezer slumped at the table next to us looked up and looked down and looked up again. It was Browne, only it took me a few seconds to realize it. He looked like he'd stepped in from a storm, hair straggled, shirt half-untucked, bleary eyed. He'd hadn't changed either – not back then.

'Joe,' he said, focusing his eyes. 'Is that you? Course it's you. How many other people could look like that and still be alive?'

Brenda smiled. Browne stood, automatically lifted his empty glass and stepped carefully over to us. He sat and put a cold hand on my arm.

'Good to see you, son. How are you getting along? How's the head these days?' He looked at Brenda then. 'And is this your young lady?'

21

'You met her,' I said.

'Did I?'

'At the fights. A couple weeks ago.'

'Fights,' he said. 'Ah, yes.'

He twisted some of the hair on his head around his finger and looked into the empty glass for his memories.

'Barbara,' he said.

'Brenda,' Brenda said, still smiling and holding her hand out.

'Charming,' Browne said, lifting her hand and putting it down again. 'I do remember,' he said, as if we were arguing with him. 'You were upset, as I recall.'

'Well...' Brenda said, glancing over at me.

'Don't mind him,' Browne said. 'He doesn't care, do you, Joe? You didn't like the violence, my dear. Was that it?'

'Yes,' she said in a small voice. 'The violence.'

Mostly what bothered her, I think, was the idea that I'd got in that ring and taken the violence.

'All that fighting, Joe,' she'd said that night, after we'd walked out of the fight and into the warm, fume-filled night.

'I'm glad we came here,' she'd said. 'Thank you.'

'What for?'

'For showing me something of your past.'

'Not much of a past,' I'd said.

'As good as any.'

We'd carried on walking in silence for a while, then she'd said, 'Tell me more about your childhood.'

'I'd tell you if I could remember it.'

'I don't think you were ever young. I think you were born old.'

She'd given me one of her smiles to let me know she was teasing. I hadn't minded. She was probably right.

Born old. Yeah, that was it – assembled on some factory floor, made up of broken parts of other machines. Broken machines.

After that, we hadn't talked much. She'd tottered along on her heels, still holding my arm tight. We'd passed a tramp trying to sleep in a doorway, wrapped up in layers of clothing, despite the heat, and lying inside an orange nylon sleeping bag.

Traffic had passed us, but it was quieter, slower, as if the heat was getting to the buses and taxis and lorries, making them all sluggish. Everything was grinding to a halt.

I heard Browne say something and looked up and saw that I was in The Fox and Globe.

'Don't blame you,' he was saying to Brenda. 'Not nice, the violence. Civilized people can't take it. Not supposed to. Not for the likes of us. For the likes of him, brainless, dead from the neck up.'

Brenda's eyes flicked from Browne to me, then back.

'Well…' she said again.

'You're too civilized for that kind of thing,' Browne was saying. 'Too tender for the tenderizer.'

I had no idea what that meant.

'You're drunk,' I told him.

'Bloody glad to hear it. I've been working on it long enough. It's quite an art, you know. Scotch is my medium, like oils to a painter. You have to drink to a certain level of inebriation – just enough to keep the effect of the alcohol from dis-uh dis-pating – and then maintain it for as long

23

as possible. Fine balance. I've been in this state now for...'
He lifted his arm and gazed at his watch. He gave up with
that and dropped his arm. 'Well, for a while.'

As Browne was letting his mouth loose, Brenda was
nodding like she agreed with him. But I'd seen what booze
did to her. She thought the drink would numb her, sock her
into unconsciousness. Instead it turned her thoughts into acid,
twisted her memories until they split and bled again.

She glanced at me, half smiled. Browne raised his glass
to the light – what light there was in that place – and stared
at the dribble of copper-coloured stuff in the bottom.

'Of course,' Browne was saying to his glass. 'The trick is
to know by how much and over what period the alcoholic
effects of... uh... alcohol will dissipate. One has to remember
also that alcohol is a disinhibitor, an unleasher of the darkness in people, the anger, the spite. It is the freer of deranged
thoughts kept in check in sober moments. And one has to
remember too that one is inclined to go too far and become
pissed out of one's brain.'

Brenda laughed. Browne looked at her, smiled, put a hand
on top of hers.

'Take no notice of me, Barbara,' he said.

Brenda nudged me and made eyes. I said, 'Huh?'

'Oh, for God's sake,' she said. Then she looked at Browne
and said, 'Can we get you another?'

She nudged me again and I had to go the bar and fetch
him some more of his fucking medium. While I was up
there, I saw the two of them leaning close to each other,
gabbing about something or other. Every now and then
Browne would touch her hand and she'd laugh. Browne

seemed good for her. I stayed at the bar a bit longer.

When I got back, Browne said, 'Hold onto this one, Joe.'

I said, 'Yeah.'

'You old softie,' he said, smiling.

I didn't mind him taking the piss out of me if it made Brenda laugh. But when I looked at her the spark had gone from her eyes, the smile had gone from her mouth and something inside me tightened up, got colder.

Browne noticed it and made a show of taking the glass from me and holding it up to the light.

'I'm the van Gogh of drink,' he said.

He glanced at Brenda, his eyes roguish. But she wasn't buying it any more, and he could see that and he became serious and put the glass down and said, 'Oh well.'

She was lost in her thoughts, tracing a line on the table with her finger, the long fingernail wiping the spilled alcohol into spikes and swirls. Me and Browne watched her do it, watched her watching the light hit the shining liquid. I realized I was still standing. I sat. Brenda didn't look at me. I had a pull of my pint and put the glass down and wiped my sleeve over my mouth. Browne sniffed. Still she didn't look up.

Finally, her hand stopped and she just gazed down, her eyes empty. Everything became still, everything stopped, as if her hand had been the only thing keeping it all moving. I waited. Browne waited. We looked at her finger and waited for it to move again.

I think we both felt it, Browne and me. The world had stopped moving – our world, anyway, whatever that was; some part of some part of some pain that we called our own.

I listened to the hum of chatter around me, the clack of the pool balls, the quiet music. Why the fuck was I here? Why had I let her bring me to this place? I knew what it would be like. I could've taken her to the West End to see a film. I could've taken her to some posh restaurant. I could've taken her to the country for a weekend, by the sea, maybe. Instead I'd let her bring me here, to my lousy past.

Brenda pulled her finger in and made a fist of her hand and looked at Browne and said, 'Why?'

'Why, my dear? Why what?'

'Why is it better to drink? Why do you drink?'

He took time to answer that. He peered at his glass.

'Well, you see,' he said, 'I feel reasonably happy most of the time, and then I remember. Then I drink.'

'Remember what?'

'Myself.'

'You drink to forget yourself?'

'Not really. I drink to forget what I've remembered, and to remember what I've forgotten. Understand?'

I said, 'No.'

I don't think either of them heard me. They'd both forgotten I was there. I didn't count. I wasn't in on this thing, whatever this thing was.

'Yes,' Brenda said. 'I understand.'

Browne turned his head slowly to look at her, and the expression on his face changed. His eyes got softer, his brow lost its creases.

'Ah,' he said. Nothing else, just 'Ah.'

And I knew that he understood, and that she knew he understood.

And I knew too that it was something I couldn't understand. And that hurt, deep, deep down.

I wanted to say something, to join in their conversation. I couldn't. I was out of it. Cold.

By now they were chatting about different stuff. I forget what. Brenda had a few drinks and lightened up. Browne was the same as always, dishing out his usual drunken bollocks.

The mood in the pub changed slowly as the day got older. Some people drifted out, some drifted in and took up their places, as if it was all staged, an act. Maybe it was. Maybe nothing had changed after all, except me and Brenda and Browne. The more we drank, the more everything seemed different. I don't know. Maybe nothing fucking changes.

I remembered how, after we'd come out of the fights, she'd pushed herself into me, gripped my arm, shivered.

'Are you cold?' I'd said.

'No.'

'What's wrong?'

'Nothing... it's just... it hurts me, sometimes, that's all.'

'What hurts you?'

'Everything. All of it. Life.' She'd pulled on my arm. 'But I have you.'

A few days later, I'd taken her to the West End and we'd walked along, her slim hand in mine. We'd walked along like all the rest of them, like the evening-dress-and-dinner-jacket mob, like anyone else. We'd walked along and looked in the windows at the Swiss watches and old oil paintings and diamond rings. People had looked at us oddly but

Brenda had been too wrapped up in the glamour of it all to notice.

So, we'd walked along and tried to pretend everything was alright. Well, for a while, maybe, it was.

Later, sitting in the Fox and Globe, it was getting too hard to pretend anything at all.

Now, years later, as me and Browne sat slumped in our seats and waited for whatever was going to happen, I saw that he was thinking of something, remembering, and his eyes went soft and sad, and he lifted the glass to his mouth.

I asked him what was on his mind.

'Oh,' he said, sniffling, 'I was just remembering that time in the pub, you and her and me. That's all.'

I was beginning to understand what Browne meant about needing to drink – the need, as he'd told Brenda, to forget what he'd remembered, to remember what he'd forgotten.

Now I wanted to tell Brenda that I knew too. But I couldn't tell her. And thinking that brought me back, and I started to lose myself again, trapped between now and then, between rage and peace, and I wanted to stop understanding and just kill.

FIVE

My head was singing when Bobby Cole came over. He swam before my eyes and, for a moment, I thought he was Dunham come to kill me. I reached for my Makarov, but, of course, it wasn't there.

He'd been in before, the day after I'd killed Paget, but I didn't remember that at the time. I was losing track, my mind slipping through the cracks between now and then and never. I didn't want to let Cole know that, though, so I sat up and let Browne do the talking while I waited for my head to stop spinning. Cole took a seat opposite me and twiddled his thumbs.

The trouble was, Cole had seen me go for my gun and he knew straight off that I was fucked up. He didn't make a thing of it, though – not then, anyway. First, he made with the chit-chat. 'How are you, Joe?' 'Take your time recovering, my son.' Shit like that, all nice and friendly. I told him I was okay, everything was fine.

We were in the lounge, and the light was dull, and Cole's brown eyes looked black. After a while, he stood and started pacing, making fists out of his hands. He'd tried the concerned visitor act as much as he could and now his patience had gone. He went over to the window and stood with his back to me, staring out. His blocky frame was dark against the light.

'We need to talk,' he said to the window.

'He's in no fit state for this,' Browne was saying.

Cole turned.

'He looks okay to me.'

'Well, when you show me your medical doctorate, I'll listen to what you say. Meantime—'

'It's okay,' I said.

Browne tightened his mouth, glared at me. Finally, he nodded.

'They're your men?' I said to Cole. 'Outside.'

'Yeah.'

They had to be his men, of course. It had taken me a while to figure it out. The fact that they hadn't tried to kill or arrest me should've told me who they were. Christ, I was slow. Fuck knows what would've happened if they'd been Dunham's out there. I probably wouldn't have made it.

'What for?'

'Protection. Don't worry, I made sure they were low-key, just to keep the neighbours from calling the law.'

'Protection,' I repeated.

'Thought you might need it.'

That was bollocks.

'Very kind of you,' Browne said. I think he was being sarcastic.

He had a point. The last thing Cole would ever bother to do would be to give someone like me protection. He might've felt he owed me, sure, but he was in the middle of a war with Dunham and he'd need all his men handy. Posting them to protect me? Never.

And yet he was here again and his face was grey. Something was up.

I told Browne to go get us a drink. He went unwillingly. When he was gone, Cole said, 'I'm taking the men off.'

'Uh-huh,' I managed to say.

'You don't need them no more, do you? Dunham won't come for you. He's not bothered with grudges when he's tryna take over the whole fucking city. Unless there's a reason I should keep them on you?'

'Is that what he's doing?' I said. 'Trying to take it all?'

He nodded. He'd turned back to the window. His shoulders were hunched, his fists clenched. There was sweat on the rolled fat around his collar. Everything was getting tight for him, even his shirt.

'I'm hitting the cunt with everything I got,' he told the window.

'Are you winning?'

He didn't say anything to that. He didn't need to. Pulling his men off told me plenty about who was winning.

Anyway, I already knew Cole was in trouble. I'd called Ben Green who'd told me about the shootings in Hackney and Leyton.

'He's getting battered all over the place,' Green had said.

I'd stayed in touch with Green. He was a useful contact. He'd been a small-timer a few years back, and now was straight. But he'd known lots of people over the years and still heard about the stuff they kept out of the news.

'There was an armed robbery on one of Cole's taxi firms,'

31

Green had told me. 'Police raids on his places. Dunham's got clout, Joe. He's got a lot of law in his pocket and they're keeping his name out of it, blaming it on rival drugs gangs.'

So, Dunham was keeping a low profile. He was living his fat life in his fat mansion and pretending to be legit. But everyone knew he was destroying the opposition.

Cole wasn't here for any of that. If he'd wanted to pull his men off, he could've done it easily enough without the act. And he sure as fuck wasn't here to visit a sick friend.

'Bother you, Joe? Me taking my men off?' he said, turning to me.

'No.'

'You think I owe you? That it?'

'I don't think anything.'

He came back and sat on Browne's armchair, his elbows on his knees, his hands clenching each other.

'Well, I made sure you were okay while you were down,' he said. 'I suppose I owed you that much.' He scratched his nose. 'Although you've plunged me into a fucking war so I don't know what exactly I *do* owe you. Maybe I should just have you shot.'

'Maybe you should.'

He sat back in the armchair and fidgeted. He was about as good at subtlety as I was. I made it easy for him.

'Why are you here?'

He looked at me long and hard, the steel in his eyes shining like blades.

He stopped fidgeting.

'I want to know what the fuck's going on,' he said, his voice low, slow, deadly.

He was scared. Cole was fucking scared. This war had shaken him; probably he was worried that things were getting out of hand, that he wasn't going to survive, that he was losing control.

'You know what's going on,' I said. 'We hit Dunham, now he's coming after us. He has to.'

'Bollocks. We hit Dunham's home, sure. I knew there'd be a comeuppance, that's not what's bothering me. What I want to know is why? Why was Dunham protecting Paget? Why am I in this fucking war? And don't tell me it's about reputation or revenge coz I won't fucking believe it.'

'You wanted Paget because he stole your drugs, your money, tried to take over your turf, sold you out to Dunham. We got him. What do you care why Dunham was protecting him?'

'I have this awful feeling that I'm being taken for a mug, that there's something else going on here that I can't see. Don't take me for a cunt, son.'

I thought about things for a moment. Well, I tried to think. Two things I knew: Cole wasn't stupid and the last thing I needed was another enemy.

The door opened and Browne tottered in, a mug of tea in each hand. He put the mugs down on the coffee table and waited there, like he wanted a tip or something. Cole didn't take his eyes off me.

'There anything else?' Browne said, eyeing Cole. 'Shall I bake some scones?'

He got like that sometimes, like a jilted bird or something. Still Cole didn't look at him.

'No,' I said.

'Fine. I'll be in the kitchen getting hammered.'

'Right.'

Browne shuffled off.

'Well?' Cole said.

I reached over for the tea, just to show that I could. It almost killed me. The pain tore through my side. Cole saw it but didn't say anything. He didn't care if I split right open in front of him. I took a gulp of the strong, sweet stuff and sat back. I could feel the sweat on my brow. If reaching for tea did that to me, how the hell was I going to go up against half of London? No, I didn't need another fucking enemy.

'You know what Paget did?' I said.

'He killed your bird.'

Just like that. 'Killed your bird.' He made it sound like Paget had scratched my car.

'Her name was Brenda,' I said. 'Remember that. Yeah. He killed her. Paget and Marriot made movies with kids. She got evidence and sent it to a vice copper called Glazer. He was bent, grassed her right back to Marriot. Then Marriot got Paget to slice her up.'

'So you wanted Paget. I don't blame you. But you haven't answered my question. Why was Dunham protecting him?'

'A film. Some bloke. I don't know who he is but he's important. Dunham wanted the DVD.'

'What kind of film?'

'The kind with children.'

'So Dunham was going to blackmail the bloke in the film?'

'My guess.'

34

He thought about that for a bit.

'Did Dunham get the DVD?' he said. 'A copy of it?'

'No. Paget must've kept it back in order to get protection from Dunham. We got to Paget while he was at Dunham's so he must've had it hidden still.'

'Right. Makes sense. He would've had to keep it back for leverage.'

Of course, I had a copy, the copy that Brenda had made and hidden in her flat. Was I going to tell Cole that? I couldn't decide, couldn't work out the pros and cons. If I told him, would he want the DVD too?

Cole leaned forward and drank some of the tea. He screwed his face up and put the mug down.

'Too much sugar,' he said.

'Your men,' I said, 'they were surveilling me? Trying to find out what was happening?'

'Surveilling. That's a big word. Yeah, they were fucking surveilling you. I wanted to see how important you were to Dunham, what he wanted, that kind of thing.'

'You could've asked me.'

'That's what I'm doing now. Besides, I didn't trust you, boy. I still don't. So, I got some of my men posted around to watch what happened. Pretty interesting stuff too. What was all that shit a few days back? Monday?'

'What shit?'

'On the football pitch.'

Football pitch? What was he talking about?

'What football pitch?'

'Boy, you hit the deck like you'd been shot. My men thought you had been. You were crawling along in the mud,

35

your hands over your head. Went on for a few minutes like that. My men went over to you to see you were alright.'

I didn't know what he was on about. It sounded like that time, a hundred years before, when I'd been in the paras, diving for cover from mortar fire. I crawled in the mud that time. I remembered that alright.

Cole leaned forward again and took the mug of tea and gulped it down. When he'd finished all that, he looked at me, his face grim, his jaw set. Finally, he nodded and stood.

'Son, you are in some confused shit.'

I had to agree with him.

'What you gonna do?' he said.

'Find Glazer,' I said. 'Kill him.'

There was sun, for once, and a breeze that didn't cut you to the bone. Maybe it was spring after all.

I checked the road. It seemed quiet. I went through the gate then moved the recycling bin a foot across Browne's path.

I had to find Glazer, and I thought I might have an idea how to start that. But, since Cole had pulled his men off, there was something else we needed to sort out, Browne and me.

I'd mended enough so that I could drive again. I walked up the road to Browne's car and drove down to the hardware store. I just about managed that without killing anyone.

I bought a hammer, four-inch nails, plywood boards and a load of other stuff. The bloke on the checkout smiled and said, 'You expecting a war?'

I said, 'Yeah.'

He didn't smile after that.

Next I went to get provisions: canned food, dried food, some first aid stuff and lots of bloody Scotch. Browne was more concerned about that than anything else. I also went to a bloke I knew in Romford and bought a couple of boxes of ammo for my Makarov, a flick knife with strap-on ankle holster. I wanted some flash-bangs, maybe a few grenades, but he couldn't get those at short notice, and I couldn't wait.

When I got back, I climbed out of the car, walked slowly along the pavement and opened the gate. It was only when I was about to open the front door that I noticed the bin had moved. I stopped the key an inch from the keyhole and looked back. I'd told Browne to stay put, and the postman had already been and gone. Yet the bin had moved.

I crept over the front lawn, around the side of the house and through the garden to the back door. I turned the door-knob slowly. The door opened. It should've been locked. I pulled my Makarov out and held it lightly in my hand and moved slowly inside.

I heard a voice, low and slow. Then I heard Browne cry out in pain. There was a crash, the sound of smashing wood and a heavy fall. The whole house seemed to shift an inch.

I crept up the stairs, keeping my weight to the edges of each step. When I got to the landing I could see into Browne's bedroom, at the far end of the hallway. It was a mess; smashed furniture, the bed upside down, broken glass. I walked slowly that way.

The man turned as I entered. He was massive, almost my height, with a bodybuilder's shape, the wide shoulders, the bulging chest. His head was a lump of rock that sat right on his shoulders. There was no neck, as far as I could see. He outweighed me by a couple of stone, and all of that was muscle. He was one of those men whose arms wouldn't hang straight down.

He held Browne up in one hand. I brought the Makarov up to my waist, just enough for him to see it.

I'd known him years before, in my old fight days. Back then they'd called him The Reaper. I don't think he ever understood why. He was huge in those days. It had been like fighting a mountain. He was bigger now. He must've hit the irons and the steroids. He had a bashed-in face, cauliflower ears, a thick, drooping mouth and dumb, heavy-lidded eyes.

He dropped Browne who stayed dropped. He stared at me a moment, then stared at my gun, then stared back at me.

'I remember you,' he said, as if he'd made some great discovery. 'We fought.'

He was wrong about that. We hadn't fought; he'd murdered me. I was old. He was younger, fitter, stronger, faster. He out-boxed me, out-moved me. And he out-hit me to hell. I got counted out in the middle of the fifth. I was still standing, but only because a boxing ring has ropes.

'Yeah,' I said.

He stared at me a while longer, like someone had forgotten to restart his brain. His mouth hung open.

'I won,' he said when the words finally came to him.

'Yeah.'

He nodded, pleased with his thinking so far.

'You were good.'

'I was old.'

He thought about that.

'You were good for an old bloke.'

'Yeah. For an old bloke.'

39

Now that he'd used up all the words in his head, he moved towards me. I kept the gun on him, but I didn't think it would be much use. He pushed past me and ducked through the doorway. The stairs creaked like they were at breaking point. The front door opened and slammed. The house moved again back to where it'd begun.

I stuck the Makarov back in my jacket pocket and looked down at Browne. He was alive. He was conscious. That was about the best I could say for him. He lay with his eyes open and gazed up at the ceiling. He had a bloody mouth, a swelling eye, and he breathed with a rasping sound.

'My God,' he managed to say. 'My God.'

'Yeah. Are you hurt?'

'Hurt? Look at me. I'm virtually dead.'

'Anything broken?'

He sighed and groaned, moving his hand to his stomach.

'No, nothing broken. Everything agony, but nothing broken.'

'He went easy on you.'

'Call this going easy?'

'Yeah.'

He tried to sit up and fell back. I went over and started to hoist him up.

'No, leave me.'

I set him back on the ground.

'What did he want?' I said.

'Just get me a bloody drink, will you?'

I went and got him his drink. He managed to sit up for that. When he'd gulped the glass dry, he wiped the blood from his mouth, touched his eye.

40

'Christ. That man was a monster.'

'What did he want?'

'I don't know.'

'Did he ask you any questions?'

'He didn't say a bloody thing, Joe. Alright?'

He didn't ask any questions. That was strange. Could it have been because I'd arrived in time? It was possible, but it didn't seem likely. From what I'd seen of Browne and the room, there had been long enough to ask questions.

I got Browne another drink and that calmed him down a bit. He managed to stand after that. I helped him downstairs and put him into his chair.

'Christ,' he said again. 'Who was that?'

'Didn't you recognize him?'

'Recognize him? No I didn't bloody recognize him. I was too busy with other things. Getting hurt, mostly.'

'Name's Roy Buck. He was a fighter. The Reaper. You probably patched him up before.'

'Wouldn't need a doctor for that. You'd need a stone mason.'

When Browne was recovered, which took about half a bottle, we set about making the house secure – well, as secure as we could.

Out back, I cut down some of the bushes he had growing. He complained about that.

'They took me years to grow,' he said.

That was bollocks. The only thing he did to grow them was not kill them yet. I told him we needed to clear the ground, the bushes could be used as cover. He still complained.

Next, I broke up the rockery and carried the rocks, one at a bloody time, and dumped them on the back patio, beneath the upper windows. Browne complained about that too. I told him it was to make it hard to use ladders.

'Men with ladders?' Browne said. 'Don't you think you're being a bit paranoid?'

'Half an hour ago you were flying headfirst into your furniture.'

'Good point.'

Those rocks nearly killed me, what with my bad arm and my bad rib, and my bad everything else. Browne watched me, but didn't help. I told him it'd be quicker if he did.

'I almost died,' he said, 'in case you've forgotten. Plus, I'm an old man. Plus, I almost died.'

Plus, he was pissed again.

Browne's house was detached, one of those middle-class Victorian places, so we had a lot of privacy out back, but there was still this old neighbour of his, an ex-army major type who watered his roses and pruned his moustache, that kind of thing. Every now and then, he'd peer out of his bedroom window and see what there was to be angry about. Browne spotted him and waved, and muttered about the old bastard being a card-carrying fascist.

I boarded up the back windows on the ground floor, nailing a piece of plywood over the inside of each one, and then doing the outside. I made sure to drill a couple of holes in the boards first, just enough to see through. I did the same around the sides, but left the front. I put some two-by-four across the kitchen door. Upstairs, I attached locks on all the windows.

After all that, I sat down at the table in the dark kitchen and tried to think what to do next, but my thinking didn't get very far because Roy Buck kept coming into my mind and fouling it up. What had he wanted? I asked Browne about it again.

'All I know is I was in the kitchen. I heard a knock at the front door. I didn't answer it. You told me not to. Then I heard a knock at the back.'

'You opened the back door for him.'

'I was stupid. I thought it had to be you. I just saw a huge shape. It had to be you.'

'And then?'

'Then I got hit by a train. I ran upstairs and locked my bedroom door. That didn't help.'

Why would Buck show up and throw Browne around, only to leave when I came back?

Browne made me a tea and sat down with a mug of coffee. I was pretty sure coffee wasn't the only thing in it. We sat in silence, the only sounds coming from the traffic outside, the hum of the boiler, the wind brushing against the outside of the house, far off now that we sat behind a wall of wood.

I knew something was on Browne's mind from the way he wasn't drinking his coffee. Instead, he turned the mug around in his hands and looked down at it as if it would tell him his future. Finally, he looked up at me and said, 'Don't you remember the letter, son?'

'Huh?'

'The letter. From Barbara. The one she left you. Don't you remember it? You read it a few days ago, man. Surely you can't have forgotten it.'

The letter. Yes, I remembered that. She'd left it for me in that box of creams and stuff I'd bought her. It was about the only thing of hers I had left, apart from my memories, which were breaking up before my eyes. I remembered the letter, of course I fucking did. I could quote the whole thing there and then. 'I'm using you,' the letter read, 'and it tears me up inside. But I do love you.'

'No,' I said, 'I haven't forgotten it.'

'"Don't destroy yourself for me" – she wrote that. Remember?'

'Yes,' I said. 'I remember that.'

'Does it mean anything to you? Do you understand what she was saying?'

'Yes,' I said. 'I understand.'

He was still turning the mug. I watched it move slowly. I thought that if it stopped moving, the world would stop spinning or I would stop breathing or the past would stop being. The wind rattled the door, the traffic whirred, the mug turned in circles.

Don't destroy yourself for me. What else could I do?

'And?' he said.

I hadn't given that part of the letter any thought. The other parts made such a screaming noise they drowned everything else out.

'I suppose you'll know by now that I used you,' she'd written. 'You asked me what I wanted, remember? You didn't believe that I could just want to be with you. Well, you were right. To begin with. I was scared, because of what I was doing and who I was doing it to. I was scared and I needed someone strong. I needed you.'

44

I needed you. Yes, I remembered. How could I ever forget? The words were scarred into my brain. Paget had carved them there after he'd carved her face.

Browne was waiting for me to answer. I let him wait.

'She wouldn't want this,' he said finally. 'You know that.'

'I know she was a good person,' I said. 'And I know she died because she was a good person.'

He dropped his head, as if he'd been defeated. But I knew him. I knew he'd come back at me. That's what he always did; every time it looked like he'd been beaten, he'd get up and go back for more beating. In his way, he was a tough bastard, tougher than any of the fighters he'd once stitched up – tougher than me.

'So is that all you care about? That she's dead?'

I couldn't answer that. I found myself watching that mug go round and round and round. Maybe, if he kept turning it, I wouldn't ever have to think what might've been.

He stopped turning the mug, stared at it for a moment, then lifted it to his mouth, drained the contents in three glugs and put it down on the tabletop.

She'd had that picture, a print of *The Fighting Temeraire* by Turner. I'd told her about the ship the first time I went to her place, about how, at Trafalgar, she'd fought two French men-of-war to save the *Victory*.

'Whenever I think of you,' she'd written, 'I think of that old ship, that warhorse… Remember you told me about it? About how, in that picture, it was being tugged in to be broken up? I don't want to think of you like that. I don't want you to go seeking revenge for what's happened to me. Please don't.'

Don't destroy yourself for me, Joe.

Destroy myself? Of course I fucking would. I'd destroy myself and everything else for her. She was gone. I hadn't saved her. But I could give her justice. I was her justice. My vengeance was justice. I'd destroy the world. What else could I do?

I don't know if I said anything out loud, but Browne looked at me with an odd expression and said, 'You know what I think? I think you want to destroy yourself. I think you don't know anything else but destruction, violence, rage. I used to think you'd destroy yourself in the process of destroying everything else, that when there was nothing left for you to wreak your vengeance upon, you'd turn it on yourself.'

He might've been right. I'd thought about it myself. He was getting close to the mark, and I didn't like it. But then he said, 'Now, I think differently. Now I think you were the target from the word go and all these others out there, all the ones you think you need to kill are just an excuse, just a means for you to kill yourself. They're your weapon, Joe. That's all.'

We sat in silence for a while, then I drank the rest of my tea and reached over and lifted his mug. I took them over to the sink, washed them up.

'Brenda,' I said.

'What, son?'

'Her name was Brenda.'

'Yes,' he said. 'Brenda.'

There was a knock at the door. In that quiet it sounded like gunshots. Browne jumped out of his seat. Christ, he was jittery. I wasn't much better. I felt coldness crawl over my skin. Browne's fear was infecting me.

'Don't panic,' I said. 'They're not likely to knock.'

'Who is it?'

That was a dumb question.

'Go see.'

'You go.'

'It's your house. It'd look strange if I went.'

Neither of us moved. We waited for the silence to come back. It was easier in the silence. We didn't have to do anything except listen to it as it sunk through us and hollowed us with our own thoughts.

But the knocking came back. In a way, it was the fact that it was now louder that set us both at ease. Maybe silence would've been worse after all. Then we would've turned to the back door and waited for someone to start smashing down our defences.

Browne stood unwillingly and doddered out of the room and up the hallway. He opened the front door. I moved out of sight and heard a posh bloke's voice.

'What's going on here?'

'William,' Browne said, in a loud, friendly way. Too loud, I thought. Too friendly. 'How nice of you to visit.'

'I don't like what's happening here,' the posh voice said. 'It's bloody funny.'

'Funny?' I could hear the slyness in Browne's voice. The old bastard was enjoying himself, relieved, probably, that it was just some old wanker, relieved that he wasn't going to get a round in the head.

'Boarding up the windows, throwing rocks around.

47

What the bloody hell are you doing?'

'We,' Browne said, 'are preparing for an invasion.'

'What are you talking about? Are you drunk?'

'Yes.'

'I might've known. And who is that ape living here? He looks like a criminal. Is he a criminal?'

'Joe? Oh, yes, he is a criminal. He's alright, though. He's a one-man war, to be sure, but he's alright.'

I cursed his fucking tongue. I wanted to go and haul him off by his neck, but that would've made it all worse. Browne hated these posh tossers who wanted England to look like something from a Wodehouse novel, as if there'd once been a time without poverty and suffering and hate. I didn't blame him for that, but I didn't need any grief. And now, because Browne was drunk, he was baiting the bloke, telling him my name, my business. But I think he was doing it to bait me too, to get his little bit of revenge in. That's why he was being so fucking loud. Christ.

'I can see I'll get no sense from you,' the bloke said.

'I sincerely hope not, William,' Browne said.

I heard the door close.

'That was the old bugger from next door,' Browne said when he came back. 'Name's William double-barrel. Major Pennington-Jones, or something. Ha. Fool. Thinks everyone who isn't a white, middle-class *Daily Mail* reader must be a criminal or part of some communist conspiracy to deprive him of his bloody right to be a bigot.'

'Don't wind him up,' I said. 'We don't need more trouble.'

'Oh, hell. He's not worth bothering about.'

With that, he made himself a sandwich, humming as he

did it. I think he'd completely forgotten what he'd said to me a few minutes before, about Brenda and death and my need for blood – mine or anyone's. That was something, at least. Some peace.

I left him to it while I went to have a shower. All that shifting stuff about had made me sweaty and dusty.

I was just finishing up in the bathroom when the bloke came back. I heard him talking with Browne, but couldn't make out what was said. It was a short conversation. Then the door slammed.

When I went downstairs, Browne was back in the lounge, a glass of Scotch in his hand. He was watching some cooking programme on the TV and I swear his hair had gone whiter, if that was possible.

'What's wrong?'

He wouldn't look at me.

'Uh…' he said.

'What?'

'He's called the police.'

I glared at him. He still wouldn't look at me. Instead, he fixed his eyes on the TV. Someone was chopping onions. Suddenly that was fascinating to Browne. I took a deep breath.

'Alright,' I said. 'He's just some nosy old geezer. The law won't bother with him.'

Browne didn't say anything to that, but he took a deep breath.

'Will they?' I said.

'Uh… well…'

'What?'

Now he looked at me.

'He runs the local neighbourhood watch.'

'Christ. And you didn't think of that when you told him I was a criminal?'

'And... uh... he's a Rotarian.'

'A what?'

'The Rotary Club. He's a member. So are lots of the senior policemen at the local stations. Or he might be a Mason or a Conservative. Or something. Anyway, he's part of the conspiracy.'

I reached for his Scotch and pulled it from his grip.

'Hey.'

'Stay sober. When they come, have a good excuse. Say you heard a bunch teenagers one night and got scared. Say I was someone you met down the pub, you paid me a score to make the place safe.'

'They'll think I'm an idiot.'

'Yeah.'

After that he sulked. I left him to it. I had things to do. I was sick of being useless.

I decided I'd better try and do something to find Glazer. My arm was okay to use and my side didn't hurt so much. I wasn't going to heal any more than I had already.

If the law was going to pay Browne a visit, now would be a good time to disappear, for a while anyway.

SEVEN

I called at the bakery in Stepney but the manager told me Green had finished for the day. I phoned Green's number, but there was no answer so I asked the manager where Green lived. I got a cold look.

'What for?'

'I need to talk to him.'

'He know you?'

'Yeah.'

Customers were strolling in, picking up the bread, bagels, pastries. There were two girls behind the counter. One of the girls was short with thick-rimmed glasses, the other was tall, dark-haired, with large, oval eyes. They both flicked glances our way. I guessed they knew something of Green's background.

'But you don't know where he lives?' the manager was saying.

I didn't want any bother here. I didn't want someone doing anything like phoning the law. I didn't think I had it in me to keep getting away from them.

'I came here a few weeks ago,' I said. 'One morning. He told me his wife was expecting so I thought I'd go see her, say hello.'

The manager wasn't buying it. He was one of those types.

'That's right,' the short bird said. 'She's got another coming.'

'Wonder who the father is,' the taller one said.

'Why can't you phone him up?' the manager said to me.

'I did. He didn't answer. I have to go away, so I thought I'd better do it now, in case she goes into hospital.'

He was a stocky man with thick black hair and a moustache with flour on it. He wiped his hands on his apron. They had thick black hair on them too, and flour.

'Well…' he said, still wiping his hands. 'I'll call him, see if it's alright.'

'I told you, he's not answering.'

The manager called him anyway. He pocketed his phone.

'No answer,' he said. 'Sorry, mate.'

The short girl looked up again then.

'I remember you,' she said. 'Yeah. Benny went out back and had a fag and when he come back he was… well, he looked a bit off, bit green around the gills.'

'I had some bad news,' I told the girl.

'Well…' the manager said again.

A few more punters had come in by then, mostly women. They eyed me up and moved past me with as much space between us as possible. The girls were hard at it now. It was lunchtime and probably their busiest period. The manager noticed the trade building up.

He went behind the counter and tore off a piece of the paper they were using to wrap stuff in. He scribbled an address and handed it to me. I don't think he cared any more about Green's privacy, he just wanted me out of his shop.

Green's place was a terraced house, just off Roman Road. It was a new-build place, one of those ones where the back garden is the size of the living room and the walls are made of cardboard. I knocked. I heard some kid shout, 'Dad.' There was some running about and then nothing. I knocked again and heard a woman cry out.

'Benny. Answer the fucking door.'

There were heavy footsteps and finally the door opened and Green was standing looking at my stomach. He tilted his head.

'Joe,' he said. 'The fuck you doing here?'

'I wanted to talk to you.'

'Who is it?' the woman called out.

'Mate of mine.'

'Well, get rid of him.'

Green sighed.

'She's pregnant,' he said. 'I told you that, right? Hormones all over the place. Let's get outta here.' He pulled the door shut behind him. 'She's driving me fucking nuts. Hormones. Fuck. I think she uses that as an excuse.'

He started walking up the road before he remembered me. Then he stopped and turned.

'I ain't eaten yet. Fancy some grub? There's a curry house nearby.'

So we went up the street, towards the Roman Square market.

We passed a lot of boarded-up shops, pawn-brokers,

pound shops. Teenagers were hanging around here and there, eyeing us up.

'Not much work for 'em,' Green said. 'There was up till 2012 and for a bit after. The Olympic stadium's near here. Everyone thought it was the start of a whatsit, rejuvenation. Now, though…' He shrugged. 'Fine for some, but for the rest of us… The money's gone and all them government tossers and big businesses are back to not giving a shit.'

He took me to a small Indian place. There was a sign outside, dirty black writing on a dirty yellow background. 'The Moghul', the sign read.

'They do buffets, all you can eat for a tenner. You got some money on you?'

We went in. I wasn't hungry going in. Then the smell hit me and I was starving. We got a couple of plates and piled food a foot high: samosas, tikka, koftas, balti, rice, nan bread. The works.

'They even got falafel.'

We took the food to a table by the window and sat down. Outside, a woman in a burkha came by slowly. She carried a couple of bags of shopping and had to keep stopping to adjust them. Then she had to stop again and adjust her burkha. It seemed like she was fighting everything just to get home.

When I turned back to Green, he was looking at his plate, his jaw tight. After a while, he looked at me.

'Look, Joe,' he said, 'I told you I'm legit now, right? I mean, I can't get involved in things like this. I got a family.'

'I just need some information.'

He sighed.

54

'Just some information. Fuck me. People are dying all around you and all you want is some information that'll probably put me top of the death list.'

'I'll keep your name out of it. I know you're straight, but you still know people. And I need your help.'

'You don't want no one's help, Joe. You never did.'

As I looked at him, I could see the fear in his eyes.

'You're right; I move and people die. And, yes, it might put you in danger, although I'll never tell anyone where I got the information. But these are people who use children and women, use them and kill them. You've got a family – what would you do to protect them?'

He sucked in a breath and shook his head.

'You cunt,' he said, a small, twisted smile forming on his mouth. 'You're a dirty fighter, know that?'

'Yeah.'

'So what do you want to talk about?' he said, picking up his fork and shovelling some food into his gob.

'Kenny Paget.'

He stopped eating, the fork halfway to his mouth. He looked around. All the tables nearby were empty. The woman in the burkha was gone now.

'You mean the man you killed?' he said.

'Is that what you've heard?'

'That and more.'

'What more?'

'That he killed your bird.'

He'd forgotten about his food now, his knife and fork resting on the plate. Then he remembered it and started eating again.

'Yeah, well, good fucking riddance to him.'

'There's more,' I said.

He stopped again.

'Yeah?'

'She was grassing Paget and Marriot up to the law. Only, she got a bent copper called Glazer who grassed her right back. That's why she died.'

'Right. Sorry about that. This Glazer – you asked me about him before.'

'Yeah. I need to find him.'

He went back to eating, pulling a piece of nan bread apart and using it to scoop up some curry. He was taking his time about it all.

'Wouldn't know how to help you there, mate,' he said around the food.

'You can tell me where Paget lived.'

He was wiping his hands on his shirt now, watching me as he chewed. I put a forkful of something in my mouth. It was hot. I drank some water while my eyes melted. Green smiled, for some reason.

'Would that be any good to you? Paget's address? Police woulda been there, might still be hanging around.'

'Maybe, but maybe they don't know about Paget. I think Dunham would've cleaned it up. So, maybe Paget's place is just sitting there.'

'Mmm,' he said. 'Possible, I guess. Okay. I'll see what I can do. How about Marriot?'

'Marriot's been dead weeks now.'

'Yeah. He's still dead, far as I know. In fact, you killed him, right? Anyone you haven't killed recently?'

56

I said, 'He's been dead for weeks and the law know about his death. So how would I get anything by going to his place? Everything important must've gone by now.'

'Well, Joe,' Green said, while that twisted smile split his face, 'you could always talk to his wife.'

Now it was my turn to stop eating.

'What?'

'Marriot. Had a wife. Son too, I think.'

It had never occurred to me that someone like Marriot could be married, could have children. Did his wife know what the old man had done? Did she care? Or did she just spend his money?

'Yes,' I said, 'get me her address.'

57

I tried Paget's place first. It was one of those modern apartment blocks, over in Muswell Hill. It had two entrances; one at the front with a keypad security system, the other a fire escape or delivery door at the back, by the car park. The front one was out. I could try to tailgate a person going in, or wait until someone came out and jump through the door before it closed. But both those would mean somebody would see me. I looked too dodgy to allow myself to get noticed. Besides, it was an expensive-looking place so it probably had CCTV cameras in the lobby.

The door at the back was solid wood with a single handle, which had a lock in the middle of it. I wondered if that meant the building had a caretaker of some sort, someone who had a key in case of deliveries.

It was a hazy day, with the sun weak in the weak sky, and still cold enough for people to wear scarves and gloves.

I saw a cafe over the other side of the road. I went there and took a seat at a table by the window. From there I had a distant view of the back of the apartment block. All I had to do was wait and see who went in and out, and then figure a way to get access. Easy.

I ordered a coffee from the girl who came up to my table.

'What kind of coffee?' she said.

'White.'

'What kind of coffee?' she said again, looking at me like I was an idiot. I couldn't think of any type of coffee except coffee.

'Tea,' I said.

'What kind of tea?'

I finally got my fucking tea. I sat and drank it. I was able to do that, at least. I looked out the window and watched the world creep by.

A woman in her fifties walked along with a toddler by her side. The woman had hair that looked like it'd been coated in wallpaper paste. It didn't move. The kid was stuffing a chocolate bar in its mouth. Every now and then the woman would wipe the kid's mouth with a tissue.

An old bloke crossed the street, hobbling on a stick. The cars slowed for him, but didn't slow that much and he had to get over as quick as he could.

An hour passed. I drank more tea then went and pissed it out. There was something in that which made me think of my life, but I couldn't tell you what it was.

The sky turned hazier, the sun got weaker still so that it became like a negative black space; a white hole in a white sky. I watched people go by. Nobody that I saw talked. Nobody did anything much except wander along as if they were all ghosts trapped in the afterlife, and I was stuck in some place between worlds, not knowing what was real, alive, and what was dead.

The old bloke with the stick came back, crossing the road with a look of anxiety in his face. A bag of shopping dangled from each hand, so that one bag kept bashing into his walking stick, making him even slower. A van slowed to a stop to let him crawl across.

For a moment I thought I smelled Brenda, felt her next to me, and I turned. There was nothing there except a wooden chair. Emptiness swept through me, and I felt as if I was being sucked into that world of the dead, shone upon by that white hole which was emptier than anything should ever be.

Movement caught my eye and I turned to look at the apartment block. The back door opened and a man came out. I shook my head, trying to clear it of the madness. I had things to do, I told myself. I had things to do, then I could rest.

The bloke was dressed in black trousers and white shirt. He was too far for me to see him clearly, but he sure wasn't a caretaker. He could've been a resident. I watched him go to a black Ford, open it and lean into the front. He stood up, put something in his pocket, closed the car up and locked it with the remote on his key. He went back into the building, using a key to open the back door.

I waited again. Nothing happened except I got more tired, more fuzzy-headed. If I waited any longer, I'd forget what I was waiting for.

I wandered over to the apartment block. I passed the bloke's Ford and gave it a good boot. The car alarm screeched. I stood next to the door and waited. People would probably be looking at me, but I just didn't care by then.

After a minute, the door opened. I shoved my way through, slamming into the bloke. He bounced back.

'Fuck,' he said.

He was dazed. I snapped a quick right cross onto his jaw and he went down, dropping his car key. I picked it up, turned off his car alarm and let the door close behind me.

We were in a stairwell, the stairs going up to the top of the building and a door leading to the ground floor.

The man was unconscious. I rolled him over onto his side and used his shoelaces to tie his wrists behind his back. Then I bound his ankles together with his belt. I tore his shirt off and tied that around his mouth.

I climbed the stairs to the third floor and opened the fire door. This put me into a carpeted corridor. Paget's place was number 3C.

I moved down the hallway, my feet silent on the thick carpet. Paget's flat was at the end. When I got there, I put my ear to the door and listened. There was no sound inside. I tried the handle. It was locked, of course. I didn't have lock picks, and I was lousy with them anyway. I put my shoulder to the door and leaned. It wasn't a heavy door, and I felt it start to give, but not enough. I took a step back, raised my foot and kicked the thing in.

Then I waited for someone to shout at me, waited for an alarm to go off, anything like that. When none of that happened, I walked in.

As soon as I entered, something felt wrong. I didn't know what it was exactly, maybe something I'd noticed without realizing it. I shook the feeling off. My mind was wandering around so much, I didn't know how much I could trust it.

I trawled through the drawers and cupboards, looking for something that would link Paget with Glazer. Anything would do, a scribbled note, a diary with Glazer's initials. There was nothing.

There was a bookshelf against one wall, paperbacks lined up. I started to pull the books off and hold them open to see if anything fell out. Then I saw it. The bookshelf was dusty, but there was line in the dust just in front of the spines of the books. Someone had already pulled the books out – pushing the dust back – and had replaced them. It wasn't much, and I might've missed it.

I knew I wasn't going to find anything here, others had beaten me to it. Dunham, I thought. Only he and Cole and me knew that Paget was dead. Well, that's how it had been and I couldn't think Cole or Dunham would've reported it to the law. Dunham must've disposed of Paget's body.

But then I realized that was wrong, and I knew what that feeling had been. The place had been done over, sure, searched from top to bottom. I'd expected that. The problem was that it had all been put back again, nice and neat. And that meant that whoever had done the searching was expecting someone to come here. Either someone had searched the place not knowing Paget was dead and expecting him to come back, or someone who knew Paget was dead had searched the place and was waiting for someone else to turn up.

Either way I'd made a big mistake.

Too late.

I saw them as I turned, saw their grey suits, their grey faces, their grey eyes watching me coldly. I went for my gun, but I fumbled it and dropped it. I saw the blackjacks they held, the Taser. I said, 'Fuck, not again.'

They hauled me up into a sitting position, one on each arm. I couldn't see them and I tried to throw them off, but my arms were tight behind my back. I could feel the plastic ties binding my wrists together, cutting into my flesh. I pulled at them anyway, knowing it wouldn't do any good.

Then a man came before me. I looked up and cursed.

He was in his fifties, dressed in a badly fitting suit and white shirt. There was a tie around his neck, but it was pulled down so far it didn't serve any function. He wiped a hand over his grey moustache. His name was Compton and he was the fucking law.

'Hello, Joe,' Compton said. 'We must stop meeting like this.'

I told him to fuck off. He laughed.

The other two moved over to stand either side of their boss. I knew them too. Bradley was tall, white and slim with thinning hair and puffy eyes. Hayward was the youngest. He was black, too good-looking for this life. If he'd taken the time to study the other two, he would've seen the haggard look he was bound for.

'You're getting sloppy, Joe,' Compton said.

Bradley laughed at that for some reason.

63

'Yeah,' I said.

'You're lucky.'

I didn't feel lucky.

'Very,' Hayward said.

'Am I?'

'We coulda been anyone,' Bradley said. 'We coulda been part of Glazer's crew, or Dunham's. What do you think would've happened to you if that'd been the case?'

I knew the answer to that.

'They'd work you over, Joe. They'd make you hurt.'

They were law, this lot, but they weren't dangerous – annoying, yes, but not dangerous. They had a habit of turning up when I didn't have any means of escape.

They were investigating corruption in the force, and had been given the job of targeting vice corruption, especially Glazer. That put us on the same side – for the time being. Well, sort of. Of course, that didn't mean I trusted them. They were still fucking law.

Bradley pulled a pack of smokes from his jacket pocket and lit one. Hayward glanced at him and moved away. One thing was for damned sure; they were in control here, far too casual.

I shook my head, trying to get it clear.

'Punchy,' Bradley said.

Hayward laughed at that. They were having fun.

'Do you lot do everything together?' I said.

'Only where you're concerned, Joe,' Compton said. 'Well, you and Glazer.'

'You were watching the block,' I said.

'Not exactly. We have friends in the local nick. Someone

saw you enter the building. They called it in, and the locals called me.'

I tried to stand again, made it up to a crouching position before Bradley put the boot in. I went sprawling backwards. I would've ripped his head off if I could've. Instead, I cursed myself.

I pushed myself back into a sitting position then managed to put one foot down, the other leg bent so that it looked like I was being knighted. That wasn't what I had in mind, though, and they knew it. They stepped back enough that if I'd tried to charge them they would've been able to move aside.

'What're you doing here, Joe?' Compton said.

I looked up at him.

'I was just passing,' I said. 'I heard a cry for help so I came in.'

Compton smiled.

'There's a bloke downstairs. We found him tied up and unconscious.'

'Yeah?'

He sighed and shook his head.

'We know you want Glazer. That's why you came here, isn't it? Anyway, we know everything. A word from us and you'll do thirty years. You know who we are, Joe. You know we've got clout.'

'I'm guilty till proved guilty,' I said. 'Is that it?'

'That's it in a nutshell, mate,' Bradley said.

'But you *are* guilty, Joe,' Compton said. 'Don't you remember?'

They were doing their tag-team thing, taking me for

some mug who'd been caught shoplifting. I pulled at the binds.

'You're not going anywhere, son,' Compton said.

'Guilty of what?'

'Oh, just about everything, I reckon. Murder, armed robbery, assault, obstruction of the law etc. etc. and so on ad infinitum.'

'That means forever,' Bradley said. 'Like your prison term's gonna be.'

'You'll have trouble proving it.'

'Fuck proof. We make our own proof. You've been around. You know how it works.'

I knew. If they'd wanted to arrest me, they'd have done it already. Which meant they wanted something. I said to Compton, 'This place has been searched. Was it you lot?'

'Maybe.'

'What were you looking for?'

'Same as you, I expect; anything that'll lead us to Glazer. Anything that'll help convict him. Anything that'll help us find him.'

'You don't know where he is?'

They glanced at each other.

'He's fucked off,' Bradley said. 'Gone to ground. And that's your fucking fault.'

'Officially, he's on leave,' Compton said. 'No one's seen him for a couple of weeks. He's supposed to be back in a few days. I don't think he will be. He hasn't been to his home, nobody's heard from him. We could do with your help there.'

Now it was Hayward's turn. He said, 'Come on, Joe. We all want the same thing. In different ways, maybe, but the same result: Glazer has to pay.'

He was putting a lot of emotion into his voice.

'You know about Operation Elena; the whole point of that was to target the immigrant sex industry, to help women, children. That's what you want too, isn't it? To help the victims.'

Now he was looking concerned, gazing at me as if to say 'I know how much you've suffered.'

'And you know they gave the job to Glazer, right? They put him in charge of the operation, and what did he do? He sold the information to the very bastards he should've been catching. That's why we're investigating it now. We aren't your enemies, Joe.'

Sure, Hayward was a decent bloke. He was on my side. He was my fucking friend.

'He's got to pay, Joe. Let us make him pay.'

I stared at him while he sympathized with me.

They'd worked out who was playing which part. Hayward drew the good guy straw.

Well, I could play their fucking game.

'You're right. I'm tryna find him.'

'Well...' Compton said, making like he was working out a plan. 'Glazer's not likely to surface, is he? I mean, Paget's dead, Marriot's dead, and Glazer knows we're after him. No, he'll keep his head down. So we need something else, another way to get him.'

'So what do we do?' I said, still playing along.

Compton wiped a hand over his moustache.

'There's more than one way to skin a cat,' he said. 'If we could find something on him, some kind of physical evidence, say, then we could cut off his avenues of retreat. His friends would soon start turning their backs on him. Once he's out in the cold, we could get him.'

'Meanwhile, we could give you protection,' Hayward said. 'From Dunham, Glazer.'

Protection? They'd give me protection? Shit.

'So? Do you have anything?' Bradley said.

'If I did, I wouldn't be here, would I?'

'Anything, Joe,' Hayward said. 'Or if there's anything you know could lead us to finding evidence.'

I tried to stand, just to see if they'd let me. They did. In fact, they helped me. Fucking coppers.

'Such as?' I said.

Now they were looking up at me. That made me feel a bit better – not much, but a bit.

'Oh, anything concrete,' Compton said.

'Just evidence,' Hayward said.

They were being cagey, which meant they didn't know what I knew, and didn't want to tell me too much. That was worrying because it might mean they thought they knew more than me. And that might mean they did. Still, all I had to do was play dumb. That was pretty easy.

'Why didn't you ask me this earlier?'

Compton frowned. It was a lousy act.

'That's a fair question. Fact is, we thought we'd have something on him by now. We thought Paget would give us something. But then, of course, Paget disappeared on us. For good.'

He gave me a knowing look here. But I knew they'd have nothing to tie me in with that.

Something was clicking in my mind, though. Something Bradley had said earlier. They could've been part of Glazer's crew, he'd said. Or Dunham's.

That meant they knew Dunham was after me. Of course, they'd probably heard that Dunham's place got hit and Paget got killed, and they knew it was me. Sure, it was logical that Dunham would want to kill me.

But that wasn't all Bradley had said. 'They'd work you over, Joe,' he'd said. 'They'd make you hurt.' He hadn't said, 'They'd kill you, Joe.'

That was ringing alarm bells in my head.

'Suppose I find something,' I said, making like I was thinking it all through, letting them see my brain working, my lips moving. 'What would you give me? Why wouldn't I just use it to go after Glazer myself?'

They thought I was dumb; fine. I could use that.

Bradley shot a glance at Compton. There was something in that, some message. I watched Compton's face, but all he did was wipe his moustache again. Bradley turned back to me.

'Look, Joe. You know we can't condone anything illegal, right? But, if you bring us something, we'll see if we can give you a heads-up, let you know where Glazer is, if we can. You understand? We'll have to go and arrest him, but if you happened to get there first and leave before we arrived, well...'

He let that hang in the air. They were offering to give Glazer to me. Now I was suspicious as fuck.

'Think about this; if you ever want justice for your woman, give us Glazer.'

I nodded slowly. I said, 'If I get anything, I'll let you know.'

Compton nodded to Bradley who pulled a lock-knife from his pocket and sliced through my ties. I rubbed my wrists to get the circulation going again. Hayward held my gun out to me. It was empty, of course.

'You're letting me go?'

'Sure,' Compton said. 'What else are we supposed to do with you?'

'We could kill him.' That was from Bradley.

'I wonder if we could. Anyway, yes, Joe, we're letting you go. Charging you at the moment would be a waste of our time and, frankly, it might be awkward. So, you run along now, and be good. We'll get Glazer. You just keep your head down, try not to get killed by Dunham. And don't forget, you get anything, you let me know.'

He handed me a card with his number on it.

They wandered off, laughing.

I didn't mind that because I'd worked out what that alarm in my head was all about. Those cunts wanted the DVD, and they figured I might have it and that Dunham knew I might have it, which was why they expected Dunham to torture me, not just kill me as he should've done if it was payback for killing Paget.

But there was more. They wanted the DVD, but they didn't want to tell me they wanted it. That meant it was valuable to them and they didn't want me to know in case I got to use it for myself.

70

I walked slowly back to my car. The idea that I was being watched, that I was not in control, sat at the back of my head, like a shadow. It had been there, casting its darkness over my actions. Every time I thought I knew where I was, what I was doing, I'd walk, blind and confused, into some dead-end. Maybe it was just getting caught by Compton that had me thinking like that. Maybe it was the whole thing, never being able to get away from it all, from the past, from the bastards out there.

Whoever they were.

Wherever they were.

I checked the motor for any electronic surveillance gadgets. These days, though, I'd be hard pressed to find them anyway. I rolled around the streets for a while, looking for tails. I couldn't see anything obvious. I drove into some big Tesco car park, pulled up and watched the entrance. Nothing came in for a few minutes. Then a red mini entered, drove past me slowly and parked. A middle-aged woman got out and headed into the shop. I waited some more, saw nothing, then headed back onto the street and drove to the address Green had given me.

When she opened the door, a gurgled sound came from

her throat. It sounded like she was being strangled. She took a step back, tried to slam the door shut. I put my hand up and threw the door back. She turned and staggered away, going as fast as her dressing gown would let her. She went into the bathroom and slammed the door. I followed her into the flat, stopped in front of the bathroom door and smashed that thing off its hinges.

I'd told myself not to lose it, to be calm, to be in control. I only wanted to ask her some questions, I'd told myself. She wasn't to blame for her husband's work, I'd told myself.

But as I'd neared her place I kept remembering what they'd done to Brenda and all that shit I'd told myself about keeping cool went out the window. So what if she was just his wife? I didn't care about any of that. She was all that was left of Marriot, she'd been married to him, must've known what he was, what he did. That was enough for me.

And then, by the time she opened the door, I'd been about ready to rip her apart.

But when I smashed the bathroom door in, all of that fell away. She was cowering in the corner, her eyes screwed tightly shut, the dressing gown twisted around her, her knees up to her chin, her arms covering her head. I could see the inside of her leg, blue veins bulging, and her shoulder blades poking through the fabric of the gown. Her hair was dyed brown, but the grey roots were showing through and had been for a while. Whatever life she'd been used to with her husband was all gone. Now she was just another old middle-aged woman, a widow, waiting her time out.

She didn't move. I could hear a sound, a whining, mumbling noise.

72

'I'm not going to hurt you,' I said. 'I only want some information.'

Now she opened her eyes. She was wearing make-up, and her mascara had streaked with tears.

'What?' she said. 'What do you want?'

'Answers.'

'I don't know anything.'

It bothered me that she was in her dressing gown. It was mid-afternoon and she was in her dressing gown. Either she'd got up late or she was going to bed early. But she had make-up on. I couldn't work that out.

Then I worked it out.

I turned in time to see him, bare to the waist, shaven grey hair, old, collapsed chest. He brought the bottle down on my head. I moved quickly, and the blow glanced off my jaw. It dazed me, but I still managed to throw out a fist and catch him in the ribs. He crumpled.

Then the pain scorched through my head and the bath came up to hit me. I put my arms out and felt them take the weight of my body as I crashed into the white plastic.

When I looked up, the old man was staggering away, doubled over, one arm across his torso. There wasn't much to him. I could see his spine ripple down his back. A punch from me should've floored him for good. Christ, I couldn't even down some thin old bloke.

I stood and the room spun. I waited for the world to slow down, holding onto the sink while I swallowed the bile that had come up. I managed to reach the door, held onto the frame and heaved myself into the hall. The front door was open. The old man had gone. I kicked the door shut. If he was off to call the law, I didn't have long.

I heard a woman's voice, low and desperate.

Then the voice changed.

'Oh God,' it said, and her eyes were on me, huge with horror.

Somehow I was in the lounge and Marriot's wife had a phone in her hand. When she saw me, she fumbled the phone and dropped it. I reached down for the phone and put it to my ear and heard no sound. I put it in my pocket.

'Who'd you call?' I said, hearing the words coming out in a slur, knowing she couldn't understand me.

What did it matter who she'd called? Whoever it was would be trouble.

The flat was small, but well decorated. It was the ground floor of a converted Victorian house, with high ceilings, coving, a fireplace – all the trimmings. The furniture was proper antique, I thought. It was rosewood and mahogany, anyway. And there was silver all over the place. It looked like she'd managed to keep some of Marriot's money after all.

There were no photos of Marriot, which was odd. Christ, he'd only been dead a few weeks. There was a picture of her as a young woman and another of her with a bloke who looked like the one who'd just scarpered. I suppose she didn't want her dead husband to ruin things. I suppose she wasn't that bothered he was dead.

'I want Glazer,' I said.

I could see the lines beneath the face cream she'd spread on. I could hear the crackling of nicotine soaked lungs.

'Glazer,' I said again.

'He... he knew my husband,' she said. 'I don't know anything else. Is this what you do,' she said, moving backwards, 'threaten women?'

She stumbled and fell, the breath leaving her in a gasp. One hand clawed at the carpet. I could see blood vessels in her yellowy eyes, as if the pupils had grown red roots.

'If I have to.'

But even as I said it, I thought, Is this what I've become? I, who was never floored in the ring? I, this monster, feared by men of power, killer of soldiers? Now I terrify small women.

Christ, the rage, the fury kept pulling me into its depths. I saw myself as I was, as that monster, but now full of the fury of impotence, standing above an old woman who was more impotent than me. I was like some mad dog, snarling and frothing at an insect.

'Policeman,' she said. 'He was a policeman. My husband paid him.'

'So, you do know more. Stand up.'

She stood on weak legs. She kept her eyes on mine all the time.

'Can I sit down?' she said.

I nodded. She sat. I sat. I watched. She watched. I let the rage sink, fade.

'I haven't had anything to do with Frank for a long time,' she said. 'We split up a couple of years back.'

'Just tell me what you know about Glazer.'

'He and my husband knew each other. He's a policeman. That's all I know.'

75

She knew I'd killed her husband and she must've thought I'd kill her. That's why I believed her.

'Your husband must've had notebooks, address books, something like that.'

She jumped up and almost ran to a tall chest of drawers. She opened the top drawer and pulled out a bunch of papers and a couple of books. She held these out to me like she was making an offering. I suppose she was.

'Go,' she said, pushing the stuff into my hands. 'Take it all and go. Please.'

I looked through what she'd given me, but it was rubbish, all domestic stuff; bank balances and car payments, shit like that.

'Where's the rest of it? His business papers?'

'It was in his office,' she said, as if it was obvious.

And, of course, it was obvious. I even remembered the huge iron safe he'd had there.

I dropped the papers on the floor and stood, suddenly weary. All the anger had slunk away and left me hollow.

'Glazer had a girlfriend,' she said. 'That's all I can remember. He used to talk to me about her.'

'What's her name?'

'Mary.'

'Mary. Is that it?'

'It's all I know.'

I walked out of her flat and up the road to my car. I fell in behind the wheel and started it up and pulled away from the curb, my mind full of nothing thoughts, all crashing into each other, leaving me more confused than ever. I had nowhere to go, nothing to go towards. I drifted, letting the car take me along to wherever it wanted to go. I was weak with it all, sick of it, old. I was dead, but too stupid to know it.

I couldn't keep the image of Brenda's blood-soaked face from my empty mind. It filled my head, torturing me. I saw her blood on my hands. It filled her eyes, her mouth. It was more than a nightmare, more than a dreamed-of horror, more than a memory. It was all of these, and more still because it had been real, and I'd done nothing to stop it. My mind was haunting itself, tormenting me with failure.

It was then I realized I was being followed.

ELEVEN

I turned left. The green car was still behind me. I slowed to twenty-five, and the car neared me a bit, then slowed too. I could see the driver, but not clearly. He was a young bloke with short dark hair. That was about all I could make of him.

It didn't smell like law, not with just one of them, and not when he was being this obvious. It might've been one of Dunham's mob, but, again, they usually went around in pairs.

I'd been turning this way and that, trying to decide what to do, and I didn't know where we were by this time. It was a residential area, quite posh. I was winding through rows of semis, cars parked in driveways, neat front gardens, grass verges.

I was going to have to find out who he was, what he wanted. That meant I was going to have to lead him into a trap. These suburban streets were fine for taking him into a cul-de-sac, but they were too quiet, I'd be too easily noticed. So, I had to lead him to where I could turn the tables. I had an idea about that.

I sped up, and drove around until I found a main road. The first shop I saw was a newsagent. That was good enough.

I pulled up opposite and went over, all nice and slow, like I was only out to buy some smokes. There was a woman behind the counter, fifty-something with a gut and a thick baggy jumper to try and hide it.

She said, 'Can I help you? Excuse me, can I help you?'

I went through into the back, past the stacks of newspapers and boxes of crisps, and out through the rear door into the loading area.

To my right was a wall. I stood on the bin next to the wall and climbed over into someone's back yard. I carried on, crossing a few more back gardens, and then went up the driveway of a house and came back onto the road where I was parked, only about a hundred yards behind my car. I was going to stroll up to this bloke's motor from behind, take him by surprise.

But he'd gone. There were cars parked in front of me, and vans, but there was no green car. I looked behind me and saw the same.

I walked back towards my motor, glancing up and down the street, natural like, so that I didn't tip him off in case he'd parked up somewhere and was watching me. I didn't see anything. I thought he must've cottoned on to what I was doing and scarpered.

If he hadn't changed down a gear, I wouldn't have looked up. He just had to have that extra acceleration. He just had to smash me to hell. The anger, I suppose. Well, I couldn't blame him for that. I understood it too well.

I was just rounding the back of my car, when I heard his engine jump sharply in pitch. I looked back and saw his car racing towards me, an animal rushing in for the kill. I hesitated, and that was dumb. My reactions were sluggish. I wasn't going to get out of the way of this now. I thought I was dead.

He was ten yards away, doing fifty, when I snapped to and jumped onto the boot of my car. Everything went sideways. I saw the street, the sky, the buildings in snapshots. I didn't hear the sound of the impact. Or, maybe I did, but it was blurred with everything else and became part of the chaos. I felt myself fly into the air. For a split second, everything was quiet. I might've blacked out again. I can't say. What I remember is that, for that instant, which went on forever, I thought, Well, I tried. I thought, Fuck it. I thought, I don't care any more.

It was over. I was dead. I knew it.

It didn't matter.

I think I was happy. I understood what Browne was talking about; the need for nothingness, the need to not exist. Only he did it slowly, piecemeal, falling nightly, drifting into the warm blanket of oblivion that he craved and out of the cold real world. He let himself slip into the darkness.

Me, I could never go that way. This was always going to be my end, or something like it – this brutal, thuggish thing. Mine would not be a slow death. It would be this; smashed into pulp between machines. And that was fine. That was what I wanted.

But not yet.

I saw the sky, grey and lifeless, and I wondered if that was what death was, just the same greyness. Forever.

Then the tarmac was scraping my body and every bone jarred with impact. The sound of crunching metal tore through my head, and seemed like some great beast tearing the cars apart in its teeth. I felt my spine bend sideways, felt my legs flail as I rolled over and over.

Then I stopped rolling. There was silence.

Something was pressing against my shoulder. There was pain in my side. I felt cold. I felt hot.

I heard a voice.

'Are you alright? God.'

I opened my eyes and saw concrete. It took me a while to remember where I was, what had happened. The voice was there still.

'I've called an ambulance,' the voice said. 'I saw him. He must be drunk.'

I turned my head. It felt light, numb. That was bad. She came into focus. She wore a baggy jumper. I'd seen her before, hadn't I?

I was lucky. If I hadn't blacked out, I probably would've been dead. As it was, my body was relaxed when I crashed into the ground. Now I lay in a crumpled heap, my head up against the curb.

I tried to stand. I remembered the pain in my side.

'Oh, God,' the woman said. 'You're hurt.'

Hadn't she said she'd called an ambulance? Fuck. That meant law.

I let the pain push its way through my body. That was good, the pain. It was something I could hold onto.

I felt her hand on my arm. I pushed her away. When I stood, I had to wait a while, just long enough for the world to settle back again.

He was a jug-eared bloke, with dark skin and deep-set

81

eyes. He was trying to crawl away when I caught up with him. I grabbed the back of his shirt and lifted him up.

He was a small boy, half my size. All I had to do was give him a right cross to the jaw and he'd go down and stay down. But he knew something. He must've done to come at me like that.

He tried to hit me and missed by a mile. I wasn't a hard target to hit. I let go and he crumpled to the ground. He must've been as bashed up as me. He looked alright, except for his blood-covered face and the blue shirt turned purple by all that claret that pumped from a gash three inches long on his forehead.

I heard sirens. I looked at the cars. His was mashed up, the front gone. Mine was bad at the back, but the boot was big and had taken the force. I dragged him over.

'No,' he said. 'NO.'

I clipped him and his head snapped back then fell forward. I threw him into the back and fell behind the wheel.

'What are you doing to him?'

The woman moved a hand to try and hold me. I pushed her aside and slammed the door. Then she was by the window. I started the car, put it into first and let my foot slowly off the clutch. There was a tearing, wrenching sound. The car shuddered and stalled. I tried again. The woman opened the door.

'I said, what are you doing to him?'

'Hospital,' I said.

That stopped her for a moment. I pulled the door shut and locked it. I put it in gear again, let the clutch out, punched the accelerator and tore loose, half a ton of metal scraping behind us. I saw the flashing lights round the corner as I pulled out. It was the ambulance. If it'd been the law, they'd have come after me, and caught me.

The car was fucked. The steering wheel was loose in my hands, the car going too far left, then way over right as I corrected it.

I heard the kid moan.

I didn't know where I was. I was just driving away from the crash scene, through more residential streets where the houses all looked alike, and then onto another main road, past shops and pubs. People were looking at the car as we went past. It must've been a sight.

'I know who you are,' the boy said, hoarsely. 'I know what you did.'

I saw a building site and swung around and rolled in past the temporary fencing. It was a housing development, half done with skeletons of buildings along a rough road. I didn't see anyone working, no vehicles parked. I pulled into one of the brick shells.

I got out the car and opened the back door. He kicked at me, opened the other door and tried to scramble free. I grabbed his foot and hauled him out. He hit the dusty ground face first. The wind was out of him. I checked him for weapons and found a phone, which was locked.

I rolled him over. He focused on me, swung a fist at my leg then coughed and rolled back over and spat dry, dusty spittle mixed with blood.

'Who'd you work for?' I said, when he'd finished retching.

He breathed heavily and looked at me sideways.

'No one.'

I kicked him in the ribs, not hard, just enough to wake him up. His face crunched in pain.

'NO ONE.'

'How did you find me then?'

'I followed you from my mum's.'

I didn't know what that meant. I couldn't work it out.

'My name's Marriot,' he said.

Now I remembered Green had told me Marriot had a son. Somehow, it hadn't sunk in, hadn't seemed real. I suppose I would've had to think of Marriot as a father, as a normal person and not as the dying animal I'd left him, blood pouring from his gut as he'd tried to crawl away from me.

Now I understood why this kid was such a lousy tail, why he was such a fucking lousy killer, missing a sitting duck, missing a mountain. Still, he'd almost wiped me out. I was getting old, dumber by the hour.

I tried to think of something to say. I said, 'Uh.'

He pulled himself up to his knees, resting on the palms of his hands. He waited there.

'Well?' he said to the dust. 'You going to kill me now?'

It was a good question. I thought about it for a couple of seconds, but the will wasn't there.

'No,' I said.

He stood slowly, keeping his eyes on me all the time. When he was upright, he was no higher than my chest. I could've killed him with one blow. I probably should've done. It was stupid to let him go, wasn't it?

The thing is, I just didn't care about him. He was nothing to me, just some nuisance. Sure, he wanted to murder me, and I cared about someone trying to kill me, but now that

84

he was there, below my chin, I just wanted him to go away. That he wanted to avenge his father didn't bother me. It should've done. It would've, once.

Maybe, too, I understood what he was after. I'd killed his old man. That was something. That was pain, maybe the same as the pain I felt.

I told him to fuck off. He looked at me like he suspected a trap of some kind. I turned away from him and went back to the car. I wiped the steering wheel, the gearstick, the handbrake, the door handles, and tossed the keys into a pile of sand.

When I'd done that, I saw the kid was still there, staring at me.

'Fuck off,' I said again.

He was deflated now, the anger gone, the fear too. He had guts, I suppose. I had to admire that.

'I don't get it.'

'What?'

'Do you know who I am?'

'You just told me.'

'Doesn't that mean anything to you?'

'Yeah. Now go.'

He wasn't what I would've thought of as Marriot's son. He had a plummy voice, like he'd gone to a public school. And there was no violence in him. There'd been anger, sure, but that had gone. Probably, it was because I'd been to see his mum and she must've called him and he'd panicked, thinking she was in danger.

He started to leave, then stopped and turned back to me.

'I want to kill you,' he said.

'Join the queue.'

'You killed my dad.'

'Yeah.'

I was waiting for him to go. Then, I'd go too, in another direction. But he wasn't budging. I stood and looked at him. He was skinny, and his clothes didn't fit him well, as if he'd been bigger and had been ill. There were creases in his face that shouldn't have been there. Yes, he'd felt pain. Maybe, he'd imagined coming face to face with his father's killer, and exacting revenge. And now, failing, and yet still living, he didn't know what to do.

'He was a good man,' the boy said. 'He loved me and my mum.'

Now I was getting tired of him.

'Your dad was a cunt.'

He came at me, head down, charging again, as he'd done in his car. I swatted him aside and he crashed into a stack of bricks. He tried to stand, and staggered and fell back to the ground, landing on his knees. He put his head down, so that it looked like he was trying to kiss the ground. I heard him sniffling. He wiped his eyes and stood and faced me. There were grazes on his hands and face, his jeans were torn at one knee, blood darkening the denim.

'You didn't have to kill him,' he said. 'You didn't have to do that.'

I said, 'He killed someone I knew.'

I thought he'd get angry again, deny it all. But his shoulders dropped and his face turned to the ground. He wasn't like me. He wasn't a killer, an avenger. He wasn't ruled by the rage that burned his blood, or by the murder that wrenched and twisted at his heart, darkening the blood with its darkness. He was just a kid who was the son of a man I'd killed, and he didn't know what to do about it.

He turned away. I think he knew what I was telling him was the truth. I think he just hadn't wanted to believe it.

'Who was he?' he was saying to the air. 'The man he killed.'

'She.'

'Oh,' he said. 'Will you go after my mum?'

'I don't care about your mum. Or you.'

Now he started to walk away, but something came to me and I called after him. He stopped, but still wouldn't look at me.

'Your old man,' I said. 'He wasn't in it alone. There was someone else, a copper, called Glazer. Remember him?'

Now he looked at me. I don't think he'd heard my question. He said, 'He loved me.'

Then he was gone. I suppose I could've gone after him, shaken the information from him, if he even knew it. I could've done, but I only watched him walk away. I think I envied him. He'd tried and failed. And that was enough. He'd tried and failed and was back to his quiet, ordinary life. Christ, what I wouldn't have given for that.

But trying and failing wasn't enough for me. Blood was enough, anyone's blood, everyone's blood. And nothing less.

TWELVE

It took me a couple of hours to get back to Browne's. I had no idea where I was, and I didn't want to ask anyone; that would put me in their mind and if the law were around investigating a car crash, someone might remember me.

So I walked, the pavement moving from time to time, getting further from me, then closer until I had to stop and wait for it to make up its fucking mind.

I found a bus stop. When I saw one for Walthamstow Central, I got on and took a seat at the back and closed my eyes.

When the bus terminated, I got a cab.

London went by in a waking dream, a group of shadows, each blurring into the other, all a million shades of black. I saw people's faces, old and tired and as blurred as the rest of it. I saw buildings that looked as if they'd been washed in dirt. I saw traffic stall and move and stall again, as if the street was coughing it all up like it was some clot.

Brenda. The name ran through my mind, but I couldn't put a face to it, to her.

Brenda.

I sat with my forehead against the window and saw it all as it slid past. And saw my life slide along with it, being coughed up by time, coughed up and spat out. Browne was right. I was killing myself. And I didn't much care.

I'd done this before, hadn't I – been like this, felt like this? I didn't seem to be living a life. I seemed to be reliving it.

I opened my eyes. I was in a car – in a cab. I was heading back somewhere, heading back to someone. Wasn't I?

I heard Brenda, speaking softly, her voice not even a whisper, more the echo of a whisper.

'Joe,' she said. 'Joe.'

But when I looked, she wasn't there, and I felt cold, although I didn't know why. I was all mixed up. I felt like I'd just come from some operating theatre. They'd cut me open and taken everything out and stitched me back up.

When the cab stopped, I bunged the driver a fistful of notes and staggered out. I heard him telling me I'd given him too much, but it didn't mean anything to me. I couldn't even work out what it was I'd given him too much of.

I had trouble getting the key into the lock. The fucking lock was moving as much as the ground was, and the door was worse. I must've made a racket because I saw the living room curtain twitch and then the door opened and I fell in. Browne heaved me along the hallway enough to close the door. I heard him curse me under his breath.

THIRTEEN

'Is it your head, Joe?' she said.

She put a hand up to my cheek and let it rest there. It felt cool and soft and seemed to take the heat from my face, the pain from my head. I wanted her to never move her hand.

'Yeah.'

She leaned in close to me. I could smell her perfume, warm and sweet, mixed with the smell of cigarettes and the wine on her breath. She smelled like comfort and all I wanted to do was sink into her and stay there.

But I had things to do. It was ten o'clock and I had to be out at midnight to meet a bloke. It was a protection job, nothing much, but he was an Arab and liked to cruise dodgy places. He wanted someone frightening with him and I'd get half a grand for a few hours work. I couldn't turn it down. I hadn't told Brenda. I don't know why. I think because I knew she wanted company that night.

She'd called me up in the afternoon.

'Will you come over tonight?' she'd said.

I knew she needed me. She'd usually say something like, 'Are you coming over tonight?' Or, 'What are you up to, Joe?' Or, sometimes, 'Hey, Joe, pop over, if you're not robbing any banks.'

She'd been drinking and was half-cut by the time I got there. Before either of us had said anything, she was in my arms, holding me tightly.

'What's wrong?' I said, thinking someone had hurt her and that I was going to have to pay Marriot a visit and settle this thing once and for all, get Brenda off his books. I think I just wanted an excuse to do that.

'There's nothing wrong,' she said into my chest. 'I just wanted to see you.'

There was a lie in there, maybe two. Anyway, something was wrong.

'I'm here.'

'Yes.'

She took my hand and pulled me into the flat. I could feel how unsteady she was. Her hand was loose in mine, as if she barely had the strength to hold on.

She pushed me down onto the sofa and then sat herself across my legs so that she could lay her head on my chest.

I wanted to ask her what was wrong again, but I'd learned that sometimes there was no answer to that question – or, rather, that she wouldn't give one. So, I just held her while she put to rest whatever horrors were assaulting her.

I don't know how long we were like that.

I kept thinking about the job. These rich Arabs splashed the money about like they were kicking dirt off their boots, and they drank when they were away from their embassies and families. If he had a few drinks and I pushed a couple of blokes around, made like they were acting dangerous, he might splash some more of his dosh my way. I could use it.

Meanwhile, I held Brenda and felt her body heat, felt her softness, felt her breath touching me. It was good. Her body was like a drug making my head clear, pain free, making me forget things.

I think I slept. I think we both did. At some point, though, I felt her shuddering. At first I thought she must've been cold, I pulled her tighter to me. Her body was limp, except for the shaking.

She looked up at me, and I never saw any adult look so like a child.

'No way out, Joe,' she said. 'No way out.'

She was still drunk, but in a sober way, not quite slurring her words, just desperate and failing to hide it, like drunks get sometimes. It was like Browne said, I suppose; alcohol, the unleasher of the darkness, the freer of deranged thoughts. Only, with Brenda, it was the freer of fear and failure.

I pushed the braids of her hair back so that I could see her face. She was looking at me, in that unfocused way, so that it seemed like she was looking at something a few inches behind my eyes.

I was starting to think I might not make the job that night. It was a lot of money to blow. Worse, it would give me a bad rep. If another job like that came up, they'd think twice about it. I didn't care. Fuck them.

'Tell me,' I said.

She put her head back against my chest. I knew she wouldn't say what was tormenting her. At the time I just thought it was her work, the johns, the films, the dirt of it all. But we'd been over that and she wouldn't quit.

I heard her speak, but it was so quiet I couldn't hear the words. I thought she must've been asleep again. But she wasn't.

'I never told you,' she said, looking up at me.

'Told me what?'

'I can't have children.'

'Okay,' I said, not knowing what else I was supposed to say.

'Haven't you ever wanted children, Joe?'

'No,' I said.

I'd never thought about it before. It was just one of those things that I never connected with myself. Kids, a woman, a home. All that stuff was for other people, normal, average people living their normal, average lives. Some of them might've been happy. It meant nothing to me. It was like asking someone doing life in the nick what he'd do if he was free; it didn't do anything except remind him he wasn't free.

We were quiet for a while. I could feel her heart beating through my chest. I could smell the sweet shampoo scent of her hair. I'd taken some pills for my head and they were making me fuzzy, but they were numbing the pain and I felt okay.

But the longer the quiet went on, the more I thought about what Brenda had said, and the more I wondered why she'd said it. Slowly, I began to think maybe her wanting to tell me that was the reason she wanted to see me. Then I started to wonder what it meant.

Then I realized something else; she was crying. I hadn't noticed because she'd been trying to keep it quiet and had hidden her face from me, burying it in my shoulder.

Only then did I understand what she'd done. She'd bared herself to me, opened herself up and let me see the thing that probably hurt her more than anything else.

It was another of those sick jokes that the world spits at you; here was a woman who loved children, who risked her life, lost her life, to protect them, and she couldn't bear any herself while all over the place teenage girls were popping them out every nine months. You saw them in the high streets, pram in one hand, fag in the other, chatting to their mates while their babies cried to be fed.

I wondered if she'd told anyone else that. I thought she probably hadn't. She didn't have close friends and her track record with men had been lousy.

And I, dumb fucking cunt that I was, had brushed her off without a thought.

I lifted Brenda off me and turned her around. At first, she wouldn't look at me, but I kept holding her, one of my thick hands on each of her slim shoulders, and she finally lifted her wet eyes to mine. They sparkled. They were wide with fear and pain and, for a moment, I was lost in them.

What I said then I knew to be true. I hadn't ever known it until that moment. What I said was, 'I would have had children with you. That would've been okay with me.'

It all came out. She laughed and sobbed at the same time. She crushed herself into my body, as if she was clinging to me in a wild storm. I think that's exactly what she was doing.

Finally, when she'd let all the grief out, emptied herself of the horrors – for then, at least – she wiped her eyes with the back of her hand, ran her sleeve over her wet nose and pushed herself away from me, her hands flat on my chest. She looked at me and smiled.

'Have you ever seen my photos?' she said.

When I told her I hadn't, she scampered over to a chest of drawers and tugged the bottom one open. She came back with an old album and sat on the sofa beside me.

Fuck the Arab. Let him trawl his dark places without protection, see how long he'd last. The rest of us had to do it.

'Look, Joe,' Brenda said.

She pointed to the yellowing photo of a young black girl with pigtails. She was wearing school uniform and a smile as wide as the tie around her neck. She stood before a front door. Her knees were together, making her look self-conscious, nervous.

'That's me,' Brenda was saying. 'My first day of secondary school. Me mum was so proud. I remember I was nervous and excited. I don't think I was happy, but I'm smiling, so…'

She started turning the pages of the old album, the thick pages making cracking sounds as they unstuck. She showed me a girl with a doll, a girl with friends at some party, a girl mixed in with a large family.

She turned another page. I saw Brenda, a young teen now, with an older woman. They were sitting on a brown sofa surrounded by wrapped boxes. Both were leaning forward. Brenda's knees were together, her hands holding each other in her lap. They were both smiling, but Brenda's wasn't the natural smile I'd seen on the first picture, not the smile she smiled to me.

95

'Me mum,' she said. 'That was my birthday. Can't remember which one.'

Then she pointed to another picture. Here, she was still young, thin. She was in a meadow on a bright sunny day. There was a man next to her. He was white with shaggy brown hair and a narrow, sharp face. He wore jeans and a T-shirt. He was ordinary looking. He could've been anything. He had his arm around her shoulders. She didn't look too different from that girl in the school uniform, only she wasn't smiling so much now. Her knees were together still, and her hands were clasped in front of her.

'Me stepdad,' she said.

She turned the pages more quickly now, racing through her life, only giving me half a chance to see it. I suppose that's what she'd always done; showed me parts, skipped over lots.

She paused for a moment on a page with two photos. Her hand covered the bottom one as her fingers stroked the top. It was a photo of two women on a beach somewhere. The sky was cloudy, so I thought it was probably in Britain. I could've asked her, I suppose, but she seemed to be lost in the picture, her eyes a bit dreamy. She was remembering the day, the moment, and, again, it was like she'd forgotten I was there.

One of the women was Brenda, dressed in red shorts and a white blouse. She had a straw sunhat and sunglasses. The other woman had pale skin and long, straight, black hair. She wore jeans and a T-shirt with some logo. She had dark glasses, like Brenda, and the same straw hat so that I guessed they'd bought them in the same place, maybe on that day.

Both women were holding ice creams.

It was a happy time, a happy memory.

Then Brenda sighed and closed the book. She chucked it to the floor and curled up and rested herself against me. After a while, I could feel her chest rising and falling, and I could hear the small bubbly noise in the back of her throat.

I carried her to the bedroom. I put her to bed then took my clothes off and climbed in beside her as softly as I could. The mattress flattened under me and her body rolled over so that it was up against my side, and I could feel her hot, soft skin. She put her hand out in her sleep and it lay on my chest, her fingertips just below my chin.

I didn't sleep so good. I lay there, afraid to move in case I woke her, and I wondered what was going on in her head. I don't think it occurred to me to ask her. I don't know why that was.

FOURTEEN

'Is it your head, Joe?' she said, her hand on my cheek, not smooth and cool now but cold.

'You're not here,' I heard myself say. 'You're dead.'

Then she was clamping my head tightly, one hand either side, and staring at me in wide-eyed dread.

'What do you mean?' she said. 'Joe? What the bloody hell are you on about? I'm right here. I'm not dead.'

'Brenda?'

Was that really her? Was this a memory? Did it happen?

'Joe?' she said. 'Joe. Look at me. What's wrong? Joe.'

There was panic in her voice, and I thought, Don't be scared. I mumbled something. At least, I think it was me.

'Joe?'

That wasn't her voice. Her face fell apart in front of me.

'Joe. Look at me.'

Everything was blurry.

'Look at me.'

Then I saw Browne standing over me. It was gloomy, but I could see him well enough. There was a look of pain on his face.

'Joe?' he said. 'Can you see me?'

I tried to speak, but my mouth wouldn't move. I nodded.

He lifted my head and put a glass of water to my mouth. I let the stuff slip down my throat. Then he took a cloth and wiped the water around my lips. He put my head down and it sank forever into the pillow.

When I opened my eyes again, he was still there, only now the pain had gone from his expression and, instead, he glared at me. I could see he was sober. That's probably why he was in such a lousy mood.

I expected a lecture. But all he said was, 'Do you know where you are?'

'Yeah.'

He bent over and looked into my eyes with one of those small torches. He moved his hands over to the back of my skull, gently probing. His hands felt like they were padded with cotton wool.

Then he moved my head. It wasn't much of a movement, but it felt to me like someone had turned the world upside down.

'You've given me something.'

'Yes. For the pain. Now don't move.'

Pain? Had I been in pain? I couldn't remember.

'What pain?'

He stood up and looked at me as if I was dying and I realized the pain I thought I'd seen in his expression was just a reflection of what he was looking at.

'You were in a state.'

'What do you mean?'

He reached to the small cabinet by the side of the bed, took out a small tube of pills and poured a couple into his hand. Then, as if he'd forgotten what he was about to do, he closed his hand and sat on the bed.

'You were screaming,' he said to the carpet. 'Calling her name. Brenda's.'

'I was dreaming,' I said, knowing it was a lie, and knowing too that he would know it was a lie.

'Yes,' he said.

He handed me the pills and the glass of water. He helped me lift my head enough to take the tablets. I didn't ask him what they were. I didn't much care.

'You hit your head again,' he said.

'Someone else hit it.'

'Ah.'

'With a car.'

'Of course.'

I tried to sit up by myself and bile filled my mouth and I threw up over the carpet.

'Idiot,' Browne said. I collapsed back. 'You know, one day you'll go to sleep and that'll be that. You'll wake up dead.'

I woke up, still alive, and rolled over and felt like someone had dumped a hundredweight of bricks on me. I usually felt like that when I woke. Just old age, I suppose. Well, that and getting run over by a car now and then.

I lay in bed for a while, trying to remember what I had to do, trying to forget what I'd done, what I hadn't done. After all that, I stared at the ceiling and let myself get things together bit by bit.

When I'd stared at the ceiling enough I tried to remember what the fuck had being going on. All the stuff with the cab and Brenda came into my mind in bits, and I tried to recall it in the way you try and hold onto a dream you've had – the more you want to remember it, the more it slips away from you. It was like trying to put a hand up and stop time moving.

And then I remembered Browne standing over me and his face telling me I was fucked, even if he wouldn't put it into words.

I hadn't dreamt about her again. I didn't know if that was good or bad. It didn't matter. It wasn't going to stop me.

There was a grey light coming in through the window.

Or, at least, something grey was coming through the window. I could feel the coldness outside. Or maybe it was inside. Maybe it was in me.

I took a shower to try and get some blood running. Then I did some exercises, as much as I could with a half-ruined body. Everything hurt, except my head. That was just numb. Maybe if my head started hurting my body would be numb. Maybe, one day, everything would be numb. I tried not to think about it.

When I felt half-human, I got dressed and went slowly downstairs. There was no sign of Browne, and I wondered if he'd finally given up on me and left town.

I made an omelette and a cup of tea, strong and sweet. I finished those off and sat and thought about things some more. Then I cleaned my guns.

It all went back to that film; Brenda and a rich bloke and a young girl. I know the way of the world, the horrors, the hate. Christ, I've seen enough, done enough myself. But when I first saw that film, it hit me like a fast cross to the jaw. It left me reeling, shaking, sick.

Marriot had set it up, and probably arranged the secret filming. Brenda had taken part in the film only to make sure she could get a copy to send to the law. She never would've allowed a child to go through that shit otherwise. Then she went and sent it off to Glazer, the vice copper given the job of nailing those responsible for the immigrant sex trade. But, of course, Glazer was bent and grassed her up to Marriot.

What Brenda did was about the bravest thing I ever heard of. But she hated herself for it. That's what she was

102

talking to Browne about, that time – the need to forget, the need to hide from something with booze. The need to hide from herself.

Two things about all that were having this knock-on effect. Firstly, the man in the film. Whoever he was, Dunham wanted him in his control, which meant he wanted the DVD as blackmail. That meant the bloke in the film was someone important, powerful, useful to Dunham.

Secondly, there were copies about. I had one, which Brenda had left me, and which I'd only recently found. Dunham knew I had that copy. That made me a target. But Paget must've had a copy too, to get protection from Dunham. I couldn't believe that Paget would be able to bluff Dunham if he hadn't had a copy. My guess was that he'd hidden it somewhere and had made a sample copy to show Dunham, enough that he got what he wanted, which was Dunham's protection from me. Paget's copy was lost, then.

That hadn't worked out too well for him. So, if I had the only copy, Dunham wanted it from me. So too did Compton and his mob, who were after Glazer as part of their anti-corruption fight. Compton had told me that if I wanted justice for Brenda's death, I'd hand over something to put Glazer away. I didn't give a fuck about their justice.

But, of course, I probably wasn't the only one to have a copy. Glazer might've had one.

When I felt up to it, I left the house and took a tour of the block, my hand on my Makarov the whole time, my eyes darting this way and that. When I saw a man walking a dog, I stopped and watched him until he was out of sight. Then I watched some more to make sure he didn't come back. When a car went by, I made a note of the make and number plate.

It was a clear morning, bright and cold with that biting air that cuts through your skin. It felt good. It felt clean. The sky was blue for once. Sounds carried on the crisp air and, as if the air was seeping into me, my thoughts started to untangle themselves.

A thought occurred to me: how did Paget find out the DVD was important to someone like Dunham? Certainly, Dunham hadn't known, so it must've been Paget who told him. But how had *he* found out? If he and Marriot had known how important their blackmail target was, they'd have used the film a long time ago.

I tried to work that out but gave up. It didn't seem important.

I'd just come back as Browne was crawling down the stairs. He was wearing blue pyjamas and a red dressing gown. The pyjamas were ten sizes too big. The dressing gown had holes and stains.

'Morning,' he said. 'Still alive, I see. Good, good. I mean, you are alive, aren't you? Sometimes it's hard to tell.'

He shuffled past me, his slippers half on, his dressing gown half off, his hair all over the place. He went to the mat by the front door and picked up *The Times*, folded it and put it under his arm. I started up the stairs and stopped and turned and looked at the newspaper.

'Since when do you have that delivered?' I said. Browne looked at the paper beneath his arm, and then at me.

'I don't,' he said. 'Not since you came here.'

He unfolded the newspaper. A piece of white card fell

out. He stooped to pick it up, read it to himself.

'It's for you,' he said, holding the card out to me.

He folded his paper up again and shuffled off to the kitchen.

The note read: 'Meet me at the usual place. E.'

It was quiet in the cafe. The breakfast trade had gone and now there were only a few punters plus the waitress, who was behind the counter putting cakes into that glass display thing they have. I guessed there was someone back in the kitchen, too.

Anyway, I hadn't seen anyone hanging about outside, and the bunch in here seemed harmless enough.

There was an old couple, silent and slow. The woman, her lunch finished, sipped her tea and stared at the floor while the man wiped bread through what was left of his egg and ketchup.

There was a young bloke, dressed in an army jacket that must've been twenty years older than he was. A tattoo snaked up his neck. He was reading a book, the plate of spaghetti in front of him getting cold.

Then there was the middle-aged bloke in a pinstriped suit and bright shiny brogues who sat and picked at a Danish pastry while he tapped away at a laptop. He was the odd one out in a place like this. He was overweight, and his suit was tight and I couldn't see any bulges anywhere. His hands were clean, his face was soft. He clocked me looking at him and his eyes widened a bit and he looked quickly back at his computer. I figured he was just what he seemed; a businessman with time on his hands and a hunger for pastries.

Eddie Lane sat at a table over the far side, in the corner, his back to the wall. There was nobody on the nearby tables. I strolled over and sat.

He was busy stirring his coffee, keeping me waiting. I let him play his game.

Eddie was Vic Dunham's right hand, and more. He was smooth and black and handsome and smart and very, very deadly.

The last time I saw Eddie and Dunham was just before I went over to Dunham's house and killed Paget and started their war with Cole.

'Hey, Joe,' he said to the coffee.

'What do you want?'

He stopped moving the spoon and looked at me, that amused gleam in his eyes.

'I want us all to be happy.'

'Right.'

Above us, the strip light flickered and made a sputtering noise.

I glanced around again, unsure of myself, of Eddie, of everything. It was like I was in some play; everyone knew their parts – everyone except me.

The old man had finished mopping up his egg yolk and now was slurping his tea. The old bird opposite watched him over the rim of her mug. How many times had she watched him eat, drink? What was it like, to be with someone for decades? To watch them grow old? I hadn't heard them speak yet.

'Are you tooled up?' Eddie said.

'Yes.'

He nodded and went back to stirring his coffee. The waitress had noticed me now and came plodding over, as slowly as she could. Her feet made a sticking noise each time they left the vinyl-tiled floor. It sounded the same as the flickering light, only slower. It didn't seem real, none of it did.

When the waitress finally made it to our table, she took a pad out of her pocket and held a pen over it.

'Something to eat?' she said to me.

'No.'

'Drink?'

'Tea.'

She didn't bother to write that down.

'You got a radio here?' Eddie said to her.

She looked at him as if he'd accused her of gobbing in his coffee.

'Yeah,' she said defensively.

'Put it on, will you?'

She plodded back the way she'd come, even more slowly, as if the sticky tiles were gradually dragging her down.

We waited, Eddie and me. He stirred his coffee. I watched him stir his coffee. We listened to the flickering light, and to the clanking of plates from the kitchen and the clinking of knives and forks on ceramic.

Eddie finally had enough of stirring his coffee. He tossed the spoon down.

'You think Bobby Cole's gonna save you?' he said, watching the waitress fade away.

'No.'

Now he moved his eyes back to me.

'Well, you're right about that. Cole won't last much longer. We've got him, Joe. Vic's got him.'

'You think I care about Cole?'

'No. I just think you'd better not get on Cole's side.'

'I don't have sides.'

'Don't you?'

The radio came on. Static-filled music came from a tinny speaker. It was good enough to cover our voices.

'So, you're gonna wait it out at Browne's for everything to cool off. Or wait for something to happen, maybe?'

'Maybe.'

'Fuck's sake, Joe. You're a stubborn cunt, know that? There's a war going on and you're in the middle.'

'You haven't told me what you want.'

'I want you to leave, go away, lie low for a while.'

'Is this a warning?'

'It's a friendly word.'

'When did you start becoming friendly?'

That made him smile.

'I'm always friendly, Joe. Aren't we friends?'

'You're nobody's friend, Eddie. Neither am I.'

'You're paranoid.'

I told him to fuck off. He smiled even more.

'Don't be like that.'

The waitress came back with a mug of tea. She dropped it in front of me and threw some packets of sugar and a spoon onto the table. Then she scribbled the bill out and put it down between us.

She looked at Eddie, and at Eddie's coffee. When she was happy she'd made the point that people like us were a waste of her valuable time, she strolled back to her cakes.

'How should I be?' I said to Eddie.

'You should be smart. Leave London.'

'Why?'

'You're dead here, even if you live, which you won't.'

Now it was my turn to stir. I picked up a couple of sachets of sugar and tore them open and poured the sugar into my tea, nice and slowly, one grain at a time. When I'd done that, I stirred. Let Eddie fucking wait.

What I didn't understand was this act of his, this friendly warning. He didn't give a shit about me, or anyone. Everything he did had a reason. Finding that reason was the tough part.

I stirred. Eddie waited, knowing what I was doing. My spoon clinked the mug. The tea whirled round and round, like my head, like my fucking life.

I could hear the sound of the traffic outside, whirring by, going around like the tea in my mug. I could smell frying fat and coffee and plastic.

I stopped stirring, put the spoon down. The tea carried on spinning. The light kept on flickering.

The old bloke spoke at last. He said, 'You want something else? Jean?'

She didn't answer him. Turning to look, I saw them side-on. The old fellow was looking at the woman, waiting for an answer. She still had the mug up to her lips, but she wasn't drinking from it. She just looked at the bloke over the rim. He gave up and went back to his bread.

There was something strange in that and my hackles rose. Everything here was weird, and I thought again that I was stuck in some play not knowing what I was supposed to do.

I tried to ignore that feeling. I turned my attention back to my tea.

'I'm staying,' I said to Eddie, watching as the brown liquid slid round and round so slowly now that it was barely moving at all.

'Leave London, Joe. While you still can.'

'Why would you care?'

'Call it a favour. Because we go back.'

'Nice of you.'

'Fine. You're not important, that's why. You're a sideshow, but Vic wants you out and he's as stubborn as you and while he's hell-bent on getting you, he's losing sight of the bigger picture.'

'So you're here off your own bat.'

'I'm here unofficially, yes.'

'What would Dunham say to that?'

I saw his jaw muscle flicker. The gleam in his eyes dimmed a bit.

'Don't push it. Like I said, I'm doing you a favour. I'm the fucking gift horse.'

'If I'm just a sideshow, why does Dunham want me?'

'Because you made him look stupid, weak. You know he can't have that. He has to destroy you, Joe. No choice.'

'He's had plenty of time.'

'I've managed to hold him off.'

'Then why don't you kill me now? Have done with it,

111

take my head back to Dunham. And don't give me that bollocks about us being friends.'

When he didn't say anything to that, I said, 'It's the film, isn't it? That's why you haven't killed me yet? You want a copy. I've got one.'

Two girls came into the cafe then and sat down at the table next to us. My skin prickled. They were both young, both had that Celtic thing going on, the white skin, the red-blonde hair.

Eddie picked up his spoon and started stirring his coffee again. One day maybe he'd drink the fucking stuff.

One of the girls had a slim, athletic figure. She had freckles on her arms and a long white neck. Her pale blue eyes seemed paler beneath the narrow arched eyebrows. Her hair was long and straight, and the colour of honey. She had a band of flowers tattooed around her wrist, as if they were her hopes and dreams and she carried them where she could see them, remember them now and then.

The other girl had curves, all in the right places. She was a redhead too, only it was darker and curly, like gold thread that had rusted. Her eyes were large and a kind of blue-green-grey, the colour changing as she moved her head. And they were soft eyes which looked as if, sometimes, they'd melt away and take her some place quiet.

When they'd first sat down, I'd thought they might be law, but I could see they weren't. They didn't have the core of decay that the police always carry with them. Even the best undercover coppers can't hide that rot, that disease that infects them, as if their soul had gangrene.

No, these girls were too clean for that. They'd just

112

straggled in and taken a seat without thinking. They were too innocent to notice what others could see; the danger that lived with people like Eddie and me, the threat, the murder in our blood.

So we said nothing for a while, me and Eddie. He stirred his coffee, gazing at the table top as if he was just waiting for a friend. I watched Eddie and scanned the cafe, making sure nobody was looking at us too closely. I could hear the girls at the next table as they chattered. They talked about clothes and music and men, laughing now and then, teasing each other.

My mind started to wander, and I thought about Brenda and me, sitting, as we sometimes used to, in a cafe like this, me probably stirring my tea while Brenda nattered about clothes or music or whatever, teasing me, as she used to do.

And for a moment – just a moment – I wanted to be at that table with those girls, just so that I could sit there and listen to them, just so that I could be normal for a while, unknown, unknowing, another mug who worked five days out of seven for forty years, and then retired and died. I wanted to be with those girls and be normal for a while, and be ignored. Sometimes that was all I wanted; to be ignored.

I noticed Eddie looking at the girls, probably wondering, like I had, if they were plain-clothes. Then he flicked his gaze over to me, and a sly glimmer came into his sly eyes.

Maybe I'd given something away, a slip, a flicker of expression.

'I have a thing for redheads,' he said. 'Their bodies are more sensitive. Did you know that, Joe? Must be their skin. You touch them and they melt.'

I had to wonder why he was telling me. I didn't care, and he knew it.

The girls had noticed him now. He flashed them his handsome, movie-star smile. They went for him straight away.

He leaned towards them.

'I'm Eddie,' he said.

The woman with pale blue eyes blushed and smiled. When she did that, her eyes got even lighter so that they were the blue of a clear summer evening sky.

'What're your names?' Eddie said.

'Karen,' said the one with pale eyes. She spoke in a Scots accent. Glaswegian, I thought. The other girl had an English accent, posh, smooth. She said her name was Vicky. Eddie told them he'd always liked redheads.

'Maybe it's a black thing,' he was saying. 'We get bored of brunettes, and blondes are a bit too common these days. It's not often you see a proper redhead. Now I'm looking at two of them.'

They watched him, wide-eyed, as if he was doing some magic trick. He did that to women, and he knew it. He said, 'My friend here's just got out of the nick, and he hasn't seen a woman for a while, so we were wondering if you'd like to join us.'

Then, as one, they looked at me, and their smiles fell away, and their sparkling eyes dulled, and all that was left was a kind of fear. I couldn't blame them for that. I knew what I looked like to people. I knew what I did to them. I wasn't the kind who could be ignored. Maybe that was my curse. I felt it, though. Somewhere inside, I felt a stab of pain.

114

The one with curly hair looked at her watch.

'Well...' she said, looking at her friend for support.

'We have to go,' the other one said. 'We only came in for a moment.'

They hadn't even ordered.

As they were walking out, Eddie turned back to me, that slyness dancing in his eyes.

'You've got a way with the birds, Joe. I never seen two women scarper so fast.'

Now I understood what he was doing. It was another of his games. He was putting me down a bit, letting me know what power he had, what I didn't have.

I tried to pretend I didn't care about all that. I had a gun, I told myself. Fuck the rest.

But that was a lie. I did care, and I couldn't understand why. Maybe it was just that I missed being with Brenda. Maybe it was that simple.

But Eddie had made a mistake. Wanting Brenda only reminded me that she was gone. And for that, people would suffer. For that, I'd make the whole fucking world suffer.

'Happy now?' I said.

'I got rid of 'em, didn't I?'

'Yeah.'

I was tired of all his shit. My head was starting to wander again. I needed it clear. I needed to know what this was really about. Things were happening in the background that I was missing. Eddie was toying with me, I knew that much. I said, 'You still haven't told me what you want? Is it the DVD?'

He leaned back in his seat.

'We want it, sure. You know that. But I don't think you're gonna give it to us.'

'Right.'

He sighed, and his sigh said I was being dumb. I wasn't doing what I was supposed to be doing. I was being childish.

'Why do you want it?' he said.

'I could ask you the same thing. You know what's on it.'

There it was again, that flicker in his jaw. He was angry about this, whatever he pretended. On one hand, he worked for Dunham, and he was loyal, I had to admit that. Fuck, I even respected it. But Dunham had given protection to Paget. And now Dunham wanted a DVD of some rich cunt with a child so that he could use it for his own means.

I think that bothered Eddie. I didn't get that. Eddie was too smart to let his conscience be affected by that sort of thing – that was, if he had a conscience, which I doubted.

'Vic wants it,' he said. 'And he wants Glazer too.'

'What do you know about Glazer?'

'Paget told us everything, so don't think you've got a lead on us there. Vic wants that film, Joe. That's all that matters.'

'Fuck Dunham. And fuck you.'

That made Eddie smile, but it was a weak smile, as if, privately, he agreed with me. He bent forward and took a sip of coffee.

'Who's the man in the film?' I said.

He didn't even bother answering that one. He just put his coffee down. That was all the answer I'd expected.

'The girl in the film,' I said, and saw Eddie's jaw tighten again, 'she's about the same age as Dunham's daughter.'

116

I don't know why I said that. It didn't make any difference, and I knew it. But, still, I'd said it. Eddie didn't speak for a moment. He gazed at his coffee. He wasn't stirring it now. He was past those games.

'We saw an opportunity to exploit a situation,' he said to the coffee. 'It's the business we're in. Don't get sentimental about these things. But you want Glazer. Why?'

'He was part of it. Maybe the worst part. If he hadn't grassed her up to Marriot, she might be alive.'

'Leave Glazer and maybe I can get Vic to leave you.'

'No good.'

'So you want it all neat and tidy and done up in a fucking bow.'

'I want blood.'

'Why, Joe? What does it matter? It's only business. You of all people should know that.'

'It's not business to me. It's personal.'

He leaned back again, a satisfied look on his face, as if he'd solved it all, proved something important.

'Personal. Yeah. That's the problem, isn't it? Since when did you start caring about things, Joe? About people?'

I didn't know what to say to that. He was watching me. I had the feeling he was trying to see how far I'd go, how much strength I had left, whether I was the same man he'd known for years.

After a while, he reached forward and drank some coffee.

'How's things, Joe?' he said, putting the mug back. 'How's Browne?'

Right then I knew Eddie knew exactly what had happened to Browne. He'd never given a shit about Browne. He wasn't

117

important, and Eddie didn't have curiosity for things that weren't important.

It was Dunham who'd sent Roy Buck. It must've been.

'He got hit,' I said. 'By a bloody train.'

'Oh?'

I watched him closely.

'Roy Buck,' I said. 'Remember him?'

'The Reaper?'

'Yeah.'

'I remember.'

'He was at Browne's place.'

'What did he want?'

I shrugged and kept watching Eddie.

He looked right back at me. He didn't twitch a muscle, didn't flicker. That amused glint was missing from his eyes. And I knew I was right. The bastard knew all about Buck.

What was more, he was letting me know he knew.

There was something wrong with that, though.

Eddie was subtle and smart, and, sure, sending Buck was the kind of thing he'd do. He knew there was something fucked up about Buck, that he'd break bones without thinking anything of it. And he knew that I'd know what Buck was capable of – Christ, he'd done it to me, hadn't he?

But Eddie also knew me well enough to know I wasn't scared of Buck, or anyone for that matter.

'I'll keep the DVD. I'll take my chances with Buck.'

'I might agree with you, but Vic won't. You know that. He'll come after you. And if he can't get you...'

He frowned.

'You'll let Buck loose on Browne.'

'Me?' he said.

'Do you think I care that much about Browne?' I said.

'I don't think anything. However, didn't we just establish that you did care for people?' He shook his head, smiling. 'Shit, Joe. You almost got me there. You want him, don't you? The bloke in the film.'

'I don't know who he is.'

'No, but you're going to try and find out. You're gonna get him yourself, aren't you? You won't. You won't even get close. You're not big enough, Joe. I'm right, aren't I? Is that what you want? His blood too?'

'I want everybody's blood.'

'Yeah. But it'll cost you. Blood for blood. Can you accept that?'

As he was saying all that, something else came into my mind. I thought back to the encounter with Buck. Had he been waiting for me to turn up? Was that the whole point of it, that it was a show of strength, a threat? Was that why he hadn't asked Browne any questions?

'Go to this place,' Eddie must've told him. 'Wait till the old man's alone and throw him around. The other man will come back. Leave when he does.'

But here was the problem: Dunham wouldn't have bothered with that shit. He would've wanted me taken somewhere and tortured or killed.

Instead of that, Eddie must've decided to try another way, a more subtle method. But he'd overplayed his hand, had been too subtle, had outsmarted himself. He was telling me he knew about Buck, sure, but he was telling me in his

119

roundabout way, meaning he wasn't telling me at all, only hinting at it, but knowing that I'd get the hint.

But I now knew that Eddie must've done that by himself, as a warning to me. And all that told me there was a split in the Dunham camp – or, rather, that Eddie wasn't happy with how things were going.

And letting me know that was his mistake.

Still, something wasn't right.

'If Dunham wants me so bad,' I said, 'he wouldn't let me leave London.'

'I told you, I could persuade him.'

'How? After what I did, why would he give me a chance?'

'He's a reasonable man. He's a businessman.'

'Bollocks. You're smart, Eddie. He's all emotion. You said it yourself, he's like me: full of rage. He'd want me dead. You know that.'

Eddie shifted in his seat.

'Yeah, well, that's a funny thing,' he said, not looking like he thought it was funny at all. 'You saved his daughter. He feels he owes you, so he's agreed to give you a chance to leave town. If you do that, he'll let you live.'

Saved his daughter? What the fuck was Eddie on about? Dunham had Paget stashed at his house and I found him there and killed him. What had Dunham's daughter got to do with that?

I remembered finding Paget, there in Dunham's huge country pad. I remembered his pale mask-face in the dark room, as it hovered, and the blade he had at the girl's throat, and her mother's scream. After that it was blood and mayhem and the two of us went at each other like madmen.

Fuck, we were mad with blood-lust, each fighting beyond our strength, fighting to the death.

He might've won that fight if it hadn't been for Dunham's wife. She was slim and young and about as close to a wisp of mist as any woman I'd ever known, but when Paget had threatened her daughter, she became ice, and as mad with the blood as the rest of us. My hand had been swollen, my gun empty and lying somewhere on the floor. Paget's blade was stuck in my good arm and I had a busted rib from one of his rounds. I was finished and I knew it and the only thing I cared about was that I'd failed Brenda, failed to feed the hunger for vengeance that bubbled inside me.

Then, at the moment when I should've been dead, Dunham's wife handed me my empty gun and I took it and smashed Paget's skull to a pulp. I suppose, in her eyes, it might have seemed like I'd saved her daughter.

As I was remembering that, something clicked in my mind.

It was that time Eddie and Dunham had tried to misdirect me, that first time I'd gone to Dunham's house when I'd been led there by Eddie. They'd taken me to the very place where they had Paget holed up and asked me if I knew where he was. That was Eddie's idea; another of his fucking subtleties.

Anyway, Dunham's wife had been there, reading a book or something. What now made that buzzing in my mind was the way Eddie had looked at her as we'd passed, and the way she'd ignored him, and the pain I saw on Eddie's face.

That was one of the things that tipped me to Paget's hiding there. I could see that she was angry with Eddie, and that it hurt him. In itself, it was nothing. But...

'It's not you, is it?' I said. 'The reason you're here. The offer to let me live if I leave London. It's not Dunham, and it's not you.'

'I'm making the offer. I told you that.'

'Yes. But when I asked if you were here off your own bat, you said you were here unofficially.'

'So?'

'It's not the same thing.'

'What are you getting at?'

'I'm getting at what the fuck you're up to.'

He sighed and leaned his elbows on the table. I heard chatter now from the old couple. The woman was talking about going to see her sister at the weekend and the bloke wanted to watch some football game on the telly.

The light flickered. The DJ on the radio talked about the pointless shit DJs talk about.

'It's her,' I said. 'That's why you're here. It's Dunham's wife.'

'Leave it, Joe,' he said quietly, looking down at the table top. 'There's stuff going on that's way above your head.'

'Dunham doesn't know you're here. He doesn't know you've made me this offer. He wouldn't give a fuck if I'd saved his daughter or not. He wants my guts, he'll try and get them. But his wife... if she thought I'd saved her daughter, she'd want to stop her husband killing me.'

'Leave it.'

'You're taking a risk, Eddie. Why would you do that?'

Now his gaze shot up, pinning me.

'Leave her out of it.'

His eyes blazed and I saw him for the killer he was.

'So I was right,' I said. 'Since when did you start caring about things, Eddie? About people?'

He tightened his fists until the veins popped out. Fuck him. Let him suffer for once.

'Shut the fuck up, Joe.'

'She hates you for what you're doing,' I said, turning the knife as much as I could, enjoying the pain I was causing, 'the people you're dealing with, the kinds of things they do to children, to girls like her daughter. She hates you and you can't stand it and she wants you to save me because I saved her daughter and you've got to do it for her—'

He shot up suddenly, the chair flying backwards and clattering a dozen feet away.

'Shut the fuck up,' he shouted.

Everything went quiet. Even the light seemed to stop making its flickering noise.

Eddie's hand had moved towards the inside of his buttoned jacket. I don't know if he was even aware he was doing it.

I knew everyone in the cafe would be staring at us, but I kept my eyes on Eddie, on his eyes, which were full of fury. I'd never before seen him lose his cool.

Christ, he was really hurting. He must've loved her and she was ignoring him, pushing him away, punishing him for what he was doing. And it was eating him up inside, the acid of despair corroding his guts so that he couldn't keep it down any more, and now he was spitting it out at me.

Then, as quickly as it came, his anger went. He smiled, but it was a strained, forced smile.

'You're not an idiot, Joe. I know that. Leave it be. Get out of town. I'll make sure you won't get hurt. Okay?'

'And Glazer? The DVD?'

'Business. That's all.'

The old lady said something then. She spoke softly to the man opposite her. What she said was, 'Who are you?'

He gazed at her with sadness. That's what it's like, I suppose, decades of life together and you end up not knowing the person sitting opposite you.

I stood to go. Eddie put a hand out and grabbed mine.

'Joe,' he said.

But I'd had enough of it all by then. I pulled my hand back.

'Fuck yourself, Eddie. And fuck Dunham too.'

He nodded, and his face was grim, his eyes suddenly dead.

'Alright,' he said, very quietly. 'You want it like that. Fine. I gave you a chance. Now you ain't got one. We want that DVD. Give it up or you'll get hurt.'

So, there it was. He'd chosen a side.

SEVENTEEN

Tina opened the door and stared at my chest. She took a step back and looked up. Her face was washed-out, her eyes wide and red-rimmed. She opened her mouth to speak, but nothing came out.

'Remember me?' I said.

She nodded and swallowed.

'Yes,' she said finally.

It'd been a few weeks since I'd seen her. Back then, I'd been looking for Paget and had been led to Tina's place, where he'd holed up for a while. Glazer had been here too, which was why I wanted to see her again.

Cole's men had been looking for Paget too, and they'd beaten me here, and then beaten her for information.

Her injuries had healed. Her hair looked bright and fresh, not that dark, lank blonde that I'd seen on her before, but she still looked thin and pale, still too frail, as if the blood didn't flow through her veins but, rather, fled from them.

After what had happened to her – first Kenny Paget appearing out of the blue, then Bobby Cole's men – I thought she'd run away screaming when she saw me. Instead, she didn't seem surprised that I was there. Maybe nothing surprised her any more.

'I need to talk to you,' I said.

'About Kenny?'

'In a way.'

She stood in the doorway, and now lifted one hand to the frame, as if to steady herself.

'Did... is he...?'

'He's dead.'

She blinked, then stood back.

'Is that why you came here? To tell me he's dead? I could've read that in the papers.'

'It won't be in any papers.'

'Oh.'

'And that's not why I came here.'

'What do you want then?'

'Can I come in?'

She didn't answer me but just turned around and walked away from the open door.

It was Tina who'd told me that Brenda had got hold of a copy of the film to use in evidence against Marriot and Paget.

'Brenda was a fool,' Tina had said. 'She thought she could out-think them, outsmart them.'

And it was Tina who'd told me that Brenda thought she was safe because she'd hooked up with some hard man, some monster.

Me.

She led me down the narrow hallway and into the small lounge. The ceiling was only a few inches above my head. I could've punched a hole through and reached right into the rooms upstairs.

The place was neat enough, but the building was cheap,

one of those prefab places, made of cardboard and only meant to last a few years but somehow standing half a century later. I wanted to smash it all down, just to get some room to move.

The children's toys had gone but the photos were still there, scattered about. There were the newer ones of her grandchildren that she wasn't allowed to see, and the old faded ones of her own kids who wouldn't come to visit.

She didn't look old enough to have grandkids. She was in her late-thirties, early forties, though, so I guess that made her old enough.

The TV was on, some woman droning on about fashion while models modelled clothes and some poncey bloke standing next to them nodded away like it was important. Tina dropped onto her sofa and picked up the remote and killed the TV. I sat opposite her.

'What's your name?' she said. 'Did you tell me? I can't remember.'

'Joe.'

'Joe. Yes. Is that it? Have you got a last name?'

'Yeah. Lots.'

'Right. So, Joe, what do you want?'

'I want to know about a man, Michael Glazer. He came over when Paget was hiding here a few weeks back.'

She nodded. 'Fat bloke. Bald. I remember him. But I didn't know him.'

'I need to find him.'

'You need to? Why?'

'He was the one Brenda sent the DVD to. He was a copper, still is. He was the one who told Marriot.'

127

She curled up, hugged her legs. Brenda used to do that sometimes. We'd be in bed, or she'd be on the sofa and I'd know she was hurting. It was in that way she hugged her legs, as if she was closing herself up, becoming as small as possible.

'You and me,' Tina had said. 'Her saviours.'

She creased her forehead and looked like a kid trying to spell its name.

'How do you know about this Glazer?'

'For someone who doesn't care, you're asking a lot of questions.'

'You want me to help you murder a man,' she said. 'Why shouldn't I ask?'

'You wanted me to murder Paget. You weren't bothered about questions then.'

'That wasn't murder. That was justice.'

'It was revenge. You should know that.'

She was quiet for a while, holding onto her legs.

'Yeah, well...'

'Kill him,' she'd said to me before. 'Kill him.'

Paget had been her pimp, back when Brenda had been alive. I could only imagine the hatred she bore for him. She wasn't like Brenda, whose anger with Paget and Marriot was a driving force. No, Tina's fury burned inside her, ate her up. She was more like me, I suppose.

Then, for a moment, it wasn't Tina I was looking at, but Brenda, and she was looking at me, waiting for me to do something, to save her. And I couldn't, though everything inside me screamed to.

'What do you remember about him? Glazer?' I said.

'Nothing.'

'You must remember something.'

'Look, he only came here a couple of times, when Kenny was here.'

'What did they talk about, Glazer and Paget?'

'How would I know?'

She didn't want to talk about Paget. Maybe she'd talk about Brenda.

'Why did Brenda give him the DVD? Did she tell you?'

She thought about that.

'I remember she said she'd heard about some police operation. A girl's name.'

'Elena,' I said. 'It was called Operation Elena.'

'And there was this copper. Was that him? Glazer?'

'Yeah. Did he ever mention where he lived? A girlfriend?'

'No.'

'Think. Mary something.'

'I told you. No.'

'Don't you want to get them all?'

'I don't care,' she said, but the tremor in her voice made the lie clear.

She had it too, I thought, that bitter black blood that flooded her body, that rage, that regret.

Maybe she knew that I knew it. Anyway, she picked up the remote and flicked the TV back on. There was a programme about cooking now.

'I can't help you,' she said. 'Please go.'

'I'm just trying to understand what's going on,' I said. 'I feel like I'm in a maze.'

She looked up at me, her lips pale.

'It's not a maze,' she said. 'It's a tunnel. The further in you go, the darker it gets. Turn back now. Please. Turn back, for everyone's sake.'

She turned to stare at the TV, and I watched her watching it and saw the tears gather in her eyes, and I thought she was a lot like Brenda, and completely different.

EIGHTEEN

I went to Brenda's flat a few days after she'd been murdered. I had a key. I could've gone any time, but I'd waited. I knew the law might be all over it, looking for something to lead them to the killer. I had to avoid the police, sure, but that wasn't what had stopped me going. I didn't like the law, but I wasn't scared of them. I wasn't scared of anyone. To fear someone, you must fear the worst they could do to you. The worst had been done to me. Even death didn't seem something to fear.

I climbed the concrete stairs, sweating in the late afternoon heat, swallowing the smell of piss in the stairways, the dampness of the air. The higher I got, the more it closed in on me so that it was like the whole block had died when Brenda had, and I was breathing in its foul decay.

I remembered the first time I'd walked those steps. Then it had been cold, now it was hot. That was how long it had all lasted. We'd been together only as long as it took the weather to change.

By the time I got to her floor, I was soaked with sweat. I don't think the heat had anything to do with that, though.

As I trudged along the walkway, it felt to me that I was carrying some massive weight, felt like my legs wouldn't get me there. A woman came out of a flat a couple of doors up from Brenda's. She lit a fag and tossed the match over the handrail. Then she saw me and dragged on her fag and watched me walk towards her.

She was somewhere in her forties, fat, with spiky black hair and a round, chubby face. Her mouth was a bitter thing, thin-lipped and wrinkled. It didn't fit her face and made her look like she'd spent most of her life disapproving of others.

She had a thing for black. There were thick black marks around her eyes, and she wore a tight black T-shirt and black leggings, which showed off the rolls of fat. She would've looked better if she'd worn a sack.

'She's gone,' the woman said as I stopped in front of Brenda's front door.

I put my key in the lock and turned it and opened the door, and smelled Brenda on the air. Something inside me cracked a little more.

'I know,' I said.

I went in. The woman came to the door.

'Who are you?' she said, peering in.

I turned away from her. I didn't think I could stop from falling apart, and I didn't want anyone to see that.

'A friend,' I said.

She laughed at that.

'Lotta friends she has.'

There was an edge of viciousness in that laugh. I felt the muscles in my back tighten. She must've sensed danger because she said, 'Nice girl. I like her.'

She kept talking about her in the present tense. Didn't she know Brenda was dead?

132

I went through into the living room. I could see Brenda sitting there, at the small table, cigarette in one hand, glass of vodka in the other, smiling slyly as she took the piss out of me. I never minded her doing that. I'd have given anything for her to be there doing it again.

Instead she was gone and the place had been smashed up. The sofa had been ripped open, white stuffing spilling everywhere, like a creature with its guts hanging out. The curtains had been torn down, the TV had been broken apart, the china shattered.

Everything I saw was destroyed. They'd left Brenda's home ruined, as if they wanted to destroy her utterly, and me with her.

Of course, I didn't know then who they were. All I knew was that she'd been killed in an alleyway, and the coppers said it was a john, some unknown man who'd wanted to kill a woman, and had chosen Brenda.

I blamed Marriot for Brenda's death, but only because she'd worked for him. Only later did I find out he'd had her killed. Only later did I make him pay. Much later.

I looked over to where the bookcase had stood. Now it was on its face, books opened up and cast around, like dead birds littering the floor. I saw the book I was after. It was one about the battle of Trafalgar. I'd given it to her a couple of days after we'd met. She'd shown me her print of Turner's *The Fighting Temeraire*, one of the saddest pictures she'd ever seen, she told me.

'That beautiful ship,' she said, 'and it's being dragged in to be pulled apart. Its time is up.'

She didn't use a bookmark, so she used to dog-ear the

pages. I opened the book and found the last page she'd read. It was page sixty-two. She hadn't even got to the start of the battle. She'd never get there, would never find out about the *Temeraire*. That poor old ship, as she called it, as she called me.

I looked around for the print and found it on the floor, the glass broken, the frame snapped. I pulled the picture away, looked at it. There was a tear across the sky, where Turner had burned the clouds.

'...something?'

It was that fat bird talking. I'd forgotten she was there. I felt her near me, her smoky breath touching my neck.

I rolled the print up and added it to the book under my arm.

'Who did this?'

'Police were here,' she said.

Now I turned to face her.

Coppers smashed places apart, sure. But not if the place belonged to the victim. This was as if they were treating Brenda like the suspect.

'Why?'

'Looking for drugs.'

'Drugs?'

'What they said.'

Drugs? What the fuck?

'What did they tell you about her? About the woman who lived here?'

'Didn't tell me nothing. Only it was drugs. Asked me who came here. I didn't tell 'em nothing.'

I saw a vase on the floor. It was a cheap thing, not worth

134

a penny, but inside it was where Brenda had saved her cash. She'd wanted to be a beautician, and that had been the money she'd saved so she could do a course. Fucking coppers, I thought. Bent, all of them.

'She's dead,' I said.

The woman backed up a step.

'What? Dead?'

'Who were they?'

'How? What do you mean?'

'She's dead. She didn't deal in drugs. She was murdered.'

She edged back further.

'I don't know nothing about that.'

'Were they drug squad, these coppers?'

'Dunno. They were coppers.'

'They show you a warrant card? They tell you what branch they were with? Were they CID?'

'They flashed something. Didn't see what.'

'Uniformed?'

'No.'

'If you didn't see their warrant cards and they weren't in uniform, how do you know they were law?'

I found myself breathing hard. I found myself closing in on her, this woman who'd had a dig at Brenda. I had to hold onto myself. Her cigarette hung limply from her fingers. I watched the smoke coil up and fade into the air.

She snapped out of her fear and started to walk away from me. She didn't go far. I rested my hand on her shoulder and she stopped moving.

'Tell me exactly what happened,' I said.

She turned. Right then, for an instant, all I wanted to

135

do was destroy, as others had destroyed. She was in my way. Destroy her, my head said. Destroy them all. She saw it in me. She pissed herself, the smell of it mixing with the heat in the flat so that everything seemed even more like it was dead and rotting around me; that smell of sweet foulness, that heat of corruption when the body fed on itself, ate itself up.

I pushed her away, sick of her, of myself.

It was my rage taking control of me again. She was a sour, mocking cunt, but that was all. She hadn't murdered Brenda.

I told her to go.

I went into the bedroom. That had been trashed too. It was worse here, more like a rape. I wanted to find these coppers and tear them apart for that, for the disrespect. Brenda had never done drugs. She was murdered in an alley, left to bleed out while the sky dripped its thin blood on her. She died smelling waste and wet petrol and slime. And now they'd done this to her, and I wanted to murder them for that, beat into them the fact that I would never see her again. And all I had now was a memory and the image of a ruined flat.

Over on the dressing table, her jewellery box had been opened and emptied. Some copper had helped himself to that lot. There was nothing of value in it for him, but for me it was more of her that had been taken. I'd wanted a necklace I'd bought her. I'd wanted the rings she'd worn.

I went over to her bed. I tried not to think of the moments we'd spent there, of the times she'd stroked me, asked me about my life. Or when, her back against the wall and her

136

knees up to her chin, she'd looked so young, so lost and I, in my clumsy stupid way, had tried to comfort her.

I tried not to think of all that but, of course, I did.

When I smelled her on the sheets, I cracked, as if some part of me had finally gone as far as it could and just broke apart, as this flat had. I was in pieces on the floor, shattered.

When I was able, I lifted myself from her bed and sat there and stared at the carpet. I don't know what I was looking at, or why. I just stared.

After a while, I realized I was looking at her underwear, scattered all over the place. I leaned over and picked a bra up and held it to my face.

And then I saw it. On the carpet, beneath the clothing, lay a photograph album. It was closed. I opened it and flicked through the pages. They were all empty.

Why would the law want Brenda's photos? Were they looking into Marriot for something and wanted evidence from Brenda? But that couldn't be, not if they were after drugs, as they'd said.

There had once been prints of photos, so maybe there were negatives. I searched, and did my own pulling apart. Brenda's place had gone, now. Brenda had gone. It didn't matter about her place any more. I tore it apart, and in doing that I tore into myself, unleashed some of the rage I felt. I ripped the mattress to pieces, as if it was the memory of her death. I flayed it. I lifted it up and threw it. I smashed the table with a blow, and then slammed my fists into the wall until the plaster fell away in chunks.

Then I really lost control. I can't remember what

happened next, only that by the time I'd finished my knuckles were dripping blood and my head was light and my face was wet. And the place was properly destroyed. I mean obliterated. It seemed the right thing to do. In a way, it was what I wanted, it was a funeral service, of sorts. She was gone, there should be nothing left. That was how I felt back then. The lousy fucking world had torn her apart, now I would tear the world apart, make it bleed.

I crumpled to the floor.

I stood slowly, gathered the book, the Turner print, and left.

As I went out the front door, I saw her, standing outside her place, fag in hand, mouth tight in hate. She glared at me.

'I seen you, you know,' she said, as I was walking away. 'I seen you with her. Just another one of her friends, weren't you?' I carried on walking, but her words cut into me. 'How do I know you didn't kill her? Who the fuck are you?'

I stopped and turned, took a step towards her. She ran for her front door, opened it and stopped to look back at me.

'I'm death,' I said. 'Remember me.'

Back then I'd cursed that woman for an idiot, then for disliking Brenda. But, mostly, I'd cursed the law for being a bunch of thieving cunts, and for being too fucking stupid to realize that Brenda was a victim, not a criminal. I'd thought it was typical law, that they'd put her death down to a drug deal or something and were more bothered about the drug angle than her.

But since then I'd learned a few things. Now I didn't think it was because they didn't give a shit or because they were dumb. Now I knew how much the law was involved in things, and to what purpose. Glazer was law. He had a reason to want to search Brenda's place.

Now I thought those coppers knew exactly what they were doing. They'd searched Brenda's flat, ripped it apart, looking for something – not drugs, though, not fucking drugs.

And that gave me a reason to find this woman again, and question her more.

So I climbed the same stairs, smelled the same damp smell, saw the same fucking graffiti. Each step took me back, back until I had to stop and remind myself that I wasn't going to see Brenda, that she wasn't there any more. It was as if the stairway itself was my history, each step marking a moment in the last six years, each one harder to climb. This step was Paget's death, this the casino robbery. Up they went. Back they went. If I kept climbing, maybe Brenda would be up there waiting for me.

I tried her place first, just on the off-chance. There was no answer, no sound from inside. I tried again, but my knocks had a dull, dead sound, as if I was knocking on rock. The place was empty.

I went further along the walkway and heard a woman's voice, sharp and loud.

'Zach,' the voice said, 'make me a drink. And put your bloody clothes on.'

I knocked. When the door opened, I saw that this was a different woman. She was about the same age as the other one, mid-forties, I reckoned, but looked a hundred times better. She had a deep tan and a spark in her eyes, and she looked like she enjoyed life, as if it was something that was there to be grabbed and wrung out. She gave me a once over and pulled a cigarette from the packet she was holding. She lit the fag, sucked on it and said, 'You're a big one. I don't owe any money, if that's why you're here.'

'It's not.'

'You remind me of my husband, only he was about a third your size. God rest him.'

I caught a glimpse of a young bloke, mid-twenties, good looking in a kind of pop star way. He was holding a towel over his lower body. He glanced at me for a moment, and there was a wide-eyed look to him, as if he'd been taken out of some other life and shoved here, and now he didn't know where he was or what he was doing.

140

'Debs,' the boy said, 'I can't find my trousers.'

The woman rolled her eyes.

'He's a bit soft, that one,' she said to me, 'but he'll do for the time being.'

She went off to help Zach find his trousers. When she came back, she was smiling.

'Bless him,' she said.

'I'm looking for the woman who used to live here.'

'Yeah?' she said. She wasn't smiling now. 'What for? You sure you're not a money collector? She owe you something?'

'No.'

'No, but you're trouble.'

'I just want to talk to her.'

'Yeah, well, there's only me here, since my husband got run over by a bus.'

She said that as if her husband had done it to piss her off. Anyway, whatever had happened to her husband, she didn't seem too bothered about it. I suppose Zach had something to do with her feelings there.

'This woman lived here about six years ago,' I said.

She took another drag from her cigarette.

'Yeah, I knew her. Bought the place from her just about then. Sour bitch. Had a face like a shrivelled twat.'

'I need to talk to her.'

'Yeah? About what? You don't look like the police, I'll give you that. So what is it?'

'She knew someone,' I said. 'A friend of mine who lived a couple doors up.'

There was a change in the woman now. The spark had

141

gone from her eyes. She came out of the flat and pulled the door to behind her.

'The girl there?' she said, pointing at Brenda's flat.

'Yeah.'

'Shame. I heard about her. All that was just before I moved here, but I remember people talked about it. Nice girl, I heard.'

There was a different kind of glint in her eyes now, and I thought this woman must feel things strongly, must be one of those honest people who don't bother with the bullshit of it all – like Browne, like Brenda herself.

I said, 'Yeah.'

Then the woman put her hand on mine. I didn't know why. I didn't know what I was supposed to do. I looked at her hand.

'Were you close to her? The girl there?'

Was I close to her? 'I'm still close to her,' I wanted to say. Instead, I said, 'I need to talk to the one who lived here.' The woman nodded like she understood it all. 'I won't tell her anything you tell me.'

'Tell her,' she said, pulling her hand away from mine. 'I don't care. Couldn't stand the cow. Her name's Maggie something. Hold on.'

She went back inside. A few minutes later she returned with some documents.

'Margaret Sanford.'

'Know where she went?'

'She said she was moving to Canada to be with her son. But that's bollocks coz I saw her a year ago in Tesco in Drayton. You know, near the Arsenal stadium.'

'You sure it was her?'

'Yeah.'

'Anyone with her?' She sucked some smoke, shook her head. 'How much shopping did she have?'

'Trolley full.'

That meant she must live nearby – or she had done a year ago. Had she gone to Canada and come back? That didn't seem likely, not for her. She was one of those fat, lazy types who could barely bring themselves to move off their sofas. So, why had she lied?

It was only then that I realized what this Debs had said earlier. My mind had been so full of holes that it had passed right through. Now it was coming back and getting stuck.

'You bought this place from this Margaret? Direct from her?'

'Yes.'

'When?'

'I told you. Just after that girl – just after your friend was killed. Six weeks, couple months after, I think. Police'd gone by then, but the odd reporter came by.'

So, the old cunt had sold up and lied about where she was going. And all that was a couple of months after Brenda had died.

Fuck.

TWENTY

The first thing I did when I got back to Browne's was to call Ben Green and tell him I needed to find Margaret Sanford.

He wanted to know why I needed to find her, said he wouldn't help me if the woman got hurt. I told him she'd been a neighbour of Brenda's, which was true, and that I wanted to ask her some questions, which was also true. Green didn't need to know the rest. I told him I'd send some money his way and promised I wouldn't kill her.

Then I waited.

It was early evening now, and going dark. I'd had a busy day, but I felt no closer to anything than I had in the morning. I had to think about things, which meant, first, I had to not think about things, let my head clear a bit.

I went into the kitchen and took a look out through the peepholes I'd made in the wooden screens. I watched the gloom for a while and then went and sat at the table and listened to the fridge drone and the odd bus or lorry rumble by.

It was darker at the back of the house because of the covered windows. I didn't want the light on. I wanted to let the darkness fill the space around me so that I could let my head float off and empty, just for a while.

Browne came in and switched the light on and blinded me. He was dressed in old slacks and an inside-out T-shirt. I saw he'd been asleep. His face was puffy, his eyes bloodshot, his grey hair wilder than usual.

He saw me sitting there and yawned and wiped a hand over his hair, making it even madder, if that was possible.

'Been back long?' he said.

'No.'

'Did you find him? This Glazer?'

'No.'

He frowned, nodded, stood watching me.

'Can't say I'm displeased, Joe.'

He shrugged to himself, mumbled something, scratched his armpit.

'Hungry?' he said, shuffling over to the fridge. 'You must be.'

He made us something to eat. Well, he took it out of a box and put it in the microwave. It was okay. After that, he sat at the table and picked up the *Evening Standard* I'd bought for him. I made tea and put his mug down in front of him. He wasn't reading the paper as far as I could see, just staring at it.

I turned the light off, returned the room to shadow. I liked that, shadow, darkness. There was something true about it, something clear.

We drank our tea. Browne pretended to read his paper by the light from the hallway, but I knew it was too dark for him to see anything.

Something was bothering him but I didn't want to ask in case he lectured me again. But there was something

145

I wanted to say to him, too. Only, I knew it was going to be hard going. My head was confused enough without all the grief I was going to get from Browne behaving like a stroppy teenager.

So, we sat in silence and I let the silence grow until I could wrap myself in it for a while, forget Browne, forget all the shit. That was something else I liked. Silence. Shadow and silence. Nothingness.

The only thing I was sure about was that I didn't know what the fuck was going on. Eddie was right about that much. I kept getting snapshots, bits and pieces. I couldn't see the whole picture because, as Eddie was pleased to tell me, I was too small to count.

A week or so ago, Browne had wanted me to give the DVD that Brenda had left me to Compton and his mob. They were investigating Glazer, after all. They were anti-corruption coppers. Surely, they could be trusted. Couldn't they?

Well, maybe. But I had a thing about the law. I knew most of them were okay, sure, but there were enough bent ones to count; you could never know which ones were straight, which were wrong. Anyway, as far as they were concerned, I was fair game, a villain. What if I handed Compton the DVD and he went right on and arrested me? I'd do thirty years. Fuck that.

Then, too, I might need the DVD myself. Maybe I'd get in a jam with Dunham. He wanted the DVD as well. We were bound to bump into each other.

Again, I had to wonder how it was that Paget had found out the DVD was valuable. He hadn't known at the time, or until recently. Marriot had done a few years inside and if either of them had known the DVD was wanted by Compton, they would've cut a deal. Instead, Paget only found out in time to use it to get protection from Dunham.

And what of Glazer? I had to make sure I got to him before Compton or Dunham. And then there was this stuff with the law searching Brenda's flat after she'd died. That must've been Glazer, and he must've been after the DVD. But why? If Brenda had sent him a copy, he must've already had one. Unless she hadn't sent it. What if the copy I'd found was the one intended for Glazer?

But no. That copy was meant for me. It was addressed to me. For Joe, it had said. She must've known I'd go there, to her flat, to her secret place, as she called it; the place where she hid things that meant something to her. The cotton dress I'd bought her, and the creams from Liberty. And the letter to me.

So, what was Glazer after?

It was a fucking mess, and the more I thought about it all, the more I got lost in it. Cole was right, I was in some confused shit.

'I haven't watered it,' Browne said.

He did that sometimes, spoke his thoughts out loud. It was odd, hearing his voice cut through the silence. I'd forgotten he was there. I think, probably, he'd forgotten I was there.

'What?'

He looked up. I could hardly see his face. I wondered how long we'd been like that, in the gathering gloom. His paper was on the table now. He must've been looking into the same darkness as me.

'Oh,' he said. 'The flower. I haven't watered it. It's been a bit dry lately.'

His voice cracked a bit with pain, and I cracked a bit with it.

He was talking about the small violet he'd found in the back garden, near the rockery. He'd come across it a little while back. Only, for him – for us – it wasn't just a flower, it was a symbol of the life of a small African girl called Kid.

Kid. Her name was Kindness, and we called her Kid, and she was tiny, no more than skin and bones and huge eyes. But she'd had courage, and more.

She'd been used by Marriot, traded by him for money and the lust of the cunts he catered to.

I'd found her when I'd raided a house. She was hiding in the cupboard. Afterwards, she'd stayed with us, and Browne had grown fond of her. And, for a while, we'd become like some freakish family; an old drunk doctor, a battered half-dead criminal and a small, thin African girl who'd experienced more terror and more pain than either of us could imagine, but who would still kick her legs on the sofa when she watched something funny on TV, or would gape at Browne when he'd had a few too many and did his Scottish dancing for her.

I remembered her, this small girl. I remembered how she would lie asleep on my chest, rising and falling as I breathed, or how she would tremble at night, as she dreamed her memories and remembered her nightmares, or how she would hold our hands – mine and Browne's – as we walked along a market, the three of us damaged almost beyond repair, but somehow finding in each other enough to carry on.

148

Yes, I remembered her. And what had been done to her.

If for nothing else, Marriot had to die for what he did to Kid. If I could, I'd bring him back to life just so that I could kill him again.

But she'd died too, caught in the savage crossfire when I'd gone to kill him.

And of all the bastard ironies in this fucked-up bastard world, the worst, perhaps, was this: storming Marriot's place and flattening it, trying to find and free Kid, killing all the blurred shapes that moved before my blurred head, it might have been me who'd fired the shot that killed her.

I'd never told Browne I might've killed Kid. I think it would've been more than he could bear. Christ, it was almost more than I could bear.

So, she'd died and Browne had found this small violet, by itself, in the garden. From then on he'd looked after it, in his own way.

'Oh, it won't last much longer,' he said quietly. 'I know that. It's such a wee thing, so delicate. It's starting to wither now already.'

Brenda was dead, Kid was dead, and Browne was dying, as slowly as he could, one glass of Scotch at a time. Even the flower was dying. And then there was me, or what was left of me, beaten and bashed, gutted, old.

But not down. Not yet.

So, there we were; me and Browne, and our memories of dead people filling the space between us and a whole load of shit going on that I didn't understand, and all the while we both knew it was only a matter of time before the war outside smashed into the house, destroyed us both.

149

I remembered my tea and drank some of it. It was cold.

'You should go somewhere,' I said, putting the mug down. 'Get out of here.'

I couldn't see his face clearly now. It was too dark. But I knew he was angry.

'I'm not running.'

'You're stupid if you don't.'

'Are you running?'

'It doesn't matter about me.'

He said, 'Tsk.'

That was it as far as he was concerned.

I went up to my room and pulled a grand from the bag. When I went back down, the light was on. He was back to pretending that he was reading his paper. I held the money out to him.

'Go to Scotland. Go to your sister's.'

He looked at the money.

'I'm not taking that. And I'm not bloody going to Scotland.'

'Take the money.'

'It's blood money.'

'All money's blood money.'

He lowered the opened paper onto the table and ran his hand through his hair.

'Well, maybe so. I'm still not going to Scotland. I'm not leaving my own bloody house.'

'I can't protect you here. There are too many of them.'

'Come with me, son.'

'I need to stay in London.'

'So you can get killed? Come with me, Joe.'

I sat back down at the table. Well, I fell into the seat.

My strength was fading.

'What would I do in Scotland?'

'Grow old.'

Grow old. Would that be so bad? End all this shit. Run away. Grow old in some out of the way place. Everyone was telling me the same thing: leave, live. Even Brenda had said it, more or less, in her letter:

'Don't destroy yourself for me, Joe.'

'I can't,' I said.

'There are too many of them, you said. Too many for even you, Joe.'

'Maybe.'

'But you'll stay, even if staying kills you?'

'Yeah.'

He slammed his hand on the table.

'You're a bloody fool. What's the point? What the hell can you prove? If this is for Brenda or Kid… Christ, Joe, they're dead. They wouldn't want you to do this to yourself for them.'

'It's not for them. It's for me.'

'Your self-respect? Is that it? Your bloody egotistical self-satisfaction? Your reputation?'

'If you like.'

Browne swung round, his face fiercer than I'd ever seen it. I didn't know he had it in him, that anger.

'You bloody idiot,' he said. 'Don't you see? You think this rage of yours, this hatred, is a weapon to turn on everything, to level the world, to flatten your enemies, like you did in the ring. But you're wrong, Joe. Hatred turns inwards and inwards again so that it's forever unfolding

151

new parts of yourself to hate. I know all about that. And finally all the years of vitriol corrode your innards and hollow you, gut you so that you're a different thing inside, hating your own existence, wanting to smash the image that looks back from the mirror.'

I couldn't say anything to that. I knew he was right.

He sighed and looked at me and shook his head slowly in that way he had. He dumped the newspaper in a half-crumpled mess, stood, trudged to the cupboard above the sink and pulled out a bottle of Scotch and a glass. He came back to the table, sat heavily, unscrewed the bottle top and poured.

'Then I'll stay too,' he said, screwing the top back onto the bottle, very carefully. 'I'll take my chances.'

'You were all set to leave a couple of weeks back.'

'Aye,' he said. 'Well…'

Well, that was before he found the flower. Before he found a purpose, however small.

'You'll get in my way. Take the money and go.'

After that, there was nothing. Every now and then he'd take a sip of Scotch. He was stubborn. And brave, in a way. Oh, he was scared all right, and he knew the dangers without me telling him, so deciding to stay took guts. I knew I wasn't going to get him to leave.

I got up and started to make another tea, but then I decided I didn't want one and I pulled a glass from the cupboard and went and sat down and slid the glass along to Browne. He hesitated, looking at me quizzically. Then he uncapped the Scotch and poured me a hefty amount and slid the glass back.

I didn't usually drink. But, now and then, I'd have some, just to dull the pain, as Browne used to say. I swallowed some of the booze and felt it burn its way down to my gut.

'I'll tell you something I've come to learn,' Browne said.

I knew I was in for one of his lectures. Somehow, this time, I didn't mind. The alcohol, probably.

He said, 'I've come to appreciate the world in a new light. Because of people like you, Joe, and the scum you know. It seems to me now that all the stuff they tell us to be – honourable, honest, kind – all that play-the-game mantra, it's all a load of old rot.'

I could've told him that when I was five years old.

'It's what they want us to believe,' he was saying, 'the authorities, it's what they want us to do, us being the weak and powerless, the meek.' He laughed. 'The meek shall inherit the earth. My God, that's another one, isn't it? Another of the lies.'

He scratched his ear.

'Everything's wrong,' he said. 'We're a country upside down, arse over tit. We've got kids getting pregnant while their parents play computer games; forty-year-old children and twelve-year-old adults. We've got bankers on the fiddle, policemen breaking the law, MPs doing whatever they want. Science and technology bring everyone closer together while governments and religion push us all further apart.'

He went on like that for a while, telling me it was all arse upwards. Then he was quiet, his fingers still attached to his ear.

'I forgot what I was saying,' he said finally.

He remembered his Scotch, though, and took a long swig

153

of it. Maybe his memories were in there somewhere, the sour taste of his own failures mixing with the acid of this new knowledge of his that the world was lousy.

'It's rot,' he said again. 'All of it.'

I'd grown used to Browne's ways, his whining, his barbed comments. He would get drunk and rant about something, or he'd be sarky, sly in his humour. I mostly ignored it all.

But now he was being thoughtful, and he wasn't drunk, yet. And somehow that made his words carry weight, as if they were final. I wondered if, by deciding to stay at home he was throwing in the towel, as if he'd decided life just wasn't worth the fight any more, wasn't worth the pain.

'It won't die,' I said. 'Wild violets are perennials. It'll be back next year.'

I didn't know if that was true.

Browne sat thinking for a while. Then he rubbed his head and smiled.

Afterwards, we went and sat in the lounge and watched something on TV. I can't remember what it was. I remember, though, that Browne wouldn't stop talking about how he was going to transform the garden. He had big plans, he said. Would I help? I said, yeah, sure.

When he shuffled off to bed, I finally got some rest. I turned the TV off and sat in the darkness again.

For some reason, I kept thinking about that evening in the Fox and Globe, when me and Brenda had met Browne in there, and he'd given his lecture about why he drank. That wasn't what made me think of it, though. There was something about the way Brenda had acted that time, something off.

154

After Browne had gone, the pub got slowly quieter. It must've been late afternoon; after the day crowd, before the evening mob.

Music was playing. It was soppy shit, but Brenda was getting drunk and she smiled and swayed to the music. Her long throat was bare and looked like carved mahogany. Her hair, done up in those thin plaits that she always had, fell down her neck like black water. But her eyes... her eyes had a glazed look, as if her smile was stuck onto a mask. She wasn't looking at me as she moved to the music. She was staring out into space, into the place between us, between everything.

Then she closed her eyes slowly, and opened them, just as slowly, and saw me and the smile struggled a bit, and her eyes got a bit wet, and she reached a hand across the table and took mine, her fingers like ice, despite the heat. I looked down at her slim hand resting on my clumsy, gnarled thing. As I closed my fingers, she pulled away from me, and when I looked up at her, her eyes had lost their softness and she was glancing over my shoulder, looking towards the bar area. The hairs on my back bristled. I thought that she must've seen Paget or Marriot. I thought there'd be trouble, thought I was going to hurt them, this time, whatever Brenda said about leaving it alone. So, I turned and scanned the bar.

There were a few people there, but nobody I knew. There was a young barman, spots and tattoos and puppy fat. There were two men in suits, sitting astride stools, their guts pouring over their belts, eyeing the woman who'd just come in, as if they'd forgotten that they were twenty years too late. There was a big bloke sitting at the far end of the bar, nursing a pint. He had shaved brown hair and a short beard and moustache. Every now and then, he'd look my way, as if he knew me but couldn't place me. When I met his eyes, he'd move them over to something else, but I knew he turned his gaze back to me a minute later. Did I know him? I couldn't remember.

Then there was the woman, the one who'd just come in. She was slim, thin, really, with pale skin and black hair which ran down to the nape of her neck and stopped there in a straight line. I couldn't see her face clearly, but I caught a glimpse of huge eyes, black holes in a white face. I could see her arm as it reached for a glass of something. It was long and thin and the colour of ivory. She wore a short black dress. Her legs were as thin and pale as her arms. It seemed wrong; her hair too black for her skin, her skin too white for her dress.

I wouldn't have paid any attention to any of these people except for the way Brenda reacted. She'd gone still and then, seeing me catch her looking over, she reached out quickly for a drink, and sipped it and smiled at me.

It was then I felt that coldness creep along my insides, and I knew we hadn't come to that pub by accident, or because Brenda wanted to get out of the flat or because she fancied a drink or wanted to listen to sad music. And, for a reason I couldn't explain, I felt the tightening of my guts, the darkness. And fear.

I turned back to look at that scene at the bar. That's what it now seemed to me; a scene, something staged.

'Someone you know?' I said.

'No.'

'Is it the bloke? That big one? Does he work for Marriot?'

'It's nothing, Joe. Nobody.'

I let it go. What else could I do? It was possible she'd seen someone she'd known. Maybe those two blokes were johns, maybe the big bloke knew Paget, maybe the woman was a pro. I didn't know and knew not to ask, but one thing I did know, if Brenda had seen something she hadn't wanted to see, we would've been out of there sharpish. As it was, she made like everything was fine. And that's what made me realize it wasn't.

I knew, and she knew that I knew because when, after I'd scanned the pub once more, I turned back to her, she was looking at me, and there was something in her gaze that made my insides crawl. Now, years later, when I think of that look, I think of it as if she was saying goodbye to me, right there and then. The sadness in her eyes was as deep as the darkness I feel when I think of it.

And then she stood.

'I'm gonna get a drink,' she said.

There was a drink right in front of her, but I didn't say anything. She wandered off. I watched her as she went slowly up to the bar. She lit a cigarette. Nobody cared about smoking, not in that place. She didn't look to her left or right and nobody paid her any attention except the barman who spoke to her and went off to get her drink. I turned away. My eyes were still sore from all her smoke. I didn't care about that, but my head hurt and that was getting to me, so I closed my eyes for a moment, to try and get the haze out of my head, to try and rid the sourness of Browne's despair and Brenda's sadness and my weakness.

When I opened my eyes, the music had changed, had become sadder, and Brenda was standing in front of me, a glass of colourless stuff in her right hand, hanging loosely by her side, a cigarette in her left, dangling in the same way. I wondered how long she'd been like that, how much time I'd lost. Seemed like I was always losing time, one way or another. So, she stood like that a while and looked at the table, at the glass already there. It was like she'd forgotten all about me. Maybe she had. Then she closed her eyes and started again to sway to the music. She opened her eyes and looked at me and smiled.

'Dance with me, Joe,' she said.

Apart from those at the bar, there were a half-dozen tables occupied, couples, small groups. But, of everyone in the place, nobody was dancing. I turned back to Brenda and told her I was too big and clumsy to dance. I told her I'd make her look stupid. I knew I was lying, but I believed it anyway.

I didn't dance with her that night, or ever. I hate myself for that.

I looked back to the bar. Everything seemed the same, stuck in a freeze frame, but also different, as if the picture had been forwarded a few frames. The young barman dangled around, waiting for an order; the businessmen faced each other and chatted, each holding a pint over his gut; the big bloke still nursed his drink, still let his glance wander around; and the woman with the short black hair and thin white arms and large eyes – she was at the end of the bar now, ignoring the occasional looks from the businessmen. She was stirring her drink with a straw while she spoke on the phone. Her handbag was on the bar in front of her. She closed it, switched her phone off and left the pub. She hadn't touched her drink.

I noticed then that Brenda was sitting down, looking at me.

'I'm sorry, Joe,' she said.

'What for?'

She shrugged.

'For being me.'

'That doesn't make sense,' I said. 'I like you. I...'

She put a finger on my lips.

'Don't.'

I wasn't sure what I was going to say. Whatever it was, she didn't want to hear it.

She looked at me. No, she looked into me, our eyes locked. There was nothing else in the world but her and me, no time but the present.

We were like that forever. And then she got up and took my hand and led me from the pub.

TWENTY-TWO

It took Green a day to find the woman.

'I got something,' he said.

'What?'

'Not on the phone, mate. Alright?'

I went cold then. Green was right, of course. I knew I might have heat on me from all over, so I should've known to be careful about the phone. What worried me more, though, was that Green was taking care about it, as if he knew something.

'Alright. Where? When?'

'Where you saw me a few weeks back. Soon as.'

'Right.'

I met him in the bakery. He wasn't working, but he wanted to get out of the house.

'She's doing my fucking nut in,' he said.

That's what he told me, anyway. I thought he was lying. I thought probably he was being careful, not wanting me anywhere near his family. That was fine. Sensible.

The bakery was quieter now. The girls had gone, but the manager was still there. Green smiled at him and led me out back, to the walled yard.

'What've you got?'

'I found her. This Margaret Sanford,' he said, lighting up a smoke. 'She ain't changed her name. We was lucky there. She must either be stupid or real sure of herself. It's been a few years, right? She probably thinks everyone's forgotten about her. That's often what happens.'

He handed me the address on a piece of paper. It took a few seconds for his words to sink into my thick brain.

'What do you mean?' I said.

'Huh?'

'Why would she be worried about people remembering her?'

'She was a grass. Didn't you know?'

I felt the coldness again, dripping down my guts.

'No.'

'That's how I found her so quick.'

I felt like I was in some kind of trap. Every time I thought I knew where I was, I'd turn around and find myself lost.

'Who'd she grass on? Who to?'

'She snouted for the local law, plain-clothes mob. As for who she grassed up, I dunno. She was nosy, saw things, heard things. Nothing big.'

And I'd walked right into her that day I'd gone to Brenda's. She must've been onto the law the moment I left.

'Is that why you didn't want to talk on the phone?' I said.

He took his time answering that. It was cold outside, but there was sweat on his forehead. He took another drag of his cigarette.

'I got a funny feeling. Things ain't kosher.'

'Why?'

'I called a few people up, asking about this bird, right? Well, they didn't know anything, but they tried a few people. You know how it works. Anyway, I get a call from this bloke, Brian Ward. Know him?'

'No.'

'I knew him way back. He didn't know anything about this woman, but he told me something else. First he says that he heard me and you were mates. I said maybe. Then he said he was in with his local Bill. I think he went to school with some of them or something. Anyway, he says to me, be careful, don't get involved. Says there's rumours going round the station that you've got big enemies. I asked him who these enemies were, but he didn't know. Told me they were law, though. He knew that much.'

'Where's he from?'

'Dunno. North London somewhere. Brent, maybe.'

It was Glazer. Had to be. But how did some plod in the local cop shop know anything about Glazer wanting me? Glazer was surely going to want to keep it quiet from his own mob. Had one of his men talked?

'Can you get hold of him again? Find out if he can get anything more?'

'Can't risk it, mate. I don't mind helping you out if it's villains we're dealing with, but not the law. I've got previous, and a family. I can't get involved if they're onto you.'

'Then tell me where to find this Brian Ward.'

'Joe, do me a favour, alright? Leave it. Get out of town for a bit.'

'Tell me where he is. I won't get you involved.'

'I'm out, Joe. Sorry.'

'What is it? What's wrong?'

He looked up at me.

'I just heard about Cole,' he said.

'Cole? What about him?'

'He's dead, Joe. Fucker's dead. They bombed his house. Fucking bombed it.'

Cole was dead. Christ. I never thought someone like him could die the same as everyone else.

And if Cole was dead, I was out of allies.

'You know what that means, right?' Green was saying. 'Joe? You understand what that means?'

'It means now Dunham can concentrate on me. I'm next.'

He nodded.

'You and anyone near you. I'm not gonna be one of them. I'm sorry, Joe. Don't call me again, please.'

He stood and dropped the smoke and, looking down at it, slowly squashed it beneath his foot as if the cigarette was his knowledge of me. Then he was gone. I didn't blame him.

TWENTY-THREE

I found her in a bedsit in Leytonstone. When she opened the
door, I thought Green had got it wrong. This couldn't have
been the same woman. She looked like she was in her seven-
ties, scrawny, skin wrinkled and paper thin.

Then I saw her mouth. It was the same bitter slash, only
now it suited the rest of her face better.

She still wore black, but the clothes were baggy on her.
Her body looked like it was made of broken wooden sticks,
and her hair was thin and white, as if it had been spun by
a spider. It was stuck to her scalp.

'Yes?' she said, looking up at me.

'Margaret Sanford?'

'Yeah.'

There was a glimmer of recognition. Her hand went to
her throat. I moved my foot to stop her closing the door,
but she didn't try. She said, 'What do you want?'

'To talk.'

'About what?'

'The past.'

She said, 'I always knew... You got any money?'

I fished a hundred quid from my pocket. Her hand came
out, but I held the money.

'If you talk.'

She opened the door and grabbed the money.

I moved past her. She closed the door and followed me into the main room.

There was a single mattress on the floor and a jumble of stuff all over the place, clothes, shoes, bags of crisps, empty bottles of booze, boxes of pills. There were two chairs. One faced the TV, a small table next to it. The table was littered with pills and odds and ends. I saw a couple of unlit joints there, sitting in an ashtray. The other chair was stuck in the corner facing the wall, as if she never again expected company. The chairs were as thin and tattered as the she was. I turned the one by the wall to face the other.

'Cancer,' she said, as I sat.

'What?'

'If that's what you're wondering. I've been ill since – well, since you last saw me.'

'Uh-huh.'

'In my oesophagus.'

Oesophagus. It was probably the biggest word she'd ever known.

'It's rare,' she said, 'apparently.'

I said, 'You remember me.'

She picked up her electronic cigarette. She'd decided to give up the fags, just as she was about to die. Maybe she was now so desperate for life that she'd do anything for a few more hours, minutes. I supposed I could understand that. I supposed we'll all be like that one day. Well, most of us.

'I remember you,' she said, dropping the metal stick onto the table top. 'You're death.'

The way she said it, I think she believed it. She was dying, anyway. Maybe I was death. Maybe I was a carrier, my blood poisoned, affecting everyone I came into contact with. Everyone I met died from something, like Brenda, like Kid, like Paget and Marriot, like this woman with her cancer.

'So what you wanna talk about?'

'You know.'

She reached down for a bottle of water, took a few sips and put it slowly back onto the floor. Then she picked up the electronic cigarette again and sucked on it and blew out smoky stuff.

'I don't know anything,' she said after all that.

She didn't even try to sound truthful. I don't think she had the strength.

'Her name was Brenda. She lived two doors up from you.'

'I remember her. So?'

'She died. Her place got smashed up by the law. So you said.'

'What does that mean?'

'It means you're a liar.'

Her eyes had been roaming the room, the lids drooping a bit. Now they snapped open and up at me.

'You can't come into my fucking home and call me a liar. I might have cancer, but I don't have to fucking take that.'

She was trying too hard.

'You were a grass.'

She tried to stand, but fell back in her seat. I could see the pain in her face, but she tried to hide it. She was breathing hard. She didn't say anything for a while. Then, with a sigh, she said, 'Yeah. I was a grass. So what?'

166

'Who'd you work for?'

She reached down for her water again and drank a few gulps, only this time it wasn't a delaying tactic. I thought she was going to throw up. When she didn't, she said, 'A CID sergeant. DS Rose.'

I'd never heard of him.

'What'd you tell him?'

'I just told him what I saw, what I heard. I'm a very observant person. I'd see people calling at some flat and leaving a minute later with a package. I'd tell him stuff like that. Didn't have much choice. I needed the money, and I had a record and Rose made sure he had his thumb on me. That flat was a housing association place and he coulda got me thrown out.'

'What did you tell him about Brenda?'

'Nothing. I swear. I didn't know anything about her. She was just this woman who lived there.'

'That's not what you said to me when I first saw you. You said she had a lot of friends.'

She tapped her hand on the arm of her chair, looked down at the floor.

'Yeah, well…'

'And the jewellery? The cash?'

Her hand stopped tapping. She looked at me now in a different way. I think she was stupid enough to think I'd been stupid enough to not twig what she'd done. She was right. I had been that stupid, or blinded by my distrust of the law.

'What?'

'I thought the coppers nicked it. That's why you made

sure you told me the law had trashed her place looking for drugs, so that I'd think they'd taken the money, Brenda's jewellery.'

'It was the law, I swear.'

'Just tell me.'

'I don't know—'

'Don't,' I said.

She sighed. When she exhaled, her body shrank and seemed to become swallowed up by the chair.

'I needed the money. She didn't want it no more. I'm sorry she died, honest. But she didn't need it no more and I did.' Her hand went to her throat again, as if she was scared I was going to attack her fucking cancerous oesophagus.

'What did you do with the jewellery?'

'I sold it. What else would I do with it? Wear it to the Queen's tea party?'

'And the law?'

'They were there. I swear to you. I didn't smash her place up. They did. And they were looking for drugs. They told me.'

That part sounded true. She was a liar and a thief, but she wouldn't smash the place up like that. There wouldn't have been any point. No, that had been done by someone searching for something. And I knew what.

'Who were they?'

'I don't fucking know. I never seen 'em before.'

'Describe them.'

'Oh, Christ. I can't remember. It was years ago.'

'Okay. Was one of them stocky, about five-eight, white,

about forty years old? He would've had short brown hair, thinning.'

'No.'

'His name's Glazer. He would've had more hair then, probably would've been slimmer.'

'No.'

'You say you can't remember. So how do you know one of them wasn't Glazer?'

She took her hand from her neck, sucked on her stick again.

'Give me more money.'

'Don't push it.'

She shrugged again. She was able to do that, at least.

'I don't have to answer your questions. What are you gonna do? Call the police?'

I fished more money out of my pocket. I had about sixty quid left.

'When you tell me,' I said, closing my fist around the money.

She thought about that for a while, but the sight of that money was enough for her.

'The bloke you described wasn't one of them,' she said. 'I remember that. There was two of 'em. One was tall, six something, about thirty, forty. The other one was older, had grey hair. Oh, and he had a moustache.'

My mind reeled. She was still talking, but I didn't hear it. I stood, not knowing what the fuck was going on. I think I said something because she stopped talking and looked at me.

'Hey,' she was saying.

She pushed back in her seat. Getting as far from me as she could.

Compton. What the fuck?

There were more things I had to ask the woman, but I couldn't get my head straight, couldn't work out an order of words to use. Thoughts were mashed up in my mind. All I could think was that Compton had been to Brenda's flat, and had been there and searched it and trashed it.

'When?' I said.

'When what?'

'This copper. When was he there?'

'I don't know. Honest. I can't remember that far back. Christ.'

'When?'

'I don't know.'

Compton. It didn't make sense. Did it?

The woman stared at me. My legs felt shaky, like I'd been floored in the twelfth by a lightning fast combination and now, with my head still spinning all over the place, I was trying to stand while the canvas tipped around me.

Compton. Christ. How far did this thing go back? How long had they been toying with me?

She called after me. I might have said something back, but I don't think I knew what it was.

It was only as I was leaving that it hit me, what she'd said. Her flat was a housing association place. I stopped and turned. She was standing close behind me, her hand out.

'My money,' she said. 'You—'

Her face fell. I don't know what she saw when she looked at me. Her death, I suppose. I moved towards her, she

170

backed away, put both her hands up to her throat.

My mind was going back and forth, from then to now, and I was losing track of when I was. I saw her, this cancerous woman, but with her fat around her, telling me Brenda was gone. I saw that other woman, Debs, telling me she'd bought the place from this bird who, as I was looking at her, seemed to be shedding her flab. I saw her telling me that her place had been a housing association flat.

She'd been a grass. She'd left a couple of months after Brenda got killed. That was nothing in itself, but she'd sold the flat, not vacated it. So, where had she suddenly got the money to buy her council place? And how could she buy it and sell it so quickly? Two months was too fast.

'Please,' she said. 'I'm dying.'

She stumbled as she backed up and fell heavily on her arm and cried out. I watched her as she lay on the ground, watched this thin, old-looking, cancerous woman at my feet.

Then I reached down and held out my hand. She took it. I pulled her up.

She rubbed her arm.

'Day before you were there,' she said.

'What?'

'That's when he was there. The man with the moustache. The day before you came. The day before I saw you.'

'Why did you tell me you couldn't remember?'

'Coz I was scared you knew I'd grassed you up.'

'What did you tell them?'

'I told them about you,' she said. 'I remembered you. I'd seen you before, with her. I'm sorry.'

'What did you tell them?'

171

'I told 'em she was your bird. I told 'em your name was Joe. I'd heard her call you that.'

'Why? Why'd you tell them about me?'

'They asked me. All I did was answer their questions. That's all. They were coppers, for fuck's sake. What else could I do?'

Fuck. She told them about me, told them I was with Brenda, that my name was Joe. And Compton had told me he only learned about me years after Brenda was killed, and only then because he was investigating Glazer and his connection with vice corruption. There were pictures of me in the file relating to Paget and Marriot, Compton had said.

What the fuck was going on? What was Compton after?

'And the money for your flat? And the clout to get it through the system so you could sell it?'

'It was him. The copper.'

'Why?'

'I told him I wouldn't talk coz you could find out and come back for me. People knew I was a grass. He came back the same day with some council bloke. They gave me forms to sign and told me I owned the flat.'

He must've had clout to do something like that; cutting through the red tape, handing over a flat.

'What did they want?' I said. 'What did they ask you?'

I took her by the arm and led her back to her seat. She sat meekly. I gave her one of the spliffs and she lit it up.

'Thanks,' she said.

She took a few hits. I gave her time. Her eyelids came down a bit, her mouth drooped, she sank back into the seat.

'I lied,' she said. 'Some of that stuff I told you. It was a lie. Now, I probably ain't got much longer to live. So…'

I nodded.

'Start at the beginning.'

'I was a grass for this copper, DS Rose, like I told you.'

'Where was he from?'

'Local nick. Anyway, all that was true. He told me to keep my eyes open, report things. There were gangs, drugs. There was a crack house a few floors below. All I done was make notes, car plates, names I learned. Then I give them to Rose. We'd meet each week in a pub near me.'

'Right,' I said, just for something to say.

'Well, one day I was in another pub, can't remember where, and Rose comes up to me. There's another bloke with him. The copper with the moustache.'

'Did he give you his name?'

'No. Rose told me to do what he said. Then he left. And this other copper, he buys me a drink and says don't bother with the drugs and stuff now. There's a woman, he says, lives next to you…'

'When was this?'

'Two, three weeks before she died.'

That would've been before she made the film.

My mind span away from me, and I felt Brenda near, saw her as I'd seen her that night in the pub, standing waiting for me to tell her I wasn't going to dance with her. I remembered what she smelled like that night; the sweetness of her perfume, the dankness of cigarette smoke, the tang of alcohol.

'Poor old Joe,' she'd say, 'heading for the breaker's yard.'

173

'He told me to keep a look out for people coming and going,' Sanford was saying, 'make notes, like I done for Rose.'

Her voice was thick and sleepy. She took another pull on the spliff, sucked it in hard and let it go in a breath of relief, as if she didn't have the strength not to.

'What did you see? What did you tell him?'

'Nothing. Really. There wasn't much I could tell him. Nothing happened. Aside from you.'

The spliff was down to its roach and she took a final hit, holding it between her finger nails, and dropped it on the carpet.

'Apart from when she was killed,' she said. 'Then stuff happened.'

'What happened?'

'They came, like I told you. The one with the moustache and the tall one. They went round there, that copper, with the other one, the tall one, and pulled the place apart. They said if anybody asked, I was to say they were from the drug squad. Then I nicked some stuff because the door was open. And that's it.'

She spread her arms.

'So you knew she was dead. When I came round that time, you knew and you pretended you thought she was still alive.'

'Yeah, that's right. I pretended. I thought you might think I had something to do with her getting killed. I didn't, but I thought you might think so.'

'What were they after, the coppers?'

'As if they'd tell me. When they were gone I went in and

174

took some stuff. Jewellery, money. I stole it, okay? I'm sorry. I'm sorry.'

There had to be more than that. Why bother with relocating her, going through all that shit with the housing association?

'What did you tell him?'

Her eyes were closed now. Her movements were slow. I put my hand on her shoulder, felt the bones through thin flesh. I shook her a little, not hard. Her eyes opened.

'What did you tell him?'

She brushed my hand away.

'Only what I saw, what I heard. Fuck. It was nothing. Really.'

'What?'

'God, I can't remember. There were blokes, of course. She'd kiss 'em. I'd describe 'em.'

She smiled, but it was a twisted, pained smile.

'And?'

'And I'd try and hear their names if I could, make a note of car numbers.'

'What blokes?'

'Ah, Christ. Please. How can I remember that?'

'You remembered me.'

'You were easy to remember.'

'Why'd you say that?'

She opened her eyes, lost some of her sleepiness.

I thought she was going to tell me I was easy to remember because I was so dangerous, so big, so fucking ugly. But she didn't. Something dark came into her face, as if a thunder cloud had passed behind me and been reflected in her eyes, and I realized it was a cloud, of sorts. It was her guilt, blocking out the light.

'You were easy to remember,' she said. 'When she kissed you she smiled.'

TWENTY-FOUR

Back at Browne's, I went back over what Margaret Sanford had told me, and tried to get it in some kind of order.

I knew that Brenda had known of Marriot's use of children in films for a while – she'd told me about it when we first started seeing each other. Somehow she got herself into one of these films. That was the one I'd seen, the one I had on DVD. She'd hidden a copy in a hole beneath her floor that she'd hoped I'd find. I did, years after she'd died. That was where I'd found her letter to me, the one asking me not to seek revenge, not to destroy myself for her.

The stuff about Glazer I'd assumed. It had made sense. He knew Paget, had hidden out with him. That I knew because of what Hayward had told me. Hayward had been undercover in Glazer's vice unit as part of Compton's investigation into corruption – or, what I had thought was Compton's investigation.

This I knew; Brenda had been murdered by Paget. She'd been murdered because she'd grassed Marriot up for what he was doing. She'd known she was in danger a long time before she'd done the film. And she hooked up with me because of who I was, who I am. She'd thought she was safe with me. I was her protection.

Some protection.

Fuck.

Browne came into the kitchen, where I was sitting, and looked at me and muttered something and left and came back again.

'What's up with you?' he said.

I could've told him about Cole getting killed, but I thought he'd just panic. That was the last thing I needed.

'I'm thinking,' I said.

'Holy Christ.'

I wanted him gone. I wanted to be alone with the past, with Brenda. I wanted to fall into it and get lost. I wanted to drown in it. But, as I knew, that way madness lay.

Browne turned to leave.

'Wait,' I said. 'Sit down.'

He came back in and sat. I told him what Margaret Sanford had told me.

'You say Compton was the one who wanted an eye kept on Brenda?'

'Yeah.'

'And he was the one who searched her place after she...'

'Yeah. He was the one.'

He thought about this.

'So, the question to ask is: what did he want?'

I looked at him. His face was scrunched up in concentration. He was trying, I supposed – in his way.

'I know that's the question,' I said.

'Yes,' he said. 'But you haven't seen how you could find out.'

If he thought I was going to corner Compton and

178

Bradley and Hayward and ask them politely what—

'The policeman,' he said, as I was thinking he was an idiot. 'The other policeman. This Rose.'

'Rose,' I said, thinking that he wasn't an idiot after all, but that I was.

'Yes. So, you need to find him, ask him what Compton wanted. Your friend Ben can help, can't he?'

'Green? He won't get involved any more.'

'Hmmm.'

Now Browne was thinking again. I was thinking too but I had the feeling he was doing it better than me.

'You said she was an informant?'

'Huh?'

'This Margaret Sanford.'

'Yeah.'

'And he was a local detective. So, he must've worked out of one of the station houses close to where she lived. That's your old patch, isn't it?'

TWENTY-FIVE

In the end, I found Rose easily. Browne was right – for once.

I was in a pub called The Grove, in Edgware. I took a seat at the table and phoned a couple of the nicks round where Brenda used to live. At the second place a woman told me Rose was now a DI and had transferred to Brompton. I called him there and when he answered I told him I had information relating to a case of his.

'What case?' he said.

'I'd rather not talk on the phone.'

'I can see you this afternoon. Come by. I promise you can talk in confidence.'

I told him I didn't want to be seen going to a police station. I said, 'Is there somewhere else we can meet?'

He hesitated. Then he said, 'There's a pub nearby called—'

'No,' I said. 'Look, there's a pub I know in Edgware, on the High Street. It's called The Grove.'

He sighed, asked again what it was concerning.

'It's an old case. A murder case.'

There was a long silence.

'Give me an hour,' he said finally.

'What car are you driving?'

'Blue Renault Laguna.'

I'd chosen the pub because it was halfway between the two of us, and because I could keep an eye on it before Rose got there. It was a large Edwardian building, stained glass at the top of the windows, lots of red brick. Inside it was roomy, space between the tables, high ceilings. It wasn't really a pub any more. Now it was the kind of place where people went to drink wine and talk about their tax returns. If you really tried, you could just about buy a pint of beer. But it occupied a good position. It was on a corner of the High Street, and it had two entrances, one on each road.

After I finished speaking to Rose, I left the pub and took a seat at the bus stop opposite. From there I could see all traffic going by, both entrances to the pub and anyone who went in.

It took him forty minutes. I watched the Renault drive past slowly, then carry on and turn. But he didn't stop. He drove off.

A couple of minutes later he came by again, parked. A tall bloke got out. He had short dark hair, a tanned face, deep-set eyes. He stepped into the pub. I gave him a minute then went over.

He was sitting at a table in the corner, back to the wall. He had a drink in front of him. I got a pint and went over and sat.

'You're Rose?'

'Yeah. And you?'

'Joe.'

'Joe. Joe What?'

'Nothing.'

'Right. You were at the bus stop as I drove up.'

He'd clocked me, then. And I hadn't noticed.

'Yeah.'

He nodded, drank some beer.

'Okay, you want to tell me something?'

'I want to ask you something. About when you were a DS, few years back.'

He sniffed, then stood up.

'Waste of fucking time,' he said.

As he was walking past me, I said, 'I can close a case for you. A murder. A long time ago. A woman called Brenda.'

He stopped, and I could see he knew what I was talking about. He looked at me again. He sat back down, drank some more beer.

'Joe,' he said, mulling the name over. 'You were a fighter. The Machine.'

'Yeah.'

He nodded.

'Yes,' he said. 'Awful. You were her boyfriend. I remember now. We looked into you but you had an alibi. You had a job in some casino, if I remember. Place was full of CCTVs. But we still wanted to talk to you. Only, you'd made yourself scarce. And now you know something.'

'What was the result of your investigation?'

'You know there were no convictions. She was a pro, so it was put down to a john. There were no witnesses, no CCTV footage, no DNA. Plenty of forensic stuff, but nothing to take us anywhere. It's still open. But you say you can close it for us?'

'I know who killed her.'

His eyes narrowed. He scratched his nose.

'Go on.'

'Give me some answers first.'

'About?'

'Man called Compton. A Detective Super.'

He drank some more beer, then took an e-cigarette out of his pocket and sucked on it. A small red light came on at the tip. While he did that, he scanned the pub, looking over my shoulder.

He blew out smoky stuff and said, 'I promised my wife. She's been onto me for years to quit smoking.'

'What about Compton?'

'I remember him.'

'Who was he?'

Rose shrugged.

'My boss came up to me one day, introduces Compton, tells me to help him as much as he wants. I asked Compton what he was working on, but he only said it was an important investigation. But I know one thing: he wasn't a copper.'

That made my skin prickle. It hadn't even occurred to me that Compton might not be law. But now that Rose had said it, something clicked in my head, and I knew Rose was right.

'What do you mean?'

Rose shrugged.

'He felt wrong. He didn't talk right, didn't know the lingo. I asked him about work he'd done and he was vague.'

'He was with another man. Bradley. A DI.'

'Yeah. I knew Bradley. He used to be Special Branch a

long time ago. That's why I found it odd that he was working on some vice thing. But, again…'

He spread his hands.

'Bradley was Special Branch?'

'Mm-hmm.'

'And what was Compton?' I said, knowing already what the answer must be.

'I'd guess political. Five, probably.'

Christ. What was this shit? MI5?

'Your boss,' I said, 'would he tell me?'

'That was my old DCI. He retired a few years ago. He's living in Florida, I think. Besides, if he wouldn't tell me then, why would he tell you now? What's this all about?'

'Do you remember a snout of yours, Margaret Sanford?'

'Maybe.'

'She lived near Brenda. She grassed for you, then Compton came and took her over. Then, after Brenda died, Sanford left sharpish. Why?'

'I wouldn't know.'

'You must know something.'

'I don't. I asked my boss and he told me to shut up and do as I was told. He said it's orders from above. I was smart enough to do as he said.'

'But—'

'I've answered as many questions as I'm gonna. Maybe you'd better start telling me something. Like who killed your bird.'

He wasn't going to tell me any more about Compton. But I'd already guessed that he'd be cagey. If I gave him something from my end, I might be able to work him back-wards towards Compton.

'It was Kenny Paget,' I said.

He shook his head, a look of frustration on his face.

'He was the first we thought of, had a bad rep and liked the blade. But he had an alibi too. Several people alibied him, in fact.'

'Marriot's men?'

'They still counted as witnesses.'

'It was on Marriot's orders that Paget killed her.'

'If you've got any evidence...'

He waited for me to say something, his eyebrows raised.

'There's no evidence,' I said.

He sighed deeply, scratched his chin.

'So what've you got? Your theory? That's not gonna do it.'

'Paget told me himself.'

'Well, I can see how someone like you could persuade him to talk, but it won't stand up in court.'

'It won't get to court. Neither will Paget.'

He sat back, sucked on his electronic cigarette. He stared at me long and hard, and his look now was flat and cold. Finally, he said, 'There's a war going on, I hear. In the East. You anything to do with that?'

'I know about it.'

'Bobby Cole's dead. They say Vic Dunham was behind it. They say Dunham's out for someone else too, someone like you.'

'Uh-huh.'

'And I heard Frank Marriot got himself killed a few

weeks back, and Kenny Paget disappeared on everyone, RIP. It's not my patch, so I don't really care. And even if it was my patch, I still wouldn't care. Having said that, I don't wanna hear no more. As far as I'm concerned, you lot can kill each other all day long.'

He gulped down the rest of his beer, put it slowly down onto the beer mat and stood.

'Good luck,' he said.

Then he was gone.

TWENTY-SIX

I had things to do. I had to work out what Rose had told me, what it meant. I had to find Compton or Bradley, put the screws on them. I had to find Glazer. I had to kill him.

But the next day, all I could manage to do was breathe in the right places and try not to drop dead. Even that was a struggle.

I was sitting with Browne in his lounge watching the TV dribble out some daytime shit. I could just about do that. I dozed on and off.

We'd been like that for a while, not speaking, not doing anything really except waiting for something to happen.

I thought I heard the phone ring at one point, but when I looked up I saw Browne where he had been. There was no sound of a phone ringing. There was no sound of anything. At least, I couldn't hear anything.

Then I opened my eyes again and saw Browne dozing, slumped down in his chair, his mouth open, his hand twitching. I reached over for the remote and turned the television volume down.

After a while the news came on and I watched as they showed people in Iraq killing each other and people in Syria killing each other and people everywhere killing each other.

Then I saw a house that had been gutted by fire, charred and razed. And I saw a fuzzy telephoto picture of a man. I recognized the man. It was Cole.

So, he was dead. And I was fucked. But I didn't care. It was as if it was all part of a dream. It was unreal and far away.

TWENTY-SEVEN

When we got back to her place, she flaked out on the sofa. I watched her for a while, thinking how beautiful she was. I took her clothes off, put her to bed.

I'd tried to speak to her about her work, tried to convince her to quit, but she'd only got angry with me so, now, I left it alone, scared that I'd push her away with my nagging.

Then I thought about what she'd said in the pub, about her apologizing for being who she was, and wondered why she'd said it. What had she been up to?

And I wondered again why we'd gone there.

When I thought she was asleep I lay down beside her. She rolled over, put a hand on my chest, moved it over so that it was above my heart. I felt my heartbeats through her hand, rebounding back into my flesh, as if she was giving me life.

'Joe,' she said, 'Joe.'

'I'm here.'

'Joe,' she said again, only softer. She seemed to be fading, going away from me, disappearing into the fog.

I put my arm around her shoulder, pulled her closer. She wrapped her legs around me. I stroked her thigh. It was warm and smooth. It was like silk, only smoother.

'Don't be afraid,' I said, not knowing why.

'Afraid,' she said, almost whispering. 'Afraid.'

Her body came out in goosebumps. I held her tighter.

'Have you ever felt fear?' she said.

'What of?'

'Oh, anything.'

Have I ever felt fear? Fuck.

'Yeah,' I said. 'I've felt fear.'

There are different kinds of fear, I told her. There's the fear that hits you in the guts like a sledgehammer when you hear the order to fix bayonets. There's the fear when you climb into the ring, knowing you're too old, too damaged to keep on fighting but knowing too that you haven't got any choice. There's the fear when you climb out of the ring and your head is fucked all ways and you don't even know who you are.

There's the fear you feel coming from others that soaks into your skin. There's the fear that spreads inside when you're alone. I knew both of those. I told her all this.

And then there's the fear, the dread I'd had when I thought I'd lost her. I didn't tell her about that one.

'I didn't think you could feel fear,' she said.

'Everyone feels fear,' I said. 'Everyone.'

She was quiet for a while, then she sat up, pulling herself away from me. She reached over to the bedside table for a cigarette. The flare of the lighter flashed onto her face and made it look pale, dead. The flickering flame threw our shadows around the room. Then it all went dark again and I heard her suck in smoke and breathe it out as if she was sighing.

'I hate it,' she said. 'The fear.'

'Most people let it rule their lives. But it's not so bad. Fear's a prison. If you want out of prison, you have to stop fear controlling you.'

'Live with it, you mean?'

I thought about that.

'Sort of. You have to know it's there but ignore it, push it aside. When I was in the Falklands we had to go forward into shelling, machine gun fire. I was shit scared. We all were. Our platoon sergeant told us we were all probably gonna die. After that the fear didn't bother me.'

She didn't say anything, but I knew she was thinking about what I'd said. I could hear her smoking, feel the heat of her thigh pressed against me.

'What are you scared of?' I said.

'Nothing.'

She didn't even bother to try and sound convincing.

'What is it?'

'Just stuff, Joe. Please.'

That meant I had to shut up, not question her.

'I feel safe with you, though,' she said. 'And, what you said, that helps too.'

I told her that was good, but I felt fear then, real, dark, thick fear.

She killed the smoke and put her head back on the pillow and folded herself into me again.

We were silent for a long time. I stared up at the greyness of the ceiling, just happy to be there, in her bed, her body and mine tied together. If I could've spent the rest of my life like that, I'd have been okay. Fuck the world.

'I remember this time with me dad,' she said, her voice low, husky. 'Me real dad, that is, when I was a kid. Long time ago, incidentally.'

'Not so long,' I said.

She snuggled up more.

'Well, anyway, I was scared of spiders. If I saw one, I'd scream and jump on my bed. They move so fast. I think it was that more than anything that scared me. There was this crack, see, in the skirting board and this spider lived there. I'd seen it go in and out. I told my dad, begged him to do something. So, he covered the crack, boarded it up.'

Now she was quiet for a moment. I didn't want to say anything. It was like, if I spoke, I'd break something. I always seemed to be treading on eggshells when I was with her.

'Anyway,' she said quietly, 'I would lie there, in bed, thinking about that spider being trapped there, starving to death, in the dark. I thought maybe it had a family and that it was just trying to feed them. And I couldn't stand it. I felt so guilty, Joe. Next day I got my dad to pull the board off. I was never scared of spiders after that.'

'What happened to him?' I said. 'Your dad?'

Her body tensed.

'He left, went back to St Lucia. Just dumped us. Never heard from him again.'

'Why did you want to go to that pub?'

She said nothing for a long time. Her body felt cold and I thought again about her face looking so pale in the light of the flame.

'The Falklands,' she said, finally. 'That was a long time ago. You don't have to do that now. You don't have to do

192

what they tell you. What scares you now? Apart from dancing with me.'

She poked me in the ribs with her elbow, making light of it all. That's how I knew it had upset her, me not dancing.

'I'm afraid you'll get hurt,' I said. 'I'm afraid it'll be my fault, that I didn't stop it.'

'Oh, Joe.'

She pushed herself into me, hugged me tightly, tighter than she'd ever done before.

'You won't let that happen,' she said.

After she was murdered, I sometimes thought that, of everything I'd done or said, not dancing with her that night hurt her the most. Maybe I was wrong. Maybe I just wanted to think it so that I could hate myself a bit more – if that was possible.

Somewhere, a phone was ringing.

TWENTY-EIGHT

I opened my eyes, saw Browne watching the TV, wondered where I was, remembered.

I mumbled something. Browne mumbled something back.

Slowly the day got older, and I got older with it, but at a hundred times the speed.

The highlight of the afternoon was when Browne laughed at some politician on the box. He was being interviewed, this bloke, and had been asked if he thought the police needed external regulation, and he'd said no, not at all. He'd gone on to say that, on the whole, the public trusted the police, just as they did politicians.

That's when Browne laughed. He laughed a lot. Then he stared at the space in front of him, not laughing at all. Then he had another drink.

I kept telling myself I had to get up and do something, but I couldn't remember what. So I stayed where I was and waited for something to happen.

Nothing happened. And then nothing more happened and I started to wonder what I was supposed to be waiting for anyway.

Then something happened.

The phone rang.

Browne glanced at me sideways, as if checking to see if I'd heard it. He got up and went out and came back.

'Joe,' he said, holding the handset out to me.

I took it and held it to my ear and said, 'Yeah?'

I heard a voice that sounded too posh to be anyone I could know.

'Is this… is this Joe?' the voice said.

Was I Joe? I had to think about that.

'Maybe,' I said. 'Who's this?'

'Marriot,' the voice said.

Marriot? He was dead. I killed him. I said, 'Who is this?'

'Marriot. Jason Marriot.'

Jason Marriot? I didn't know any Jason Marriot.

'I want to help you,' he said.

'What?'

'You said you knew someone who… who died.'

'I've known lots of people who've died,' I said, thinking someone here was going mad.

'Look, I don't know how to do this. I don't… Look, you told me about a woman you knew. If she died, it was Kenny Paget who killed her.'

'Yes,' I said, knowing now who he was, remembering what I'd told him. I knew a woman.

'I know that my dad was somehow responsible. I know that. But there were others, right? It wasn't just him.'

'Right.'

'And Paget's one.'

'Yes.'

'And you'll go after Paget? I can help. I know where he lives.'

195

'Paget's dead,' I said.

There was a long silence.

'I see,' he said.

Only now was my head beginning to work properly. He wanted to help, he'd said. Was this a set up? Who was he working for?

'Why do you want to help me?'

For a few seconds all I could hear was a kind of buzzing sound. Then his voice filled my ear, and I could make out the pain in it.

'I spoke to my mum,' he said. 'I spoke to her about my dad. I know what he did.'

After I'd hung up, Browne handed me some tablets.

'Take 'em,' he said.

I explained to Browne that the boy was Marriot's son, and that he might help me get to Glazer, and that he'd tried to kill me.

'That's how I hit my head again,' I said.

Browne sat and listened to all that, and then he sighed and shook his head and said, 'I don't know why I bother.'

I didn't know why either, except that he couldn't seem to help himself.

When the knock came, Browne answered it and led Marriot in. He seemed younger than I'd remembered, not much more than a teenager. He was thin, his jeans and plaid shirt too baggy. There was a plaster on his forehead, and a smudged blue-yellow bruise on his chin.

'Come in, son,' Browne said to him. 'Can I get you a cup of tea?'

'Uh, yeah. Yes, please.'

Browne wandered off and Marriot came further into the room, looking at me side-on.

He sat in the chair opposite me, and leaned forward, his arms on his knees. He seemed about two miles away, and yet his face was a few feet from mine.

We waited like that until Browne came back with a mug of tea. Meanwhile, Marriot had clocked Browne's Scotch, and Browne noticed him noticing it.

'Would you like a bit of something in your tea?'

Marriot nodded. Browne topped the tea up from his half-bottle.

Browne and me watched him sip the tea, then gulp it down.

'Take your time,' Browne said.

'I didn't know what to do,' the boy said, lowering the mug and wiping his mouth on his shirt sleeve.

'What do you mean?' I said.

'Look, what you said, about my dad, what he did...'

He looked down at the mug in his hands.

'It wasn't your fault,' Browne said. 'You can't be held responsible. Or your mother.'

I thought Browne was talking bollocks there, but he gave me a look that said, Right, Joe?

'Right,' I said.

'My mum,' Marriot said, 'she thinks you'll come back. I want you to promise you won't see her again, won't hurt her.'

Browne was looking at me the same way the boy was. They were waiting for an answer – would I promise not to hurt a woman? Did Browne think I might?

'I don't care about your mother,' I said, looking down at my hands, which were huge and ugly and brutal, the bones made of iron and the skin made of tree bark.

'Promise me you won't touch her.'

'Yes,' I said, not able to look away from those hands, 'I promise.'

'May I have another tea, please?' he said.

Browne took his mug, looked at it, looked at me, looked at Marriot.

'How about a glass instead?' he said.

The boy nodded. I'd never known Browne to hand out so much of his booze, except when he knew I was fucked in the head, or injured, or missing Brenda or Kid, or whatever.

Anyway, he went to the cabinet, pulled out a glass, dusted it off and handed it to the kid, along with his bottle of Scotch.

When he'd had another swig, Marriot shuddered and said, 'I know my dad was involved in crime.' His voice was thicker. 'I think I always knew it. But I didn't really understand what, exactly.'

'And now?'

He didn't answer that.

'You asked me about a man called Glazer,' he said, looking up at me and Browne as if he wanted us to smile and pat him on the back.

'Yeah.'

'I remember him. His name was Mike. He'd come around the house sometimes. Him and that… that bastard, Paget. Look, it was them, all right. Not my dad.'

198

'I don't care about that,' I said. 'I just want Glazer.'

Browne glared at me again. I didn't know why.

'You said you could help me,' I said to the boy. 'How?'

'My dad had a safe,' he said, 'in his office.'

'Yes,' I said.

'After he died, it was unlocked. The solicitor had to get someone in from the safe company. There wasn't much in there, but what there was went to my mum. She didn't know what to do with it, so I took it. I've had it in a shoebox in a cupboard.'

'Where is it now? This stuff?'

'In my car.'

'Go get it.'

He didn't move.

'Finish your drink first, son,' Browne said.

The boy nodded, tipped the booze into this mouth, shuddered again.

'This must've been hard for you,' Browne said. 'Coming here, telling us what you have.'

'It was.'

Browne glanced at me. I saw his jaw flex, something flicker in his eye. He turned back to Marriot.

'Why don't you go, son,' Browne was saying, 'take that stuff to the police? Let them sort it out.'

'What?' I said.

'The police?' Marriot said.

'You seem like a decent man,' Browne was telling him. 'Don't get yourself involved any further. Just take it all to the police, make a clean breast of it.'

I tried to stand up, but went dizzy half way and fell

199

back again. It wasn't the usual kind of dizziness. I looked at Browne, understanding what he'd done.

'What were those pills?' I said.

'Sedatives. They'll wear off. In a while.'

I swear there was a smile on his face.

'You planned this.'

Browne ignored that. He turned back to Marriot who was looking at us both with his mouth open.

'I don't understand,' Marriot said.

'This world,' Browne was saying, 'these people, Joe, here, look at him, you don't belong in this, doing what they do. Go live your life. Be good.'

Browne had done me properly. Him and his bloody morality. The boy was unsure now.

'And you?' he said. 'What about you? Why are you here? It doesn't make sense.'

'I've learned too late.'

'Well…'

I shook my head.

'Give it to the law and they'll be all over you,' I told Marriot. 'And your mum. Glazer's one of them. They protect their own. You know that.' His eyes flickered from me to Browne and back again. 'And if they do investigate it, your dad's name will be shit. Your mum's too. Browne may go for that innocent line, but the law won't.'

Browne stared daggers at me.

'My mum didn't know what my dad did.'

'Uh-huh.'

'She didn't know.'

'Maybe, but it'll take a lot to convince the law about

that, even if you found ones who weren't going to grass you to Glazer. You want to protect her, don't you?'

I expected a fight with Browne, but he sighed and said nothing. We all said nothing, then Marriot got up and left.

Browne watched him go, then dropped his head. He thought Marriot would be back. I wasn't so sure.

Silence filled the air between Browne and me. I was angry. Browne knew I would be, of course, which is why he'd doped me.

'What was all that about?' I said.

'You don't get it, do you? You just don't understand.'

'No. I don't.'

He sighed, shrugged. Another failure. Another one to chalk up.

'He phoned when you were asleep, told me who he was. He said he wanted to talk to you, to help you. It occurred to me that he might have something to lead you to Glazer.'

'So?'

'What would you have me do? Help you kill a man? You don't really think I'd go that far, do you?'

He was right, of course. I hadn't thought about it. Browne was a fuck-up in a lot of ways, but he'd never hurt anyone so far as I knew, even the ones who deserved it. And he would never let someone be hurt if he could avoid it.

So, he saw an opportunity to prevent me doing harm. All he had to do was give me some sedatives and try to convince Marriot's son to walk away.

'What else can I do?' I said.

'The police, Joe. Let them handle it.'

'Police? What police? Glazer is a policeman. Compton is. You think you can trust them?'

'They can't all be bad.'

'Tell me the ones that aren't. Christ, Brenda went to the fucking police, and they murdered her for it.'

'I know, son,' he said, quietly. 'I know.'

We heard the front door close. The boy must've put the latch on.

He walked into the room holding a shoebox. He held it out to me, but kept his eyes down.

'I don't care about anything,' he said, 'except my mum. Leave her alone, that's all.'

I opened the box and started to go through the stuff inside. Browne watched in silence. He filled his glass.

There was a ledger. Names, numbers, amounts, credits, debits. I saw Glazer's name there. He was getting a grand a month from Marriot. There were other names, some I knew, most I didn't. That ledger would send a lot of people down, if the law got it. The right law, that was. But it was no use to me. I tossed it aside.

There were papers, deeds, documents relating to this and that. Marriot owned a lot of stuff; properties around London, Scotland, Spain. There were memorandums of association, articles of association. Marriot had companies doing all sorts of shit – on paper, at least. Paget's name was on a few of them, listed as a director. So were a few other people, most of them dead. None of these helped me.

It was the address book that did it. As soon as I saw it, I grabbed it, opened it up, went straight to G:

Glazer, M.

202

But the entry had been crossed out.

I called the number anyway. A child's voice answered, said he'd get his mummy.

'Hello,' the woman said.

'Is Mike there?'

'Oh, no, sorry. You've got the wrong number.'

So, that was that. Another dead end.

I looked through it anyway, from the start. A, B, C, on and on.

And then I got to S.

Sutton, Mary

I was about to turn to the next page when I remembered what Marriot's wife had said. Glazer had a girlfriend, she said. Mary something.

'What's this?' I said to young Marriot.

I held the book out. He looked at it, shrugged.

'Dunno.'

I called the number. A woman answered. I said, 'Is Mike Glazer there?'

'He's not here at the moment. Can I ask who's calling?'

It took me a moment to register what she'd said. After all this time, I'd found him. It didn't seem real. I said, 'Do you know when he'll be back?'

'No. Who's calling?'

I killed the phone.

'Got him.'

'What are you gonna do?' the boy said, his face suddenly white.

Even Browne raised an eyebrow. If the boy had only just realized I was going to kill Glazer, he was a fucking idiot.

Maybe he'd just wanted to pretend that I was bluffing.

'Bush Hill,' I said, 'where's that?'

'That's only a couple of miles away,' Browne said, shaking his head, staring, perhaps, at the stupidity of it all.

A couple of miles away. Christ. I could've walked there in half an hour.

'What are you gonna do?' the boy said again.

'Go home,' I told him. 'Go back to your mum.'

'Find him, then,' Browne said to me. 'But if you kill him, you'll betray her. You damned well remember that.'

204

I was going to have to be careful I wasn't followed. No one must know I was going to Glazer. I decided I'd use public transport, hit the city, mix it up a bit. It's hard to follow someone when they can jump on a bus, hail a cab and head off through London traffic.

There was a young family at the bus stop. The woman had long blonde hair and huge blue eyes. She was rocking a pram. Inside were two small babies, both wrapped in rainbow coloured blankets, both staring up at her with blank open faces as she looked back down at them, smiling. The bloke next to her wore an Aston Villa shirt. He saw me come near and stepped closer to the woman.

The woman turned, then, and watched me as I took a seat. The bloke relaxed a bit when I did that. I don't know what he expected me to do. Kidnap the babies, probably. On the girl's T-shirt were the words 'Help... Twins'. She turned back to the children. Her husband looked up the road, waiting for the bus, his eyes flicking over to me every now and then.

I found myself looking at the two babies. They both had wisps of blonde hair falling below woollen hats. On one hat was the word 'Imogen', on the other, 'Jessica'. They moved lazily, one lifting its arm up out from below the blanket, reaching for something in the air, the other stretching its mouth. I sniffed, and that brought their attention to me. They stared, mouths open, eyes wide, as if they were looking at something new, something that didn't fit.

I saw that the woman was looking at me again, her large eyes soft. I thought, clocking me looking at her babies, she'd move away, pull her children nearer. Parents protected their young as a matter of instinct, and people always looked at me as a threat.

She didn't move away or pull the pram closer. Instead, she carried on rocking it. A bus came up the road and the bloke said something to her. They lifted the babies out of the pram, the woman and the bloke each holding one of them. Then the bloke collapsed the pram. The bus pulled up. The door opened. The bloke got on, but the woman paused and turned and looked back towards me. She didn't seem scared or horrified or sickened. She seemed interested.

Then she did something odd. She smiled. I didn't know how to respond to that. I think I smiled back. The bloke was eyeing me up from the bus. Maybe he saw something in me that she didn't. Maybe it was the other way round; she seeing something that he didn't, or couldn't.

Then they were gone.

I sat there for a while, watching the world wander past. I was supposed to be scoping the scene for tails, but my mind kept going blank, and out of the blankness I'd think about that woman smiling. Then I'd think about Brenda smiling and the two would become one and I'd see Brenda with a pram, rocking it gently, letting the babies see her face, her smile, her wide open eyes.

When a bus came, I got on it, not bothering where it was going, not checking for tails.

I wondered what that blonde girl had seen. What had been on my face as I'd gazed at her and her babies? Had I let it slip for a moment? Had I seen Brenda? Had I seen something I'd lost, forgetting that I'd lost it and seeing it as if it was real?

I looked out the window. We were heading along the Mile End Road. I must've been sitting on that bus for half an hour, but it felt as if I'd only just got on. I had no idea now if I was being tailed.

I got out at the tube station, and took the Central line to Liverpool Street. There'd been too many people on the plat-form for me to see if I'd been followed onto the train. I stood in the middle of the carriage, having to bow my head. I held the hand grip tightly and looked up and down the carriage, trying to see if anyone was deliberately avoiding my gaze. As far as I could make out, everyone was doing that. In fact, everyone was avoiding everyone's gaze. Some were reading books or newspapers, some were texting, some sitting looking blankly into space while sounds went along the wires attached to their ears. It was like we were all part of a funeral cortege, only nobody knew the deceased or any of the other mourners.

The train driver did his best to break my neck, but somehow I made it to Liverpool Street in one piece. When I got out, I took a few seconds to straighten up and breathe air that wasn't full of heat and eye-stinging perfume and body odour and silence.

I went up to the mainline concourse and then through

that and up the elevator to the gallery bit, which, at least, was open to the outside. The cold air seeped in and made me feel clean again, even if it was filled with grit and fumes.

I stood there a while, watching the grey shapes flow below me. It felt like I was in a different world; all these people moving around like parts in some great machine, each thinking they were their own person, each thinking they were important.

I saw men in suits and long coats, and women in suits and short coats, an endless line of people who didn't do anything for anyone except themselves and others like them – not unlike my kind, except those like me knew we weren't kidding ourselves. We took what we could, how we could, and fuck you. This lot did the same, but less honestly and without guns.

Except for a few teenage lads in black jeans and leather jackets, there were no kids, no old people either, no disabled or slow or poor people. I saw a few builders wander around, walking more lazily than the rest. I saw tourists and some single young people with backpacks and suitcases heading home, or back to college or wherever. Mostly, I saw a name-less, faceless grey-suited horde, swarming and buzzing, heading in a mass to one exit or another. I hated them all, the whole fucking lot, except maybe those kids in black or the single people with suitcases and backpacks. The rest I hated because they didn't know what they were.

And I wanted to be like them.

I didn't see anyone who stood out, though. I didn't see anyone who looked at me for more than a second. I didn't see anyone who didn't seem to be going somewhere or doing something.

There was a pub outside, next to the station. I went in there and stood at the bar and watched the entrance to see if anyone followed me in. Nobody did. I took a pint, went outside with the smokers and waited until everyone I saw hanging around had gone or met up with someone else.

After that, I hailed a cab and told the cabbie to take me to Piccadilly Circus. Anyone following me now would have a hard time.

I wasn't being paranoid, I told myself, I was just being careful. Dunham wanted Glazer as much as me, or, at least, he wanted what Glazer had. So did Compton, I thought. I'd have been stupid if I hadn't taken precautions.

When, finally, I was sure nobody had followed me, I told the cabbie to pull over. I paid him, then got another cab and told him to take me to Bush Hill. He twisted around and looked at me suspiciously.

'That's gonna be a big fare, mate,' he said.

I gave him a score up front. After that, he was okay.

I kept a lookout through the rear window while the cabbie told me why United had fucked up this season and how the country was letting in too many immigrants and why his wife was a selfish cow.

After a few years, we pulled up outside a detached house on a quiet suburban road. I paid the cabbie and got out. I waited until the taxi had turned a corner, then I waited some more. Nothing moved. There were no people around, no cars rolling by.

The house was smart, without being posh. Still, in this

area, it was probably the top end of a million. The place was about a hundred years old, one of those red-bricked things with large bay windows and high chimneys. In front of it was a large lawn with a cherry tree. I could see Browne living in a place like this, if he'd been reasonably successful as a GP. Either Glazer had done well out of corruption or his girlfriend was loaded – or both.

I touched the Makarov in my jacket pocket and walked up the driveway, the gravel crunching beneath my feet, past a silver S-Class Merc, brand new. I felt alert. Something inside me stirred. I was about to end it, kill the last one who'd killed Brenda. I was going to close the circle, at last. Adrenaline started to flood me. I felt my muscles tighten, my heart race.

I rang the bell, waited, rang it again. There was no sound from inside, no movement that I could see. I took a step back and kicked the door open. I had about twenty stone behind that foot. The lock smashed apart. The door flew back.

I had my gun out now, held low. It felt good. It was cold and heavy and endless. It was death, and I liked it.

I stayed where I was, in the doorway, and waited for sound, movement, something. Still nothing. I stepped inside. Ahead of me were stairs. To my right was a door, closed. To the left was a doorway leading to the lounge. I went that way, moving quietly, the carpet softening my steps, just in case nobody had heard the door smash off its hinges.

I saw the woman as I went into the room. She was on the floor, blood dripping from the gash in her head, soaking into the blue carpet making a small black pool. Her hands were tied behind her back, her eyes closed.

I took a step forward. And stopped.

Her blood was still dripping. The bloodstain was small. Fuck.

I turned.

He was a yard behind me. He swung something dark and heavy and missed and grunted with the effort. If I hadn't turned he'd have caved my head in.

I saw then what he was holding. It was an assault rifle with a collapsible stock. He brought it up and tried to swing it in my face, but he'd forgotten that the stock was back. And he'd forgotten that I used to be a boxer. I stepped outside him and he swung and hit air and staggered forward, unbalanced. I threw my free fist into his kidney and his head snapped back with pain and shock. He dropped the rifle, fell to the ground and whimpered, squirming around. I kicked him in the head. Then I saw shadows and threw myself aside as the bullets tore the place apart.

I rolled and turned and emptied the magazine from a kneeling position, both hands holding the Makarov. I hit space. They were gone.

I heard a screech of tyres. I jumped up and ran to the front window. Two men dragged a struggling figure towards a white van, while another helped the bloke I'd floored. The back doors of the van opened and they threw the struggling man in.

I recognized the figure. It was Glazer. The bastards had got him.

I was out the front door as the van was pulling away. I got the last three letters of the number plate. I cursed myself for not driving. Tails. Fuck. They didn't need to tail me.

211

They knew where Glazer was.

But I knew something too. I knew who they were. I recognized the man who'd tried to hit me with his gun; he worked for Vic Dunham.

It crossed my mind that I'd been set up, that Marriot's son had wanted vengeance on me and had arranged this. But no. He wouldn't have sent me here. He'd have sent me to a corner of some wasteland. And, besides, Dunham's men would've finished the job. As it was, it looked like I took them by surprise. Maybe it had been coincidence.

I rushed back in. The woman's eyes were open now, but they were empty, blank.

'Car keys,' I said.

She mumbled something but I couldn't understand her.

I went through the ground floor until I found the kitchen. I threw open drawers, tore through the place and found nothing. Then, I stopped and thought about it. I went back into the hallway and saw a coat stand. I saw a man's jacket and put my hand in the pockets and found them.

I was on my way out the front door when the image of the woman on the floor came into my head. I don't know why that was, and I don't know why it made me stop, but it did.

I went back, and cursed myself for doing it.

Her eyes were closed. The blood had stopped flowing, which might've meant she was dead, or that the blood had congealed. I knelt down, checked her pulse. She was alive. I put her in the recovery position, got the phone from the sideboard, dialled 999 and asked for an ambulance.

212

I left the line open, wiped the phone down and left it on the floor, near her.

Browne would've been proud of me.

The Merc span as I pulled out of the driveway, the wheels throwing gravel all over the place. Dust filled the rear-view. I fishtailed across the road and straightened it out. Thank Christ I was driving an auto.

I gunned the motor down Bush Hill Road. It was mostly residential, and traffic was light, although the parking was a bastard and I had to weave my way through it, and all the time I was looking for a white van – in London. Fucking brilliant.

I had to slam on the brakes when I got to the bottom of the road and some delivery van was backing out of a parking bay.

Then I hit red lights at the junction with the A105. I pulled the car to a stop and thought. Which way now? Left? Right? Straight on?

I had an idea where they were going. Or I thought I did. Surely they wouldn't take him to one of Dunham's homes. So, they'd probably head for the club, go in the back way. I had to head towards the West End, then. That was easy. And I had a fast car. And they were in a slow van and wouldn't want the law stopping them for speeding or running lights, not with a kidnapped copper in the back.

The A105 went to the North Circular, which was to the right. But I could get to the North Circular by the A10 too, which was straight ahead.

The bloke in the car behind blew his horn. The lights were green. He blew his horn again. People were looking.

Central London was south of us, and to the east. They could take the A10 to the City, or to the North Circular. Either way, they'd use the A10 for a bit.

I had to take a chance on that. I slammed my foot on the gas and left the bloke behind sitting there as if someone had glued his car to the road.

I weaved through the traffic, always looking as far ahead as I could, trying to make out anything white, anything big.

I was going through suburban streets, large semi-detached houses on both sides. The road was wide, few parked cars. The Merc was a cinch to drive, smooth, powerful. All I had to do was move my foot, move my hands. I'd swing past one car, floor it, feel the motor scream, then bring the whole thing back down when I was about to pile head-on into something coming towards me.

It was fine. Except for one thing: there was no white van – at all.

I hit the A10 junction. I didn't bother stopping for the red light this time. The car slewed across the lanes, ahead of a jack-knifing truck, and onto the two-lane. I had to throw the wheel over to correct the back end, but I brought the motor round, just missing a white-faced woman in a Honda.

Then I really opened the Merc up, foot to the floor; fifty, sixty, seventy. The traffic was heavier here, but my adrenaline was high, rising with the speed, the thrum of the engine feeding blood to my body, my heart pumping, my head clear. Eighty.

The steering wheel was easy in my hands, and the car was smooth, like I was driving on ice, sliding between

214

cars, vans, buses. It felt like I was slicing through the world, through all the bollocks, through my own impotence, pounding the engine, hearing it roar, gritting my teeth, squeezing the steering wheel as if it was Glazer's neck, Paget's, Dunham's.

I was going to catch the van, ram the Merc right into it, smash the cunts to pieces and fuck everything else. Fuck it all.

Right then, with that adrenaline pumping, I felt good, my head clear, unclouded, and I wanted to kill. I ached to murder.

Anyone.

Everyone.

I saw white vans, but they all had something wrong with them; too dirty, too small. I saw one up ahead, about two hundred yards. It was the right size, shape, everything. I closed on it in seconds, and saw the registration was wrong.

I saw another van in the left lane and pulled in, but when I closed the gap enough I could see it had writing on the back door, some plumbing firm. I smashed the accelerator and flew past it.

I was running out of space, closing in on the North Circular. If I didn't get the van soon, I'd have to give it up. It could go right at the North Circular, or it could carry straight on. I supposed, at least, that I knew where it was heading. If I lost it, I could look to find it again nearer Dunham's club.

The traffic was getting thicker as we neared the North Circular. I knew the roundabout up ahead. It was a bastard.

There were coaches in the way now, and everything was slowing down. I got the finger a few times, got flashed and hooted at. I saw a cop car pass on the other side of the reservation. He wasn't going to be able to cross over for a while, but he might radio ahead. I was driving a stolen car belonging to a kidnapped copper. And I was armed with a pistol that could tie me into crime scenes all over London.

And then I hit a clear stretch and forgot all about the law. Up in front, nearing the roundabout, was a white van. I eased closer and saw the last three letters of the number plate.

KJP. That was it. That was the van. As soon as I saw it, I eased back, pulled into the left lane, let other cars overtake me. The van was sticking to the speed limit and pulled into my lane when they'd gone past an Astra. That was fine. I backed off a bit more and a small Ford overtook me, came into the lane.

I could see the top of the van above the roofs of the cars in front. I had them, but I had to keep them. There was no way I could get to Glazer like this. I had to wait until they came to a junction or lights, and then ram them at speed, which meant I had to follow them for now, and try to anticipate when they might stop, then move into position.

Then movement caught my eye and I was looking at the back of the Ford, at a young girl, staring at me through the back window.

She was about nine, ten. She had large eyes, dark skin, dark hair. And for a moment, for just a beat of a heart, I was looking at Kid, and she was looking back at me in that way of hers, eyes wide with a kind of wonder, a kind of fear.

Then the line of traffic moved forward, slowly, heading towards the roundabout. I was just starting to edge out to overtake the Ford when I saw the van go over to the left. That was wrong, surely. If they were taking that slip road, then they were going to take the North Circular east, not west, as they should've done.

So now I had no choice. I had to close in and wait until they hit a junction, then ram the fuckers. They weren't going into the City. I no longer knew where they were going. If I tried to follow and lost them, that would be it.

The van slowed as it neared the North Circular. I tried to move past the Ford, but there was no room. We were all stuck in the same long, thin limb of traffic, all part of some massive animal, barely crawling along because it no longer had the life to do anything else.

My eyes went back to the girl again. She wasn't looking at me now. She was gazing out of the side window, hypnotized by the slowness of it all, by the endless fucking pointlessness. Or so it seemed.

The Astra right behind the van was pulling out now, deciding it didn't want to take this slip road. The Ford moved up, and I moved up with it.

I was twenty yards behind the van. They weren't going to be able to go anywhere quickly. All I had to do was stay cool, stay alert, wait my turn. All I had to do was make sure they didn't see me.

They saw me. The driver glanced in his wing mirror, then looked forward, then looked back. He spoke to someone next to him. A few seconds went by. Then the passenger door opened and a man got out and started to walk towards me. It was the man with short blond hair, the one I'd hit back at the house. He brought his assault rifle up. He had the stock locked open this time, and there was a smile on his face and I knew he was going to kill me if he could.

I had a chance if I got out on my side of the car and went down low, took his legs out.

I saw movement. The girl in the Ford had turned back and was watching me, a frown on her face. She was right between me and Dunham's man, right in the path of fire. The adrenaline froze in my blood and turned my insides to ice, and all I could see was the girl, Kid, killed in the crossfire when I'd taken Marriot out, killed, perhaps, by me.

For half a second I couldn't move. I had to do something, and I had to do it quickly. I should've pulled my gun, got out of the car and killed the man walking towards me. But it was already too late. I'd lost it.

Then he opened up.

I didn't hear the gunshots. But I heard the rounds hit the car, felt it judder under the impact, as if the sky was raining rocks.

The windscreen broke into lots of spiderwebs. Something buzzed past my ear and cracked into the metal door frame. I ducked, shoved the gearstick into reverse and floored the accelerator, slamming into the car behind me. I kept on, wheels spinning, burning rubber pouring out from beneath and clouding the view out of the side windows. The car behind me was screeching back. I could hear shouting. I could hear panic, other cars trying to pull out of the way of the automatic fire.

Then everything was different and I realized the car wasn't getting peppered with bullets. I looked up and through the laced windscreen and saw the van mounting the kerb and racing off.

I glanced back at the Ford, scared suddenly that the girl would be on the floor, another innocent victim of my life.

A woman was holding the girl tightly, her hands about the girl's head. The girl was unhurt, but she was staring at me, her eyes wide, fearful and yet, I thought, angry, condemning.

I thought for a moment about going back to Glazer's place and speaking to the woman there, but then I remembered that I'd called an ambulance for her. By now she'd be surrounded by law.

In the end, I wiped the car down and walked away. Someone shouted after me, but I didn't stop and nobody followed me.

I walked. I heard sirens, lots of them. I kept walking, cursing myself for hesitating, wondering why I'd done it, wondering if I'd lost it, somehow.

'This can't go on, Joe,' Browne had said.

He was right. It couldn't go on. Something was going to give, and I was starting to think that it might be me.

I heard more sirens, further in the distance now. After a while, I heard a helicopter. I knew it was the law without looking up. It was looking for me or the van.

It was circling above. I walked with my head down.

THIRTY

By the time I got back I was shattered, wasted. I'd lost. Dunham had killed Cole, got Glazer.

He'd won.

The adrenaline had gone, and failure filled its place.

I dragged my body into Browne's house and closed the door carefully, closed it finally, on everything, on the past, on justice, revenge. Whatever.

It was late afternoon. I think. There was still sunlight, anyway. I trudged through to the kitchen and fell onto one of the wooden chairs and rested my arms on the table.

I thought about losing Glazer. I wasn't sure how I felt about it. I was angry that Dunham had beaten me, sure, but that was something else.

Browne wandered into the kitchen. He stopped, looked at me.

'Well?' he said.

'Glazer's gone. Dunham's got him. He wants the DVD.'

Browne thought about that for a minute.

'But that doesn't make sense,' he said. 'Doesn't Dunham know you have a copy?'

'Yes.'

'So, any copy he gets is useless if you still have one.

If you gave it to the media, his copy would be valueless.'

He was right, but I was too tired to care.

Browne made me a cup of tea and put it down on the table. I tried to drink some, but my hands were shaking too much.

Browne sat with me for a while, but I didn't say anything more, and he didn't push it.

After a while, he got up and went off and came back with an armful of stuff.

He'd got it into his head to do some work in the front garden. I think he just wanted to get out of the house and stretch his legs, but he was afraid to go too far. He hadn't gone into the back garden since we'd sealed that part of the house. I don't know what he thought was going to happen in the middle of the day. The precautions we'd taken were for a night attack. They weren't going to be hiding in the rose bushes. On the other hand, I couldn't blame him for being scared.

I told him again to go somewhere – his sister's or a hotel or something. But he still wouldn't listen.

'Things might get heavy,' I said. 'You'll get in the way.'

'This is my bloody house,' he said.

Anyway, all the gardening tools were in the shed in the back garden, so Browne used a carving knife, a pair of scissors, a pickaxe he'd found in the hall cupboard – and a comb. Fuck knows what that was for.

He went out there looking like he was going to break into a prison and cut someone's hair.

I rested my head on the tabletop. I didn't have anything left in me. I didn't know what to do.

221

She stood by the window of her flat, one hand holding a cigarette by her side, the other holding the back of her neck.

She'd slept badly, dreaming about something, mumbling in her sleep, tossing around. There was darkness in her mind, torment.

I hadn't slept at all. I'd watched her toss and turn, wishing I could do something to ease her. Instead, I'd felt the weight of my weakness.

I'd thought about things, and kept thinking about them until my head was dizzy. I'd tried to remember what I could about the evening. The way Brenda had acted was wrong. All of it was wrong; the pub we'd been to, the people there – those fat businessmen, the heavy-set bloke with a beard, the thin woman with white skin and black hair.

If I asked her about it, she'd clam up, like she always did, and I'd be further from her than I wanted to be. So, I thought about it and went round in circles. Always fucking circles.

At some time in the early hours, Brenda had woken, breathing heavily. She'd pulled a cigarette from the pack by the bed and stood and gone over to the window. She hadn't said anything to me, hadn't even looked at me. I had no idea how such a small thing could hurt. It was as if she knew I couldn't help, knew I'd fail her. She was alone with her nightmares, which were worse when she woke.

The room was lit by the moon which poured its pale light onto the walls, the floor, and made the cigarette smoke shimmer silver. I watched it fold and curl and fold again into circles. I looked at Brenda's slim body. The moonlight made her curves shine, as if she stood in a halo, but it also made her dark skin look livid.

'Joe,' she said, looking up at the moon, 'have you ever thought about when we go out together? We always go out at night. Did you realize that?'

'We've been out in the day,' I said.

'Well, it's usually at night. Anyway, it always seems so.'

I told her I hadn't thought about it, but it made sense.

'We live by night,' she said to the stars.

'We both work at night,' I said. 'That's all.'

'Exactly. We live under a dark sky, our sins to best conceal.'

I said something – I don't know what. It didn't matter, she wasn't listening anyway.

'Funny,' she said, 'coz I love the sun. Isn't that funny? I never thought about it before.'

'It's better at night. No people.'

She turned and watched me for a while. I couldn't see her face, but I could see the light glancing off her skin. She seemed lost.

She opened the window and tossed the cigarette out. She came back to bed. I put my arm around her shoulders.

She moved close to me. I felt her warmth press against my cold chest.

She said, 'Whenever I look up at the moon, I'll think of you. It shines so beautifully.'

'It's dull,' I said, 'and dead.'

'It's beautiful. "We all shine on." John Lennon sang that.'

'Who?'

Now she smiled, and that spark was in her eyes, brighter than any stars, brighter than the sun. She knew I was taking the piss. She knew I couldn't be that stupid. She was the only one who did.

She turned her face back to the window, to the dark sky, to the bright moon. Her eyes were so black in its light they seemed to be reflecting the black and endless night, or perhaps they were just reflecting something inside of her, as black, as endless.

Now, years later, I felt old and grey. I felt like the moon, dull and dusty and floating around out there. And she'd been like the sun: brilliant, glorious.

And if she'd ever looked at me and seen me shining, it was only because I'd reflected her light.

THIRTY-TWO

I woke when I heard the front door bang shut. It took me a moment to remember where I was, what had happened. It took me a moment more to remember that the woman I'd remembered was dead. I had a good memory for once.

I got up and went slowly out of the kitchen and into the hall. I saw Browne, standing by the front door. He looked more confused than usual. I thought, He can't be pissed already.

But he wasn't.

He dropped the pickaxe and brushed some rain from his coat.

'Strange,' he said.

He kicked his shoes off and put his slippers on. I waited for him to finish, but it looked like he'd forgotten what he was going to say. He was probably talking to himself.

'What's strange?' I said.

'Huh? Oh. William.'

'Who?'

'My neighbour. William. Remember? He came over the other day. Complaining about all that stuff you made me do outside. Said he was going to call the police.'

'Yeah. The Rotarian. What about him?'

'Oh, nothing really. It's only that just now he was so nice. Said he hadn't meant to offend me. Apologized. Very unlike him. He can't stand me.'

I didn't think much of it then. It seemed odd that this bloke would suddenly change tack, sure, but so what?

It was when I was halfway up the stairs that the thing hit me. I remembered what Browne had said to me a while back, about how even if Dunham got hold of a copy of the DVD it'd be useless because I had a copy.

I looked down at Browne, who was standing by the front door, scratching his head, still confused by his dumb fucking neighbour.

'When was this?' I said.

'Huh? Oh, twenty minutes ago. I saw him peering out of his window. I thought about what you'd said to me, about not wanting to annoy him unnecessarily. So, I went over to apologize.'

'And?'

'Well, he was nervous, wanted to get rid of me I think. That's when he apologized.'

Browne's hand stopped moving over his hair. He looked at me with wide eyes. Now he was getting it.

'What's wrong?' he said. 'Joe. What is it? Christ.'

I jumped down the stairs and went into his front room. He came with me, still asking me what was wrong. I looked out the window. It was just getting dark. There was no traffic, no people.

'There's something I didn't tell you,' I said. 'Cole. Dunham got him.'

'Got him?'

226

'He's dead.'

'Oh Christ.'

'You said this bloke, your neighbour, he's friends with some copper?'

'What? Yes. He's a Conservative, or on some board of something. He knows the local police people, the high rankers.'

I thought about that.

'We've got to go,' I said.

'What? I—'

That's when the front door smashed inwards. If it'd happened a minute earlier, me and Browne would've been finished.

A handful of dark figures burst through, shouting, holding their semi-auto rifles up, barging each other, swarming all over the place. Browne had frozen, his face white.

They didn't see us at first. They had those helmets on, and those dark visors, and their vision was limited.

I'd made a mistake. I'd secured the place from an attack by Dunham, but not by the law. For Dunham I needed a fortress. They'd try and break in and I had to hold them off long enough for them to realize the danger of exposure was too great. But the law was the law. They could stay outside as long as they wanted. For them, I needed an escape. And I didn't have one.

I saw them through the lounge door, and they were pouring up the stairs, along the hallway towards the kitchen.

I thought at first that it must have been Browne's neighbour, William. He'd gone and told his friends at the local nick that there was something going on, and they'd looked into it and found me.

But as I watched this mob, I realized there was something wrong. Either they were stupid, or they were badly trained. They should've fanned out straight away, clearing each space as they came to it. Instead, they were falling over themselves to get into the house. There was no order there.

Then I knew they weren't there to nick me. They were there to kill me.

I shoved Browne aside, slammed the door shut and braced myself against it.

It was a stupid thing to do. We were trapped now, in the front room. But I couldn't think of anything else.

'Take cover,' I said to Browne.

He looked at me with a blank face.

'What's happening?'

'Take fucking cover.'

He backed up against the far wall, as far as he could go from me.

Someone had now noticed that the door was shut. They were hammering into it. There must've been two or three of them. Each time they rammed the door, it slammed into my shoulder, thrust me back a couple of feet. I'd set my weight and shove back. At some point, someone would decide to riddle the door with automatic fire. I had to think of something. Anything.

I couldn't think of a fucking thing. The only way out was the front window, and that would take us right out into them.

Meanwhile, they kept smashing that door, and I was getting weaker, or they were getting stronger. They must've had three men there by now. They were bashing the door regularly, in, back, in, back, every second.

All this time Browne was still up against that back wall, pressing himself into it, staring at me, at the door.

'They're police.' he said.

I had an idea. It wasn't much, but what else was there?

'Joe, they're police.'

I let them hit the door another time then waited and snatched it open. One of them fell right in. I kneed him as he fell and he went straight down. I grabbed him, yanked him in and slammed the door on another bloke. I think I broke his arm. I broke something, anyway. The one who'd fallen in was trying to get up. He was onto his knees when I kicked him in the face. He went down for good after that. I pushed his body up against the door. I had a few seconds, at most. I hauled the sofa over and threw it against the door, on top of the bloke.

Then I got the chest of drawers that Browne kept his papers in. That went onto the sofa. It was made of oak, and weighed a fucking ton.

The bloke's gun was still under his hand. It was a sub-machine gun. I pulled it from his grip. I unscrewed the silencer. Fuck their games. Let's have some violence.

The gun was heavy, dead. Then I touched it and gave it life, and it kicked and bucked and struggled in my hands, fighting to break loose, spitting its fury. But I held it tight and let its fury speak for mine.

The noise of the gun was one endless explosion. It

bounced off the walls and hit me. It was thunderous, crashing into my ears. The rounds smashed through the wood of the door, through the wall, ripping into the plaster, throwing up dust, brick.

When the magazine was empty, I ditched it and reloaded with one from the bloke's black vest.

In the pause, Browne scrambled over, felt the man's neck.

I heard shouts out in the hallway. But then Browne was at me, clawing my arm.

'This man needs a hospital,' he said. 'Joe. For God's sake. You're going to kill a policeman.'

'They're not coppers,' I said.

'I don't understand. Who are they?'

'Dunham's.' I grabbed Browne by the shoulders. 'We've got to go.'

'I don't understand.'

'They're Dunham's men dressed as the law.'

I held the suppressor for him to see.

'They've got silencers on their weapons. It's a hit. He wants me and he's disguising it as a police raid. And if you're in the way, you'll be dead.'

They were bashing the door heavily now. They must've woken up to the idea that it was shut for a reason.

'Dead?'

'We haven't got time for this.'

'I don't understand.'

'Christ. They want to kill me, but they want the DVD first. They came in here like the law so they could take me out and make like they'd nicked me. After that...'

'My God.'

230

'Dunham must've put the fix in, got the local law to play ball. That's why your neighbour backed off; he must've been told to keep his mouth shut.'

'But why?'

'You said it yourself; grabbing Glazer doesn't do him any good, as long as I've got the DVD. But if Dunham kills me, finds the other DVD…'

'What're we going to do, Joe? What can we do?'

It was a good question. They were bashing hard against the door now, getting some movement from the furniture I'd piled up. It wouldn't take them long to get in. I looked around; walls, walls, walls. Window.

I put my arm across Browne's chest, pushed him back.

'Cover your face.'

I levelled the gun and let it go, firing the magazine off in one long burst, moving from one side of the window to the other, spraying that glass until it was powder. Splinters flew all over the place. I felt cuts on my hands and face, as if someone was sandblasting me. I hoped that would clear out whoever was on the other side.

But it was no good. I saw figures out there, and I heard shouting, and the door continued to get bashed. I wasn't going to be able to get them all. I'd had it. I was finished. The bastards had won.

I turned to look at Browne. He was huddled in the far corner, his arms over his head. I wanted to apologize to him for getting him in this spot, for putting him in danger.

I'd hidden the DVD. Browne didn't know where it was, but Dunham would use him as leverage to get me to talk. I'd have to hand it over.

231

As I was thinking that, I noticed the door was no longer slamming against the furniture I'd piled there. That meant they were going to try something else. I reckoned they'd come in through the window.

I braced myself. The gun was out of ammo, but I held it still. That might make them hesitate, at least. And if not, it might make them shoot me. That was probably best.

I waited, my body tense, sweat on my brow, my neck. I wasn't scared, I wasn't angry.

I felt something else, and I didn't know what it was – sadness, maybe.

I'd failed her, Brenda. I'd failed Kid too. And now I'd failed myself. It didn't sit well with me, failure. I didn't like it. I wanted to grab it by the neck and squeeze it to death. But how can you kill something that's already killed you?

I waited to die.

Browne was up, now, standing by me. I think he knew what was coming. I think he was trying to protect me.

I thought about her again, or tried to. But she wouldn't come to me. I couldn't see her. I could only see the ghost of her. And that was how I was going to go out, seeing a ghost. I think that hurt more than anything.

I still waited to die. Browne was waiting with me. I was beginning to get bored.

'I can't hear anything out there,' Browne said.

He was right. I couldn't hear anything either. It was worse like that, not hearing anything, not knowing when they were going to come.

Then we heard a banging on the door. Browne jumped a mile. It wasn't the smashing, though, but just a knock,

232

like someone wanted to come in. Then I heard a voice. But it couldn't be. I was imagining things again.

'Joe?' the voice said. 'You in there?'

'Don't open it,' Browne said.

He must've been thinking the same as me; it was a trap, it had to be.

'Joe?' the voice said again.

It was Cole. But it couldn't be. He was dead.

'I'm here,' I said to the voice.

'Open up the fucking door. It's safe.'

It was Cole alright.

'What happened?' I called out.

'We turned up, they scarpered.'

I pulled the cabinet off, then the chair and dragged the bloke away. Cole opened the door, stepped in. There was a bunch of his men with him.

'What are you doing here?' I said.

'You're welcome.'

Cole looked around at the mess, at the bloke on the floor who still wasn't doing much, except lying there. I said, 'I thought you were dead.'

He looked me up and down, shook his head.

'Well, if I was, I'd still be better off than you.'

'Your house got bombed.'

'Really? I wondered why it looked so flat.'

'I heard you were in it.'

He nodded.

'I got my wife to report me missing. I knew it would take a while for them to go through the house wreckage. The rumour mill took it from there. Bought me some time.'

'You sound desperate.'

'Dunham's been pulling me apart at the seams, boy. But I ain't finished yet.'

Another man came in. I knew him. He was called Gibson. He was small and had a gammy leg and a flat fighter's face. He waved smoke and dust away from his face.

'Gone,' he said. 'Legged it. They were Dunham's lot, though. I recognized one of them.'

Browne looked at Cole, looked at Cole's men, looked at me. Then he shook his head as if we were all just a part of some bad hangover.

He got on his knees and checked the bloke on the floor, pulled off his helmet, opened his mouth to let him breath, turned him on his side, in the recovery position.

'How did you know?' I said to Cole. 'About this?'

'When I told you I was taking my men away, well, I didn't. I kept a few men on you, one at a time, round the clock. If Dunham wanted you, I wanted to know why. I knew you weren't telling me everything. I'm not a mug, son.'

'Right.'

I still kept expecting to get killed. It didn't seem right that Dunham's mob would just roll over and leave like that. I glanced at the men Cole had brought with him. They were standing around in the hallway, lighting up, relaxing. Dunham had more men than Cole, but they weren't as good.

'My man told me there was a build up of the law,' Cole was saying, 'armed police, cordons, the works. I get hold of a copper I know, and he tells me he'll look into it. Meanwhile, we're on the move. Then he calls back, this copper, says there's nothing in the offing. So, I think about

234

things. And I charge in. If it's the law, I'm in shit. Only, it ain't. They see us and scarper. My feeling is nobody told them there'd be a lot of armed men to deal with. Dunham?'

'Eddie, I reckon.'

'Yeah. Lane's a canny bastard alright. I might have to kill him one day.'

'Good luck.'

'What was their idea? Dressing up as the law?'

'They knew I'd be hard to kill, that I'd probably be ready. They needed to get me out, alive, I think. It doesn't matter. This way nobody round here's gonna call the law; why would they? As far as they knew, the law was already here.'

I wondered if Eddie had wanted this for another reason. This caper had his mark all over it. I thought he might be playing his own game now. I knew about him and Dunham's wife. I suppose he might've thought I could use it against him.

It was like me and Eddie were fighting our own fight. Cole and Dunham were outside the ring, ready to mop up the blood, but me and Eddie were inside, and we didn't care about anything else except killing the other one. And he was young, fast, smart.

But I didn't go down easy.

Cole was looking at me, his eyes hard.

'And why would they want you alive, boy? What aren't you telling me?'

'The DVD,' I said. 'The one Brenda made, the one she sent to Glazer as evidence against Marriot and Paget.'

'Go on.'

'There's a man on it. He's important. I've got a copy and Dunham knows that.'

Cole sighed.

'So, I was right. There was something you weren't telling me.'

'Yeah.'

He shook his head sadly.

'Sometimes, Joe…'

He left it there.

I climbed the stairs and went to my bedroom. On the shelf on the wall were a bunch of books I'd bought since leaving my flat, and one I'd given Brenda about the battle of Trafalgar. I turned to page sixty-two and took out the DVD.

It wasn't much of a hiding place, but it seemed right.

I went back downstairs. Cole's men watched me with empty eyes.

Back in the lounge, Browne was still kneeling next to Dunham's bloke. He was checking his pulse, holding his wrist.

I held the DVD up.

'You know what this is worth?' I said to Cole.

'Your woman died for that, right?'

'Yeah.'

'Then it's worth a lot.'

'It's worth more than that.'

I held it out to him. He made no move to take it.

'You're giving it to me?'

'I can't get him. I know that. And I don't trust the law. So, yeah, I'm giving it to you, because you can use it to get at Dunham.'

'What makes you think I won't use it for myself?'

236

'You're a bastard, but you're not a cunt. You've never used women or children. Anyway, if you used it for profit, I'd come after you.'

'What if there are copies?'

'Doesn't matter. Just by having the DVD you'd ruin anyone's plans to control the man on it. All you'd have to do is threaten to send it to the papers.'

He looked at me, held my gaze, then took the disc and put it in his inside jacket pocket.

'Who is he?'

'I don't know. I don't care any more. But there's one condition to this. You destroy him. The man, whoever he is. Destroy him.'

He glanced at Gibson, who moved his head up a bit.

'Okay,' Cole said. 'If I can, I'll get this cunt. Meanwhile, it could buy me some more time as far as Dunham's concerned.'

'A bit of time,' Gibson said. 'That's all we need.'

Dunham's bloke was moving now, but Browne was still fussing over him. Cole surveyed the room, pushed some plaster with his foot, wiped some dust off his coat.

'I heard about that stuff with Roy Buck,' he said. 'And those other blokes. One of my boys recognized him. Why was he here? To threaten you through Browne?'

I stopped breathing. Browne stood slowly, forgetting about his patient. He looked at me. I looked at Cole.

'Other blokes?' I said. 'What other blokes?'

'There was no one else here,' Browne said.

Then I understood. You had to admire Eddie, the way his mind worked. I looked around the lounge, pulled pictures

237

off the wall, unscrewed the lightbulb, lifted the furniture.

I found it on the inside of a Chinese vase that Browne had kept on a chest of drawers in the corner and was now smashed on the floor. I held it up for the others to see. It was broken.

'Bugs,' I said, closing my fist slowly around the thing.

Cole smiled. He got it. But Browne looked as lost as ever.

'It was a decoy,' I told him. 'Buck was a decoy. That's why he came in when I wasn't here. That's why he didn't ask any questions.'

'A decoy for what?'

'While he was upstairs beating you, Eddie had other men come in and plant bugs around the place. He knew I was after Glazer, and he wanted him too. If I got any intel, he'd get it. Then Marriot's son came round and Dunham found out where Glazer was. That's how he got to Glazer before I did.'

'Maybe I won't kill Lane,' Cole said. 'Maybe I'll hire him.'

Damn, Eddie was a smart bastard. He knew if anyone came into the house, I'd be suspicious. So, he thought out how to put someone in the house that I wouldn't question. He sent Buck, because he knew I'd take it as a threat and wouldn't think anything more about it. And he was right. I didn't look any further than Buck.

'We've gotta move,' Cole said. 'They might regroup and come back. You two coming?'

'I'll not leave,' Browne said. 'There's an injured man here.'

'A man who would've killed you,' I said.

'Nevertheless. This is my home, Joe. I told you I'd not leave it.'

Cole put a hand on my arm.

'They want you dead,' he said. 'Not him. Don't worry, I'll leave some men here.'

'Okay.'

'What about you? You coming with us?'

'I've got stuff to do.'

'Well, if you're still alive when this has finished, get in touch,' Cole said.

'Right. I need a car.'

He glanced at Gibson who handed me some keys. Cole spoke to a couple of his men, told them to stay near Browne. Then he was gone.

I hung around Browne's for a while, but I was still a target and if I stayed, that would put Browne in danger.

So I left.

THIRTY-THREE

Tina opened the door, looked up at me. Her eyes were huge.

'I wondered if you'd come back.'

She was pale, paler than ever, as if she was fading into the air. She took a step back, then swayed and fell forward. I caught her, lifted her up and carried her through to the lounge. She weighed nothing. I put her on the sofa, checked her pulse.

I wondered if she'd taken pills. I slapped her, brought some colour back to her cheek. She rolled over, tried weakly to push my arm away.

'I'm okay,' she said.

'Have you taken anything?'

She shook her head, silver-yellow hair fell over her face. Gradually, she came back to life, and sat up. She lifted a hand and slowly brushed her hair aside.

'I'm okay.'

I gave her some room. She sat forward, at the edge of the seat, put her knees together, and held them, and bent her body so that she was looking down. She didn't want to look at me. I could understand that.

'Why have you come here?' she asked her feet.

'I need somewhere to stay for a while.'

'They have hotels for that.'

'There are people after me. They'd find me in a hotel.'

'But why here?'

'It's the only place I could think of.'

Now she looked up at me.

'The only place?'

'You're the only person I could think of to come to.'

'You know other people, don't you?'

'Yeah. But other people know the other people I know.'

She reached down the side of the sofa, pulled a pack of cigarettes out. On the floor, beside her foot, was an ashtray, mostly full, and a lighter. She put a cigarette in her mouth, taking a long time to do it.

'They'd find you, these *other* other people?'

'They'd find me, eventually.'

'Are you scared of them?'

'No,' I said, knowing it was the truth. 'I'm just tired.'

She nodded. I had the feeling she understood exactly.

She lit her cigarette, inhaled and blew the smoke out in a sigh, as if she was relieved at last to be breathing deadly air.

It looked strange, her smoking. It looked like a child playing at being an adult.

'Who are they, these people? Who's after you?'

'Everyone.'

She rocked back and laughed. I suppose it was funny, when you thought about it. Funny in a fucked-up way.

'You don't mess about, do you?' she said.

'No.'

She laughed some more. When she'd finished, she leaned back, looked up at me.

241

'You know how to make coffee?'

'I'll work it out.'

I made coffee for her, tea for me. We sat and drank our drinks and she smoked her smokes and I kept expecting her to scream and run from the house or call the law or something. But she didn't.

We talked a bit. She asked me where I came from, what I'd done, things like that. She told me a bit about herself.

She'd hooked up with Paget out of desperation, she said.

'He was flash, had money. I was young, stupid. I was doing tricks for twenty quid a shot. He told me I could do a hundred a time, few hundred quid a night. Course, he didn't tell me how much I'd have to shell out to Marriot. I think I made more money by myself. I was safer, too. By the time I realized that, it was too late. Nobody left Marriot. Not if they wanted to keep their looks.'

All the while we talked, there was a hole there, in the air, between us, between our words. We both knew what that hole was, we both pretended it wasn't there, but I felt it pulling me in.

We moved onto booze. I went down to the offy and got some beer for me, some mixers for her. She already had plenty of gin and vodka. The smell of Tina's G and Ts took me back to Brenda. After a few beers, I was feeling a bit drunk. I'd started out sitting on a chair, opposite Tina. Then I moved to the sofa. Then, somehow, she was nearer, and I could smell her perfume and, Christ, it was the same as Brenda used.

Every now and then, I'd close my eyes, smell her cigarette smoke, her gin, her perfume, and I'd think I was with Brenda.

But then I'd open my eyes and see a thin, pale blonde woman with huge eyes, instead of a thin, black woman with huge eyes and a huger smile. The pain would hit me. She saw it.

'You loved her, didn't you?'

I didn't have an answer for that. I didn't know what love meant. I had nothing to compare it with.

'If I could, I'd swap my life for hers,' I said. 'I'd tear the world apart to give her a minute more life. I'd tear myself apart too.'

'That's love,' she said.

Was it love? Could it be? It felt like fury to me. Maybe that was as close as I could get to love.

She moved closer to me.

'I loved her too,' she said softly.

She moved closer still, so that she was touching me. I wondered about that and thought it must've been the drink. What else could it have been?

'You said you were tired,' I heard her say, though her voice was even softer now, fading into the air along with the rest of her.

She pushed herself into me, reached her hand out to touch mine. I didn't move my hand. I wanted to, and I couldn't.

'Yeah.'

'Tired of what?'

It was a good question. I don't think I knew exactly. I just felt that I couldn't go on. My blood was running thin. I thought about what Browne had said to me once, 'You want to vent your fury, your wrath, like some god who destroys everything, innocent and guilty, anything to serve your will.'

243

'Rage,' I said to Tina. 'I'm tired of the rage. There was a time, not long ago, not long at all, when I wanted to set the world on fire, when I wanted blood, everyone's.'

'And now?'

'I don't know any more. I don't think I know anything any more.'

'Could you stop? I mean, just give it up?'

Could I?

'Brenda used to talk about it, about me stopping, about us going away somewhere, starting again. I would've done, I think.'

'But?'

I knew I shouldn't drink, what with all the pills Browne kept giving me. But I didn't care. It felt good to not care. At least my head wasn't hurting. It was buzzing a bit, but that was okay. Wasn't it?

'Joe?'

'Huh?'

'You alright? You were saying why you couldn't stop, with Brenda.'

'Was I? Yeah, Brenda. She wouldn't stop. I asked her to a couple times. She wouldn't, and wouldn't tell me why. I know now.'

'Because she wanted to get Paget and Marriot.'

Paget and Marriot. They were dead, weren't they? I could see their blood on my hands. What did they have to do with Brenda? What was the question? Who was I?

'Joe?' Brenda said.

But it wasn't Brenda. It was someone else, some slim pale woman with Brenda's smell.

I said, 'Yeah. No. I mean, she did, but she wanted to protect the children. It was always about them, more than Paget and Marriot, more than her. More than me.'

I closed my eyes, and I could feel Brenda next to me. My head was floating away. I could smell her. But I knew something wasn't right about that and I didn't dare open my eyes. I felt her arm on my chest, her head on my shoulder.

It's not real, I told myself. Keep your eyes closed, I told myself. Just for a moment.

But I opened my eyes, looked for Brenda, saw blonde hair, white skin.

'Joe,' she said.

I felt her breath on my chest.

'She couldn't stop herself,' I said. 'It was in her nature, I suppose.'

'It was suicide.'

'Maybe. It was something she had to do.'

'She's gone, Joe.'

'Yeah.'

'I know you cared about her, but you've got to leave it behind you. It's all in the past. It's gone.'

Gone. Was the past ever gone? My past was all around me, all through me. It was in my blood. It was my very life. I'd turn a corner and face it. It controlled me. Could I let it go?

We were quiet for a while. I drank my beer and, when I finished, Tina got up and went and got me a refill from the fridge. When she sat down again, she didn't make any pretence. She folded herself into me.

I felt good. I felt free. Dunham had Glazer, would do a deal with him, or kill him or whatever.

And I...

I pushed away the thought of my failure. Well, I tried to.

'It's gone,' she said again. 'For both of us.'

'Yeah.'

'Do you care about anything, Joe? Anyone?'

'Not any more.'

'Could you? I mean, could you care for me?'

I thought she must've been taking the piss. Why would she want someone like me?

But her hand was on my chest, and her face was looking up at me and her eyes were so big, so pleading.

'I could be her for you,' she said.

I reached my hand out, touched her cheek. But I didn't know if I was touching her or Brenda. I didn't know.

And I don't know if I cared. Part of me hated myself for that. Part of me didn't care.

I was going back again, or I was going forwards, just to go back. Or something. I was lost, wherever I was, whenever I was.

I no longer knew what I was. I'd been confused before, sure, but I'd always known what I was, at my heart; I was the machine, the Killing Machine. I'd fought a war, battles, a hundred men. I knew that world. I knew rage and pain.

But this...

I was lost.

She leaned forward, brushed her lips against mine.

246

We lay on our sides, facing each other. We hadn't spoken for a long time. I felt okay, no tiredness in my limbs, no fuzziness in my head, just some pain here and there. It was alright.

But there was a part of me that wasn't there. It was a small part, but it nagged at me and whispered in my ear and told me that this was all a lie, even if I wanted, for now, to believe in it.

After a while, she ran a finger along my brow. Her finger traced the line of an old scar. I'd forgotten it was there. Her finger moved slowly, tracing my history, my path through life. Her finger was like a drop of rainwater sliding down a window.

'You've got a lot of scars,' she said.

'Yeah.'

'What's this one?'

'Fight.'

'Fight,' she said, trying the word out. 'And this one?'

'Knifed.'

'Knifed. Just that? Knifed?'

'Just that.'

'Tell me about it?'

'Why?'

'Why not? Scars are interesting. Each one has a story.'

'Scars are damage, that's all.'

Her hand moved to my shoulder, and the scar there, still raw. Then to my back where her hand moved in a kind of zig-zag.

'What are these ones?'

'Shotgun.'

'And this one?' she said, moving it back to my torso.

'Fight.'

'Fight. Shotgun. Is there any part of you that's not scarred?'

'Somewhere, probably.'

'Seems like it's only scar tissue holding you together.'

'That's what Browne says.'

'You talk like you don't care.'

'I don't.'

'And this one? Sorry.'

'It's alright, just tender still. That was Paget.'

'When you…'

'Yeah.'

She was quiet for a while, moving her finger over my scars, as if, in the still of the night, in the darkness, she was reading my body, finding out what I was.

'I remember Brenda talking about you, well, about this fellow she was seeing,' she said. 'She called you the Killing Machine. All these scars; looks like you were the one getting killed.'

'I'm still here,' I said. 'It was a joke between us. That was my nickname in the ring. I never used it. She used to take the piss out of me. That's all.'

'The Killing Machine,' she said.

248

Brenda used to smile when she said that, a spark in her eyes. Tina's voice was flat, though. There was no smile in it.

She sighed, gave up tracing the scars and flattened her hand on my stomach.

'I thought I'd escaped all this. I thought I'd found a small, quiet, boring place to do small, quiet, boring stuff. I thought I'd forget, or I'd be forgotten. But then Kenny came back, and you and all the rest of them. Everything came back. You don't ever escape. Life is the killing machine.'

I said, 'Yeah.'

'Is there a way out, Joe? Could there be?'

I'd been asking myself that.

'I dunno.'

She got up on one elbow. I looked at her face, it was wreathed in shadow. Her eyes were black holes.

'There could be, couldn't there? We could leave here, start again somewhere. You and me. I'd give it all up if you could. You said you were tired of it. Are you really?'

She sounded like Brenda. Or, at least, the words were the same, but with Tina there was an edge to her voice. It sounded like desperation.

THIRTY-FIVE

She slept, her body resting on mine, her leg and arm across me, as if she was trying to stop me from leaving.

I heard a slight snore, felt her body rise and fall in slow rhythm. And, while she lay on me, thoughts lay in my mind, and pulled me into their depths.

The way she'd talked, I wondered if I could put everything behind. Could I hide here? Then, when the heat was off, go somewhere, with Tina, maybe? Could I take off, start again, as Brenda had wanted us to do?

I thought about that girl I'd seen at the bus stop, the one with the twins. I thought of the bloke with them. Could I be like him? How did I know he hadn't once been like me? Could I have a future? Other people did, why not me?

But, then, other people weren't on a death-list, they weren't wanted by the law, by mobsters, by anyone with a gun. Other people hadn't killed, hadn't seen death at close hand, hadn't had people they'd cared about cut to death, shot to death.

I tried to imagine myself as a free man. I tried to think how it might be if I could've sat in that cafe – with those two redheads on the other table – and not been wanted by half of London, and not felt old and ugly and tainted by death.

I tried, but it was no good. Once, maybe, escape could've happened. With Brenda it could've happened. I could've hung up my gloves, my guns. We might've made a go of it some-where, away from London. We might have had a family.

But Brenda was dead and that was why it could never happen, no matter how much I wanted it. It didn't feel right. Brenda was dead, and I'd failed and I could try to pretend as much as possible, try to ignore that dark hole and make plans and whatever. But, at the back of it all, I had a debt to settle. I had something I had to do. Even back at Browne's place, knowing it was all over and waiting with an empty gun for them to come and finish me off, even then it felt wrong. I just wasn't that kind of person. I couldn't give up. I was a machine, after all.

I got carefully out of the bed and started to dress.

'Are you going?'

I turned, saw Tina resting on one elbow, her hair falling in front of her face, hiding it in a curtain of silver strands.

'Yeah.'

'Why?'

'I have to.'

She nodded.

'It's suicide,' she said.

'Maybe.'

'But it's something you've got to do, right? It's in you, part of your nature?'

There was a mocking edge to her voice.

'Yeah.'

'Don't you care, Joe?'

Don't you care, Joe? That was what she said. Don't you

care, Joe? That was what I said to myself as I buttoned my shirt.

'No,' I told her. 'I don't care.'

I was damning myself. I knew that. And, no, I didn't care.

THIRTY-SIX

Tina was right. It was in me, part of my nature. Fuck, it *was* my nature. Browne knew that.

Suicide, Tina had said about Brenda's need to fight it to the end. Yeah, that was it. Suicide. A death wish.

Once you understand, it doesn't matter.

Fuck it.

Anyway, I realized there was one person who could help me get to Glazer. One person, who could and would help me. Just one, and it was Eddie, of all people, who'd told me.

I called Ben Green.

'I told you I was out, Joe.'

'I know. Dunham's got Glazer. I'm going to fuck Dunham up and I want your help.'

He swore, called me every name under the sun. Then he hung up.

He came back to me ten minutes later.

'She's in their London house,' he said. 'With their daughter. But not Dunham. He's somewhere else. Dunno where. Nobody does. And I don't know why his missus ain't with him, or out in the country where she could be safer. And the kid too.'

I knew why. After what had happened with Paget, I wondered if she'd ever set foot in Dunham's country pad again. I couldn't ever imagine her going in that room again. It must've taken days to clean it of the blood and gore. And she'd hate Dunham for what he'd done.

'Only,' Green said, 'she's not alone. She's got a handful of bodyguards. So you're not going to get close to her. Unless you phone her up.'

I had thought that Dunham would have someone with her, but not a whole bunch. That was going to make things difficult.

Still, as Green had said, I could always try phoning.

He'd given me the number for the London house and I dialled it. It rang, and I tried to figure out what to say to her. Then a man's voice answered and I hung up and cursed myself for a fucking idiot. What if I'd said something? What if my voice had been recognized?

I was going to have to do it the slow way.

THIRTY-SEVEN

I was in the doorway of a small cafe, opposite the school, but on the same side as the car, about twenty yards behind it.

It was a small place, one of those village tea shop type things, with lace tablecloths and china teapots that they brought to you on a tray. We were still in London, but the people here didn't want to be a part of the city. They wanted to think they were in a small market town in the country.

It was open for breakfast trade, and I'd gone in early and bought some grub and a cup of tea. I'd had a paper with me and I'd pretended to read it. After a while they got the idea I was just a bloke starting his day. I'd gone out front, telling the waitress I was going for a smoke. There was a small courtyard out back, she'd told me. I said I was waiting for someone and wanted to make sure they didn't miss me.

So, I stood there and waited and smoked a few tabs from the pack I'd bought earlier. Then the car came by, on my side of the road, and slowed and stopped out of my sight, a dozen yards or so away from me.

I heard the car doors open, and slam shut. Then they walked past me, Dunham's wife and daughter. I pushed myself back in the doorway. They crossed at a zebra crossing, and walked past the iron railings separating the playground from the street.

Dunham's wife kissed her daughter on the cheek, said something to her and swept some of the girl's golden hair aside. The girl wandered off, her satchel slung over her shoulder and her eyes glued to the phone in her hand, reading some text or playing a game or whatever it was kids did these days. Dunham's wife watched her daughter all the way to the school building and then, after the girl had gone in, she watched some more. Then she watched the closed door, as if thinking that her daughter might come back any second. And then she turned and walked away, head down, hands in the pockets of her long camel-hair coat.

There were a few other women there, dropping their kids off. But Dunham's wife didn't stop to chat with any of them, didn't say hello, didn't even nod or make eye contact.

Beneath her coat, she wore a white blouse and blue jeans. She wore no make-up and her hair looked like it had been thrown back quickly and tied, strands of it floating around her head. She looked haggard, like she'd just got out of bed, and yet still she was beautiful, beyond normal women.

I felt further from her, further from all people, than I'd ever felt. Next to her, I was a vile thing, huge and clumsy and ugly as death.

I checked to see if she had a bodyguard somewhere. Then, when I was sure she was by herself, I watched her walk, just for the hell of it.

She dawdled, turning now and then to look back at the

school, as if she thought that her daughter might've come out again to see her. I thought she didn't want to go back to wherever she'd come from. Then she turned away and crossed back over the road.

When she got closer to me, I could see that her skin was pale, even though her cheeks glowed in the cold air. Sunlight had broken through the clouds and gave her a silver halo. There was something in her eyes, too, as if she was thinking of things far away, or long gone.

She reminded me of Brenda. There was that same calmness, as if the world wasn't really there at all, or, maybe it was more like the world was real, but she was a ghost floating through it.

Whatever it was, it was something that I used to see in Brenda. There were those moments when she'd seem to drift off somewhere, when her eyes would glaze over and she'd forget about me, about everything around her. I think I knew, in those moments, that she expected to die. Tina was right about her. Suicide was bang on. Sadness clung to Brenda like a shroud.

And the only thing, really, that stopped me hating myself more than I did was that, sometimes, when she'd been with me, she'd forget herself and be happy.

That sadness was in Dunham's wife and Brenda. It was in Tina too. I suppose it was to do with the men in their lives. Paget, Marriot, Dunham – even Eddie, even, maybe, me. The women had children, or wanted children, and the men took them away, hurt them, used them.

I wasn't like that, at least. Maybe I wasn't so ugly after all.

257

When she was a few feet from me, I stepped forward enough so that she'd see the movement, but not enough so that the driver could see me.

'Hey,' I said.

She stopped and, for a moment, she froze and stared at me.

'Look in the window,' I said. 'Turn away from the car.'

She didn't move and I thought I'd blown it. I heard a car door open and a man's voice.

'Mrs D?' the bloke called out.

She flinched.

'I need your help,' I said.

She looked at me blankly, and I braced myself, sure now that I was going to have to tackle the driver, and lose my one good chance. But then she blinked, and turned away from me, towards the voice that had called.

'It's okay, Tom,' she said, smiling. 'Just a minute.'

She turned to look in the cafe window. I waited until I heard the car door close. I said, 'There's a garden out back. Go tell your driver you're going to get a coffee.'

She didn't move, or even look my way, but I could see in her eyes that she understood, and that she would do it. I hadn't been sure she would. After all, she was running a risk. I had to hope I'd been right about her.

After a while, she walked on, out of my sight. I heard her say something. I braced myself, hand on my gun, just in case she'd grassed me up. But nothing happened.

She brushed past me and into the cafe. I followed and we went through and out the back door.

She glanced round at the walled courtyard. She shivered,

258

held her arms around her. It was drizzling and fine drops of rain clung to her hair.

'I had to tell them I was using the bathroom,' she said. 'Otherwise they'd have come in to wait with me.'

'They?'

'In the car. Two of them.'

I'd missed the second bloke. That was sloppy.

'But they'll come looking for me soon,' she was saying. 'One of them is young and a bit stupid. The other's not stupid, though.'

'You remember me,' I said.

'Is that some kind of joke?' she said. 'I'll never forget you.'

'You know who I am?'

'You're my husband's enemy.'

'You know he wants to kill me?'

'Of course. That's how Victor treats enemies.'

She put the tip of her ring finger to the corner of her eye, and seemed to wipe something away. There was nothing there to wipe away, as far as I could see.

'They're not supposed to let me out of their sight. You've done well to see me alone. You've outwitted Victor. He doesn't like being made a fool of. If he ever finds out, he'll be angry.'

'He wants me dead, how much angrier can he get?'

Her eyes sparked for a moment, and I saw fear and fury.

'I meant he'd be angry with me. Do you understand what that means? What do you think he'll do to me if he finds out?'

She held her arms tighter about her body, but I didn't think it was the coldness that made her do that.

259

'I don't know what I'm doing here,' she said, looking back towards the door from the cafe. 'I can't help you. No one can.'

She started to walk away. I grabbed her. She stopped, looked at my hand on her arm.

'What are you gonna do?' she said. 'Kill me?'

I took my hand away. Then I took a step back. She could've left if she'd wanted. But she didn't move. She felt inside her coat pocket and took out a pack of cigarettes and a lighter. The cigarette trembled as she put it to her lips. I took the lighter from her and fired the smoke.

'Why did you come to me? What makes you think I'd help you?' she said, letting smoke fall from her mouth.

'The same reason you tried to stop your husband from having me killed.'

'How did you know about that?'

'Eddie gave me a choice.'

'I asked Eddie to stop Victor,' she said. 'Or to help you. Did he?'

'He tried, but not too hard.'

She nodded. I wasn't telling her anything she didn't already know.

'Why did you do that?' I said.

'You saved my daughter. My husband brought that man – Paget – to our house. He knew what he was, what he did.'

'Eddie knew too.'

'Eddie. Yes. Eddie knew.'

She said it softly. That spoke volumes. She expected her husband to be ruthless, but Eddie... that hurt, that was betrayal.

260

'You said you needed my help. How?'

'I need to find a man called Michael Glazer. He's a copper.'

'I've never heard of him.'

'Your husband has. He's got him somewhere.'

A car horn blared twice.

'Oh Christ,' she said. 'They'll come soon. I have to go.'

She dropped the cigarette, stamped it out.

'I have to go,' she said again.

'Glazer's in danger. He's got something your husband wants, and your husband will get it from him. Now, you know something important. You could go to the police with what I've told you, but that would end in a bloodbath at worst, imprisonment for your husband and Eddie at best. I'd go in quietly, get Glazer out.'

'Why would I help you? Aren't you just the same as the rest of them? As Victor and Eddie? Why would you risk your neck for this man Glazer?'

'I knew a woman once. Paget killed her.'

It wasn't an answer, and I thought she was probably too smart to fall for my spiel. What choice did I have? If I'd told her I wanted to kill Glazer, she'd have run a mile.

She looked at me, into me.

'Yes,' she said. 'I remember what you said to him, to Paget. She was someone you loved?'

'Yes,' I said. 'She was.'

She nodded.

'Paget... he mocked you for loving her.'

I don't know why that mattered to her, but it seemed to. Then we heard a creak and we both looked at the back door. The handle turned and I threw myself back against the wall of the cafe, to the side of the door. I pulled my gun and held it at head height.

The door opened and I heard a man's voice.

'What are you doing, Mrs Dunham?'

The doorway was recessed and the door opened inwards. Flat against the wall, I couldn't see the man. Dunham's wife stood directly before the doorway, her face white, her eyes fixed. If the bloke moved forward a step, he'd see me.

'I, uh...' the woman said.

Then another voice; this one younger.

'She's not in the bog,' the voice said. 'Oh, Mrs D. You said you were gonna use the bathroom.'

'I just wanted some fresh air. And a moment to myself,' she said, her voice tight.

'We're supposed to be with you all the time, Mrs Dunham,' the older voice said.

'I know, Matt. I'm sorry. But this is just a walled garden out here. And I'm by myself, so it's okay. You go back to the car, I won't be long.'

The men didn't move, didn't say anything. I wondered about that and my hand tightened on the grip of my Makarov.

'Oh for God's sake,' she said. 'I just wanted a moment by myself. I'm surrounded by you lot day and night. The only person I can talk to is my daughter, and she'd rather be at school with her friends. Just go back to the bloody car. I won't be long then you can lock me in and throw away the key.'

The older man cleared his throat.

262

'We're only doing what we're told, Mrs Dunham.'

She sighed.

'I know, Matt. I'm sorry. I didn't mean to take it out on you.'

'We'll grab a coffee inside. We'll wait for you there, alright?'

'That's fine. Thanks.'

The door closed and I let my gun down.

She took out another cigarette and lit it and stood in the middle of the yard, looking down at the paving stones and the weeds pushing their way through the cracks.

'Shit,' she said, brushing some of her hair back.

I stayed with my back against the wall, watching her.

'I heard Vic on the phone,' she said finally. 'He was talking to Eddie. He said, "We've got him at the factory."'

'What does that mean?'

'I don't know. Vic's got lots of places, all over London and Essex, but I never heard of a factory.'

That had been my fear. She couldn't help me, even if she'd wanted to.

'Does that help?' she said.

'No. I don't know where that is. I could try asking around, but it'll take time.'

We stood there for a while. The drizzle was getting heavier. Those two inside would start to wonder why Dunham's wife would want to stand out in the rain.

'You'd better go,' I said. 'Or they'll come back for you.'

'Yes,' she said.

She dropped her cigarette and let it fizzle out on the wet floor. She wrapped her arms about her again and started to walk towards the door. But then she stopped and turned to me.

'I could find out where it is,' she said. 'If it's important. If you can help him, the man, Glazer.'

'How?'

She shrugged.

'I'll ask someone. There's no reason why they shouldn't tell me. There's a man called Andrew. He's a business manager.'

So, she called this Andrew and asked him about any factories her husband owned. She told him she wanted a list of her husband's properties. That was all she had to do. She wrote an address down and gave it to me.

'Your husband will find out you were asking about it,' I said to her.

'I know.'

'You'll be in trouble.'

She laughed at that.

'I've been in trouble a long time.'

Now, standing in the middle of that walled yard, with her arms wrapped around her like that, she seemed more alone, and I thought again of Brenda and wondered how alone she'd been, even when I'd been with her. Is that what we did to women – me and Dunham and Eddie and Paget and Marriot, all hurting them, making them suffer alone?

Here I was, lying to the woman, letting herself offer to get into the worst trouble with a violent man just so that I could exact my revenge on the man she thought I'd try to save.

264

Yes, that's what we did. We made women suffer. We made them suffer alone. It's what we've always done.

'Tell them I had a gun,' I said. 'Tell them I threatened your daughter. They'll believe that.'

THIRTY-EIGHT

It was past eleven by the time I found the industrial estate. The midday traffic was building up and my head had started to throb again. There was a dark, rainy sky, the lights from cars and lorries bouncing off the wet road and splintering into my eyes, the fumes smothering me, the engine noise drilling into my head.

It was a relief to get off the busy roads and into the estate.

I drove slowly, scanning the lock-ups and warehouses and the odd power generator. No vehicles passed me, there were no lights on in any of the buildings. There were no people that I could see, no sounds of industry. Some of the places had been closed up, wooden boards over the windows, graffiti on the walls.

There were trees around, and areas of overgrown grass and, running through the site were potholed roads. No repairs had been done to the roads in years. The whole place was rotting into the ground.

It was near the River Lea, so half of the estate faced a path with the river, straightened up into a canal, beyond. It seemed that the Lea had once been used here, maybe for transport, maybe for water or waste.

Plot 36 was at the end of one of the roads. There was a wooden sign screwed to the building. The paint had flaked, but the sign was still readable. 'Curran Automotive Engineering' it read and, below that, in smaller letters, 'custom fuel systems – bespoke carburettors – fuel injection systems'. This was the factory, then. I stopped the car, reversed slowly and parked out of sight. Then I got out and neared the place gradually, the Makarov in my hand.

There was an eight-foot high, spiked, galvanized steel fence going around the whole lot, except for the opening for vehicles. In the middle of the plot, surrounded by tarmac, was a stubby single-storey building that looked like some kind of government place, council offices or something functional like that.

The brickwork was a dirty brown colour, the mortar almost black. The windows were large but divided into small panes, and the glass itself was frosted so that the whole building looked like a prison.

The fence and tarmac were a problem. I wasn't going to get through that steel fence and getting over would be difficult. Even if I did that, I'd be exposed for ten seconds while I ran across to the building. If there were sentries, I'd be dead before I got a dozen yards. I could wander in through the vehicular entrance, but, again, I'd be exposed.

Because it was at the end of the estate, the river ran two sides and the road one side. The fourth side bordered a set of garages, all of which looked like they hadn't been used in twenty years. The roof of one had fallen in, and a few broken cars lay about, their skeletons rusted, weeds growing up the sides. The earth was dragging them back.

On that fourth side, the windows of the building were small, narrow and high up, and I thought they probably belonged to the toilet block or something like that.

The garages were open to the road, no fencing or anything. I went into that lot.

I waited for a few minutes and watched. There were no CCTV cameras that I could see in plot 36, no patrols came round. For a moment, I had the feeling that it was all a trap, that as soon as I entered the building I'd be caught. But that was just panic. I got hold of it and got hold of my Makarov and felt better.

There'd be men inside the building, sure, but nothing I couldn't handle. But then I noticed that there were no cars parked, and that only made sense if nobody was there. Dunham's men would've come by car in case they were called away suddenly. Maybe Dunham's wife had lied, or got it wrong. Maybe they'd come and gone. It always seemed to be too late.

I looked around the garage lot and saw something I could use. Over by one of the garages, half-covered in a tarpaulin, was a pile of tyres. I went over and tried to lift the first one. It wouldn't budge, had become glued to the one below by years of decomposition. I kicked at the pile, using the flat of my foot and all my weight. A crack appeared between the first and second. I tried to lift it again, and this time it came.

It took a while, but it was quiet work, and, over that side of the building, I was sure I couldn't be seen. Finally, I had a pile of tyres five feet high, standing next to the galvanized fence. I climbed on top of them, stepped up onto the top of the fence and let myself drop down to the other side, bending my knees to soften the impact. I landed quietly and stayed like that, in a crouched position. I'd stowed the Makarov. Now I reached for it and held it ready. Nothing happened. Nobody shouted. No sirens went off. No security lights came on.

I thought again about the lack of cars. They would've needed cars to get to a place like this, and there'd be at least one here if Glazer was here too. It had to mean I was too late.

There were two doors, one front, one back. Both were made of the same grey metal. Both were locked. I went around again, checking the windows this time. Mostly they were shut tight, with no way to open them from the outside short of smashing them, but there was one on the far side that had been broken and was an inch ajar. It was a large window, and the bottom of it was only waste high. I put my fingers in the gap and pulled. It was tight, and it creaked as it opened. I froze. To me, in that quietness, the noise had sounded like a tree falling.

After a while, when there was no other sound, I opened the window more, pulling it quickly this time. When the gap was wide enough, I climbed in and found myself squatting in a small, carpeted corridor, with white walls and a couple of doors leading off. The carpet was good quality and meant my footsteps were noiseless. I'd bought a small torch with an adjustable lens to make the light larger. I opened the first door slowly, my gun ready, the light from my torch bouncing around. It was a small room, windowless and empty. Probably it had once been a storage room. I tried the next one and this was about the same, only smaller.

I moved down the corridor and through a fire door. I went through into a big space. This had to be the workshop. It smelled of metal and dust. It felt empty, gaping and cold.

I levelled my gun and moved the torch's beam around. It was a long room, maybe fifty feet by twenty, and must've taken up half of the building. The ceiling was high and strip lighting ran the length. There were long metal benches along both sides of the room, and twisted metal shavings on the floor. There were small holes and angular patches where machinery had once been bolted to the benches. There was metallic dust all over the floor, and footprints in the dust. They could've been there years – or not.

I gripped the Makarov tightly, and moved forward slowly, listening, waiting.

When I'd gone the length of the room, I came up against the back wall, windows high up, too dirty to let much light in. To my right was another door, thick and heavy. I opened it slowly and stopped. The light here was enough so that I could see clearly.

The room was bigger than the workshop, and the windows larger. Probably it had been a place for fixing the motors; there was space for several cars. It was damp and cold and empty – except for the thin, metal-framed, plastic chair and the man tied into it.

I waited in the doorway, expecting someone to move or say something. As I waited, and looked at the man in the chair, the place become darker, foggier, colder and I saw that Argentinean conscript again, lying in the mud a dozen feet from me, watching me, smiling at me in his death.

He came to me like that, in the darkness, in the quietness, when I was myself closest to death, closest to that time, when I'd been a kid, no older than the conscript, tasting the sourness of blood and fury and fear and murder for the first time. Another flashback, as Browne would say. And yet, it was more than that. It was as if that kid was now a part of me, and lived, even in his death, while I lived. He shared the darkness with Brenda, shared the same air and space and nothingness that lived in that hole inside me.

And then I was back in the factory, in the room, staring at the man in the chair.

I turned the torch onto the wall and saw the light switch. I tried it and the ceiling lights flickered then came on. I saw him clearly now.

His body was slumped forward, as far as the rope would let him, and his head was bent. It seemed like half his face was hanging off, blood congealing all over, a dark pool gathering on the concrete beneath. That must've been how Brenda's face had looked by the time Paget had finished with her.

Both his eyes were swollen shut, his mouth was split open, his nose was smashed in. Looking at those injuries, I thought he must be dead but I watched him closely and saw his chest move in shallow breathing.

So, here he was; the man I wanted to kill, the one who'd finish this cycle I was stuck in. Glazer – all neat and tidy and done up in a fucking bow. That would've made Eddie laugh. All I had to do was push his head back until his neck snapped. It would be so fucking easy.

I put my hand onto his forehead. Push, I thought. Push and be done with it.

He mumbled something, the sound coming out in bubbles through his broken mouth. I didn't hear what he was saying. I didn't really care. All I could think was that I was here, at last, with the last of them, the last who'd killed Brenda, or had a part in her killing – or, anyway, that's what I was telling myself.

'Don't know,' he said. 'Don't know.'

What didn't he know? What did Dunham want? The disc, probably. Well, I didn't care about that. I'd come to kill him and here he was.

So what was I waiting for? Why hadn't I done it already? It was easy. Push. Snap. Go home. Go back to Browne and tell him it's over, and see the disappointment creep into his face, and the resignation. Watch him open another bottle. Go back to Eddie and Dunham and tell them, 'Fuck You,' and sit back while they hit me with everything and destroy all around me. Go back to Tina and tell her, 'It's over, I killed again, can I stay here? Can we be together? Is there a life for us?'

Yeah, sure, easy. Did I give a shit about any of that?

'Since when did you start caring about things, Joe?' Eddie had said. 'About people?'

And still Glazer sat before me, slumped, bleeding. All I had to do was push, or squeeze his neck, or smack another across his jaw. Anything. I could put a round through his brain.

272

And then I saw that Argentinean boy again, lying out there, almost within my reach, but beyond anything. And I thought what I'd thought a million times before: I was the last person to see him alive. I was the last thing he saw. That was our meeting, our departing. We were nothing to each other. We were life and death to each other. And why? Because we were doing the bidding of our overlords, our masters who wore their pinstriped suits and mouthed their lies while their eyes told the truth, and who, months later, would have cocktails with each other.

Lift the gun, put the muzzle an inch from his head, put my finger on the trigger and squeeze. I could do that. It was easy.

What would I do now, I wondered, if that Argentinean boy was in front of me? Would I kill him? Could I do it again?

And still, part of me was screaming: end it, kill him, close the cycle, get your fucking revenge.

Instead, I found myself putting my hand under his chin and lifting his head. I don't know why I did that, except that I couldn't shake the image of the Argentinean boy from my mind, as if it was him, not Glazer in front of me.

He looked at me through the swollen eyes – or tried to. I must've been a blur to him, just a shape. He tried to pull away from me, but it was a weak effort and he gave up. I let go of him and his head fell forward again.

I watched him as a man watches a dying insect. The insect doesn't mean anything to the man, but he watches it anyway.

Glazer stirred and mumbled.

'Don't know,' he said.

I looked at him and saw that he was trying to open his eyes.

'Don't know what?'

'Don't know. You can't do this. I'm the law.'

'Yeah,' I said. 'You're the law and I'm justice.'

I don't think he heard me. He'd slumped forward again. I pushed him back.

'Look at me. Look. You know who I am?'

'Don't know,' he said.

I took my knife from my pocket and sliced through the swollen skin above one eye. It seemed important to me that he knew who I was. My bloody ego, I suppose, as Browne would say.

The blood drained down his face. I wiped it out of his eye as best I could, then I cut through the ropes. He fell forward and I caught him and pushed him back onto the seat.

He looked at me drowsily. Blood dribbled from the corner of his eye.

'You know who I am? Hey.'

I slapped him a couple of times. He shook his head.

'Yes,' he said. 'You're him.'

'You know what I want?'

'I don't know where it is. I don't know.'

'What? Where what is?'

'The disc.'

'That's not what I want.'

He retched, throwing his head forward. Bile and blood mixed into a dark mess and fell over his legs.

274

'Brenda,' I said. 'Remember her?'

'Brenda.'

'Six years ago. You were in vice. She worked for Marriot. She made a copy of a film and sent it to you and you grassed her up to Marriot and he had Paget kill her. Remember her?'

'And now?' he said. 'Now you're going to kill me? You're with them?'

'I'm with nobody.'

'Where are they? They were here. Where are they?'

'No one's here.'

'Where is he?'

'It's just me.'

He moved his head back, and focused on me, saw my face. Then he understood.

'I know you,' he said. 'I remember her. Yes, I grassed her up to Marriot. She contacted me, told me who she worked for. I told Marriot, but I didn't know what they were going to do to her.'

'That doesn't matter.'

'I know.'

Kill him, my brain said. Kill him. End it. Take his blood for Brenda's.

But I didn't move. I didn't squeeze or push. I just stood there, dumb and stuck.

I couldn't do it – not like this. Maybe it was too close to murder. Murder has a different taste from vengeance. It makes you sick.

Or, maybe, after all, it was what Brenda had written in that letter: 'Don't destroy yourself for me, Joe.'

I'd thought she'd meant don't end up like the ship in that print of hers – Turner's *The Fighting Temeraire*, that once glorious ship, that deadly thing, now being pulled to its death by a dreary black tug.

'Poor old Joe,' she'd say. 'Heading for the breaker's yard.'

She was right, of course. But I don't think she'd meant that.

What had she meant? What did it mean? Destruction. I could be alive, sure, but I might end up being what she hated, a thing full of acid, spewing it out at the world, at all my enemies and then, when there was nothing left outside, the acid would start to eat me alive from the inside. That's what Browne had said. I might live, but I'd be dead. The Killing Machine would've destroyed itself – an empty hull, not worthy of her memory.

I knew now, standing above Glazer, that if I killed him, I'd be doing just that: destroying myself. And I couldn't live like that – not because I cared about Glazer, or Browne, or even myself.

But I cared about Brenda – what was left of her, which was nothing but my memory, fading all the time, but still there. If I killed him and became as Dunham and Paget and all those, I'd lose the right to remember her. I'd have destroyed something inside, a place where she lived still.

'Don't destroy yourself for me, Joe.'

That wasn't it, after all. It was her that I couldn't destroy – what was left of her.

Glazer mumbled something.

'I haven't got it. I never had it.'

'What?'

276

'The disc.'

It took me a moment to understand what he'd said.

'You had it,' I said. 'Brenda – she sent it to you.'

'Never had the disc. Never had it. Don't know where it is.'

That didn't make sense.

'She sent it to you.'

'She contacted me, said she could get evidence. But I never saw it, didn't know what it was. Then she was killed. I never got anything.'

'You're lying.'

'I know you. I know you'll kill me anyway. Why would I lie about that but admit I told Marriot she contacted me?'

'You're lying,' I said.

But even as I said it, I was unsure. It was hard to look at Glazer and believe he was lying. He'd had all the lies beaten from him. There was nothing left.

And, as he said, why would he lie if he'd already admitted that Brenda had contacted him and that he'd told that to Marriot? He already expected me to kill him.

But if he hadn't had the DVD, that meant something else was going on, had been going on for a long time. And I was starting to understand what it was.

Dunham's men would be coming back to finish with Glazer. Maybe soon. And that made me think too; where were they? Why weren't they here? Why hadn't they left at least one man as a guard?

I stashed the Makarov in my jacket pocket, and held him up with one arm while I finished cutting his legs free.

I'd come here to kill him, and now I was saving him. That would've made Eddie laugh even more. Still, fuck

Eddie. It would've made Brenda smile, and that was all I cared about.

I put the knife away and put the gun back into my hand. I lifted Glazer and saw his eyes widen and knew I'd made a mistake. They *had* left someone. I swung round and slammed into a wall.

I tumbled back and crashed into the floor. Glazer landed on me and pushed the air from my lungs. I heard him scream out in pain as he bounced off me and hit the concrete. I heard my gun clatter away somewhere. My head banged into the ground and I felt an electric shock spurt down my spine.

My skull was ringing from the punch. The side of my face felt like someone had set fire to it. I tried to focus, but I couldn't control my eyes and felt them go up into my head as the world started to spin away.

Then I heard the count. Six. And I could feel the canvas beneath my fingers and I could taste the salty, metallic blood in my mouth and I could hear the crowd jeer. Seven. I'd never been floored in the ring. But here I was, on the deck thinking that Browne was going to have to patch me up pretty good later, thinking I was finished, at last.

Eight.

Then I looked up and saw him looming, staring down at me with his dumb mouth open.

Roy Buck.

Nine.

And I felt a surge of anger. Buck. I was damned if he was going to KO me. The Reaper? Fuck him. I'd show him what death was.

I rolled over onto my hands and knees. Buck should've come in and finished me. But he just stood there, waiting.

The counting had stopped and I remembered where I was.

'I was having some grub,' he said, and I cursed myself for not searching the whole place. 'I heard something.'

And still he waited, staring at me in that dumb, open-mouthed way of his. Maybe we were back in the ring after all. I didn't know any more. It seemed every time I thought I knew where I was, when I was, I'd blink and find I was wrong.

Buck. Yes, of course he'd wait. He'd fought me in the ring, and beaten me. Now he could do it again.

Now I understood why there'd been no cars outside. Buck couldn't drive. It was too difficult for him. They'd come in cars and left Buck to finish the job on Glazer. And he'd wait until they came back for him. If he had to wait a year, he'd wait because he was too fucking dumb to do anything else.

'I know you,' he said.

'Yeah. We fought. I was the old bloke.'

He thought about that for a while, as much as he could think about anything.

'The old bloke,' he said. 'Joe. The Machine. I remember. The Killing Machine.'

I stood slowly, expecting him to rush me while I was getting up. That would've been the smart thing to do. Instead, he waited and I had the feeling he was enjoying this, wanting the fight, as if it was all a bit of fun.

I glanced towards my gun, and he stepped that way, not trying to get the gun, just making sure I couldn't.

279

'Do you know where it is?' he said. 'The DVD?'

He wasn't taking the piss. He really wanted to know.

Lots of us old pugs walked around with our brains scrambled from half a life of being pummelled a couple of times a month for a few hundred quid a go. But Buck's head was wrong in a different way. It was more as if he didn't have anything in his head to mush, but rather had a lump of concrete that someone had once poured in there.

So, Eddie or Dunham had told him to find out where the DVD was. They'd pointed him at Glazer and let him get on with it. They'd chiselled the order into his concrete head, and now it was there for all time. Where's the DVD? Where's the DVD?

Whatever I said now didn't matter. He'd work on me like he'd worked on Glazer.

'The DVD?' I said. 'I know where it is. Dunham's got it.'

I saw the confusion as it crossed his brain. It was enough. I stepped in to him, and smashed his face with a quick combination; left cross, right hook, left again. It rocked him and he stepped back. Then, as quick as he'd been caught by surprise, he recovered. He spat blood, raised his hands. And I knew I'd blown it and all I could think was that I had to get to my gun. But there was no chance of that.

I went in again and threw a right cross, as fast as I could, trying to catch him off guard, but I was too late for that. He stepped back and watched my hand pass his face. I'd put a lot into that punch, and I wasn't as quick on my feet as I used to be, and even then, I wasn't quick. I staggered as I hit air and almost lost my balance. When I straightened

280

up and turned, he was looking at me as if he was trying to work something out.

Then he smiled.

'Not bad for an old bloke,' he said.

I'd landed good solid punches on his face. There was a lump on the bridge of his nose, blood dripped from it. I thought I'd broken it, but he didn't seem bothered.

Then he came at me and I couldn't believe the speed. His blows hammered into my face until I couldn't see straight. I tried to turn and glance him off, but I was too slow, too dazed. I put my head down, my arms up in a block and he switched to my body and I felt a shrieking pain in my kidney that paralysed my entire side. I went down on one knee, and he pounded my head until it went numb. Somewhere inside I was scared. It was like a far off shudder. Another blow could finish me, Browne had said. Another one? Fuck. Buck's fists were thudding into my head faster than I could think. And there were things I still had to do. That was what scared me, knowing that I was so near to finishing it, and so close to the end of living.

I had to move, block him, get away, anything. I tried to stand and my head snapped sideways from a hook. I didn't see it. I didn't even know what direction it came from. I saw the room spin around.

There was no escape. I knew I was dead unless I hit him back. I swung blind and missed and tried again and hit something. I saw a blur as he came and went from my sight. I lashed out again and felt my arm bounce off him. Then came another flurry of blows, but he was hitting my body and that was a mistake. At least it gave my head a

281

chance to clear up. I tightened the muscles in my torso, tucked my head in and hoped he'd punch himself out.

But he just kept on pounding until my guts were twisted up and my rib cage was about to cave in.

And then, as suddenly as he'd started, he stopped. I staggered as I swung. I couldn't see him. All I could see was that fucking room, spinning around me. For a moment, I thought I'd lost all feeling, that he was still pummelling me, that something had snapped and my neck had broken. But I fell forward and hit the ground and I fucking well felt that.

Then I heard a voice, Buck's voice. It said, '...you going?'

I turned enough to see him standing over Glazer who was crawling away from us. Buck put a foot on Glazer's back and pressed him into the ground.

'Where is it?' Buck said.

Now he'd remembered what he was there for. He had to question Glazer. He had to find out where the DVD was. It was scratched into his brain. And Glazer was trying to get away, so he had to stop him. He forgot about me. I was nothing.

Glazer wasn't going to be able to speak soon. He wasn't going to be able to do anything. Buck didn't know that, or didn't care. He'd go back to beating him. One more blow to the head and I was finished, so Browne had thought. Well, I wasn't. But Glazer would be.

I tried to stand, but the room was all over the fucking place and the floor hit me smack in the face. The gun was behind me. Buck was in front of me, hauling Glazer up by his neck.

282

I wouldn't get to the gun before Buck had killed Glazer, but I'd get there, and then I'd let the Makarov do its stuff and everything would be just fine because everyone would be dead, except me – or maybe including me.

I could make it to the gun, too, because Buck was busy with Glazer. So…

All I had to do was let Buck kill Glazer. That was fine, wasn't it? What did I care about Glazer? I'd come there to kill him myself, hadn't I?

Hadn't I?

Fuck.

I got up to my knees. Buck had Glazer tight in his grip. I couldn't understand what I was going to do, but I was going to do it anyway. It didn't make any kind of sense. Even Brenda would've understood if I'd let Buck kill Glazer so that I could get to my gun.

It was madness.

I ignored the gun and put everything into my legs, pushed and hit Buck at the knees. We went crashing down, all three of us. I had nothing to use against Buck. My fists weren't enough and the Makarov was out of reach. But then I remembered my knife. He was on his knees. If he got back to his feet I'd be finished. Glazer moaned and rolled over. Buck saw him, and smashed a right against Glazer's jaw. That was Buck's mistake. He should've left Glazer and concentrated on me. The punch threw him off balance for a second and I pulled out my knife and opened the blade with my thumb and jammed the thing into Buck's right leg, at the back of the knee, and tore it through with everything I had. He screamed and his eyes opened wide in shock.

I rolled away, out of his reach. He tried to stand but his leg gave way and he fell, hamstrung.

I crawled away from him, away from the carnage and over to my gun. When I turned, he was standing, his right leg hanging uselessly, blood soaking the trousers. He looked down at his leg, then over to me, as if he was trying to work out how he was going to get over to finish me off.

Then he saw the gun and his face went white. He was stupid, but even he could figure out what was coming. I emptied the magazine into his body, the rounds making small black holes in his torso. Then, as he grappled with the small holes, his shirt stained with crimson and the blood spread out from all parts. He tried to come at me, death in his face, rage in the muscles of his body, his fists balled tight. He put his bleeding hamstrung leg out and collapsed.

I think, in that final moment, he tried to do the only thing he knew: hurt, kill. Maybe he finally understood what his nickname meant.

I rolled over onto my back and felt the pain start to overcome the shock. I don't know how long I lay there, waiting until I could manage to get enough strength to stand. I know I blacked out a few times because Brenda came to me, out of the darkness. I couldn't hear her or smell her or taste her. I couldn't see her. I couldn't touch her. I just felt her, as if she was behind me, maybe, or next to me in bed, her asleep and silent, me awake, staring into the space above my eyes, the night's dark upon us.

When I opened my eyes, I looked into that space and wondered if I was really with her.

Then pain screeched along my nerves and I remembered.

I forced myself up and saw Buck's body in a thick pool of his blood. Glazer was a few feet away, lying face upwards, staring with blank, dry eyes at nothing. He'd probably died while I'd been on my back staring at the same nothing. He'd died while I'd tried to save him, maybe wondering, as I had, what this madness was.

THIRTY-NINE

It took me half an hour before I could even roll onto my side. That was the easy part.

I spat blood, waited for my face to feel normal-sized again, then stood slowly and walked out of the place.

I got back in my car and drove to Tina's. I didn't know where else to go.

She was waiting for me. I stepped up to the front door and it fell open and she stood there in a pale dress, the light coming through it from behind. Her head was bowed and her hands were behind her back, like she was a child waiting to be told off. I moved inside and closed the door behind me. She took a step back. I wondered why that was. She still hadn't looked at me. She was trembling. I put my hands on her shoulders. She looked up then, with those wide, empty, washed-out eyes.

I could taste blood, my ears were ringing so that sound came muffled to me. I was fuzzy in the head – more so than usual. But I didn't feel much pain up there, and that was worrying me.

'You're alive,' she said at last.

'Just.'

She put a hand to my cheek.

'My God, Joe. What happened?'

'I found Glazer. I talked to him. Someone else was there. Someone dangerous.'

We stood there for a while, neither talking. I supposed I'd disappointed her. I could've given up on Glazer, stayed here, maybe started again. Instead, I left and more people were dead.

'I was making something to eat,' she said.

Her hand dropped away and she turned from me, floated off, as if she was sleepwalking.

I closed the door, went into the lounge. I heard her in the kitchen.

I looked around, looked at the small, cosy world she'd made for herself in this small, cold house. I saw the photos she had on the wall, the windowsill, the shelves. There were pictures of her children and grandchildren. There was an old one of her in a bridal gown standing beside the man who would later leave her.

I opened a drawer in the cabinet, took out a photo album. I flipped it open, started to look through. The album told the same kind of story that all photo albums tell: a happy child, a holiday, smiling relatives, some of whom were now probably dead. There was a whole past life there; time was frozen forever, or, at least, until the fading colours faded away completely.

Tina said something, but I didn't hear it. I went into the kitchen. Her hands were on the counter, her elbows locked. There was an onion on the chopping board, half-diced, and a kitchen knife in her hand. I could see the tightness in her shoulders. I don't think she'd heard me come in. I put my hand on her neck and she flinched.

There were tears on her cheeks. She wiped them away with the backs of her hands. She pulled away from me and went back to chopping the onion. All that time she hadn't spoken, hadn't looked at me. Her actions were mechanical.

'The onions,' she said. 'They make me cry. Do you want something to eat?'

'I'm okay.'

She chopped, and rested the blade of the knife on the wooden board.

'Why did you come back? You left. Why did you have to come back?'

There was nothing I could say to that. I went into the lounge. Something had been in my mind, as far as anything could be in that swampy, floating mess. But it was there, clinging on and I had to seek it out. Then I remembered what it was: Tina's photos.

Seeing them had made me think again about the ones Brenda had in her flat, the ones that Compton and Bradley had taken. Why? Why were they taken? What value were they to anyone?

Tina put the radio on and I heard a thin, far-off voice talking.

The photos. What was it about them?

Compton and Bradley had been in Brenda's flat after she was killed. They hadn't taken the cash or the jewellery; Margaret Sanford admitted having taken those. But the photos had been missing. They must've been taken by Compton and Bradley.

I didn't understand that. Why would they take Brenda's photographs? Unless there was a picture of one of them in there. But I'd seen those photos. Brenda showed them to me. Compton and Bradley weren't in any of them. They were just pictures of her and her family and her friends – the few she'd had.

I opened Tina's photo album again, flicked the thick page over, saw a young girl with white blonde hair, saw a teenager who was too thin and wore too much make-up. I turned another page and another.

Why had Compton taken the photographs? And why all of them?

I turned another page and saw a woman with white skin, black hair, ice cream in her hand, smiling at the camera.

But then I thought, Suppose I take one of these pictures, one from Tina's book. If I do that, someone might know which one I'd taken. Then they'd wonder what it was about that particular picture that was so important.

I kept turning the pages hoping the answer would come to me from the images of a young, blonde, pale woman. Here was one of Tina with a baby, the bright sun making her hair shine. Here was one of a young couple, in a pub, the bloke, with a smile on his red face and Tina on his knee, her arm around his neck.

In other words, if Compton had taken one photograph, I might've known which one had been taken. Then I might start remembering something about that particular photo. To hide one, Compton had to take them all.

I stopped, and turned back a couple of pages and looked again at the woman with dark hair and an ice cream.

I thought about Compton and one important photograph. And I thought, I've seen her before, that pale woman with dark hair. I'd seen her at the pub that time.

I turned. Tina was behind me, her hands behind her back again, her eyes looking down.

'Who's this?' I said, pointing to the woman with dark hair. But even as I said it I could see who it was.

'I'm sorry,' she said.

I opened my mouth to ask why but the only noise that came out was the sound of my pain as she pushed the knife into me.

'Another scar, Joe,' she said.

The blood drained from her face as it poured from my wound. And all I could think, stupidly, was that I could smell onions.

She took the knife out as easily as she'd pushed it in. I know that because I watched her do it, watched the blade come out, watched my blood come out with it. You have no idea how red blood looks until you see it against steel and pale skin. I looked at its redness.

For a second I didn't feel anything. It was like watching it all happen to someone else. Then I felt it, the shock of it, the acid burn of it.

She backed away from me, still holding the knife in her left hand. Our eyes were locked together. I understood then what she'd done.

I put a hand onto the wound, tried to press as much as I could to keep the blood in. But the blood didn't stay in. I felt its hot wetness wrap around my fingers. She could've killed me at any time. All she had to do was walk forwards and plunge the knife in me again and again and again. It's funny that I, this monster, this Frankenstein-like creation of muscle and scarred tissue and sinew and massive bulk could be cut down by a small, thin, pale thing like her. Fuck, she was almost transparent. I could've destroyed her with the swipe of my hand.

Instead, as she backed and backed away, I staggered forward, trying to catch my own blood, trying to keep from crashing down. If I fell it would be for good. I couldn't let that happen.

So, I walked on soft legs and saw the room begin to spin and took deep breaths, in, out.

I grabbed one of Tina's cotton blouses, which had been hung on the back of her chair.

At least I understood, finally. I knew now what had happened. I knew it all – at last.

Then I was outside and the fresh air helped, but now my head was beginning to get hazy and things were fogging up.

All I had to do was make it to the car. I could do that, right?

FORTY

The cut in my side was deep, leaking blood all over the place. But, on top of all that, there was a pressure inside my head. I thought Buck might've done something bad, something I wouldn't recover from. I had to end this now, while I was still able to walk and talk and know my name.

I was about out of strength.

I had an idea, though: maybe I could get them to finish it for me.

I stumbled out of Tina's house and aimed myself at the car which moved up and down, along with the rest of the street.

After a week, I made it to the car, got inside and pulled my jacket and shirt off. The blood looked black in the moonlight. I tore Tina's blouse into strips, then took a piece of it, wadded it up and packed it against the wound, holding it as firmly as I could while I wrapped the strips around my torso and, with difficulty, got them tied.

I fished Compton's card from my inside jacket pocket, called him.

'Joe?' he said.

'Yeah.'

'What's wrong? Where are you?'

'I know where Glazer is,' I said.

I told him about the industrial estate, Dunham's place there.

'Is something wrong, Joe? You don't sound good.'

I hung up.

Next I called Browne. I told him I knew where Glazer was. I told him it was in a place owned by Dunham, a factory place off the North Circular. I told him I was meeting Compton there.

At the end of that, Browne said, 'What the bloody hell are you on about?'

'In case I don't make it back.'

Then I started the car and pulled out. The straight road snaked in front of me.

'Poor old Joe,' Brenda said.

She was sitting by my side. She touched my hand.

'That poor old ship,' she said.

'I'm breaking up,' I told her.

'Joe,' she said. 'Watch out.'

A car horn screamed at me. I didn't know why. I moved the steering wheel and felt the world slide under my car wheels.

I pulled up, opened the window and sucked in cold air, felt it grate my lungs, felt the sweat on my brow turn icy. It cleared my head. I turned to the passenger seat, but Brenda was gone.

The pain in my side wasn't so bad now. The cut must've closed up a bit. Maybe I was bleeding inside, but I didn't think so.

I set off again, putting all my strength into my

concentration. I had one thing left to do. One thing. I couldn't stop now, couldn't let my body crash when I was so close.

Keep it together, I told myself.

'Not yet,' I said to no one. 'Not just yet.'

When I saw the factory, I turned the car into its car park. This time there were other cars there, two of them.

They were waiting for me, scattered around the large factory room.

Their clobber was the same as always; shabby, grey, ill-fitting suits like you'd get off a rack at a discount shop in a retail park, and their faces were grim, tired, strained.

The room seemed thick with sweat and smoke and five-quid aftershave. They'd been there a while, waiting for me. Then, there was the smell of blood. And, underneath all that, there was a far-off stale smell, as if the air had died long ago and was hanging there, waiting to be chucked away. It made me want to smash a window open and ventilate the place, even if it was with that bleak, damp, fume-filled stuff that hung around London.

The bodies were still there. That meant I was in time; Eddie and Dunham didn't know yet. They probably still thought Buck was working on Glazer, that they'd get an answer soon. Well, Dunham might've thought that, but Eddie would've started to worry, after my phone call to Browne.

I was hiding the knife wound as best as I could. My jacket was buttoned and the dark material had soaked up the blood. I held my gun by my side. I felt cold, and I thought the rip in my side had opened again. And then,

294

too, I was still feeling the beating I'd got from Buck, some swelling around my right eye, my left ear ringing.

There was nothing in me, no strength any more. But I didn't want them to know that.

I hadn't known if Tina would call them, but if she had, I thought she wouldn't say anything about stabbing me. Now, though, seeing them standing around trying to look casual, I knew Tina hadn't told Compton anything. Why would she? She hated him as much as she feared me.

So, as far as they all knew, this was the first time I'd been here.

They clocked the gun as soon as I went in, but they didn't make a thing of it. I put it in my waistband, just to play along for the time being.

Compton waited, wiped a hand over his moustache. Hayward was back against a wall, arms folded, ankles crossed. It was a good act, all this, but I could see the sheen of sweat glistening on Hayward's dark face. I could see that shake in Compton's hand. The bodies of Glazer and Buck must've scared them plenty. That was good. That was what I wanted; to snatch some of their control from them.

Bradley pulled a pack of smokes from his jacket pocket, opened the pack, put a cigarette in his mouth and lit it with a lighter. He did all that without taking his eyes off me. He'd smoked a half dozen already. The butts were strewn about. This was a crime scene, and these were coppers, and they didn't give a shit. I doubted these deaths would ever get reported.

'Well, Joe,' Compton said at last, 'have you come to give us something? Tell us something, perhaps?'

295

I was supposed to roll over now, be a good dog. That was the cue.

I said, 'No.'

Compton's jaw twitched. Then he shrugged. That's okay, his shrug said, we don't really care.

Bradley nodded, half smiled. I think he wanted me to fight just so he could kill me. He'd probably been telling Compton not to trust me from the start.

Hayward just looked baffled, but didn't say anything. He couldn't take his eyes off the bodies on the floor, the pools of blood that shone like dark mirrors.

'Looks like we're all too late,' Compton said, walking over to one of the corpses. 'This is Glazer. Or was. Blood's still wet. Must've died recently.'

'Know the big bloke?' Bradley said.

'Yeah,' I said, without looking at the body. 'His name was Roy Buck.'

Hayward unfolded his arms. His jacket was buttoned. I could see the shape of the gun beneath.

Bradley didn't move, but he was staring hard at me. Compton just nodded, as if I'd told him it might rain later.

'Any idea what happened here, Joe?' he said.

'Buck killed Glazer. I killed Buck.'

Bradley flicked his eyes over to Compton. Hayward ran his tongue over dry lips.

'Okay, Joe. What's this all about?' Compton said.

'It's about someone I knew. Someone I—'

My throat seized up. What I wanted to say was that it was about someone I'd loved. Maybe, after so long, the idea that I could love anyone was too difficult to believe. Who was I that I could love someone? How can a machine love?

And yet the pain of losing her was so deep it couldn't be known. It was more than in me. It was of me, it shaped me.

Maybe I felt the loss more than I'd felt love for her when we'd been together. You don't think of it when it's there as much as you feel the loss of it when it's not. It was like standing in the shadow of an eclipse of the sun, feeling coldness and seeing darkness and knowing that the warmth had gone. A forever eclipse, that's what it was.

I couldn't say any more, things had become too mixed up, the memory of her swamping and drowning everything else.

I tried to push the memories away but they wouldn't go. They were caught about the hatred; memory and loathing feeding off each other, each pushing the other further in.

Browne was right; the hatred was killing me.

And I didn't care because without it, I had nothing. Browne was wrong about that; I wasn't gutting myself. I was already gutted. I was that body on the slab, moving but dead, bloodless and grey.

I realized then, at that moment, in front of these cunts, that I'd never told her what I felt for her.

'Fuck,' Bradley said. 'Will you look at that? He's human after all.'

'Let him speak,' Hayward said.

I think, of all of them, he understood most – maybe because he had a woman.

'It's about someone I knew. Her name was Brenda.'

'Yes,' Compton said. 'You told us about her.'

297

'But I didn't need to tell you about her, did I? You already knew.'

There was silence for a moment. Then Hayward broke it.

'John?' he said.

Nobody paid him any attention.

'You were there that time,' I said 'at her flat, after she'd been killed. I know you were because there was a witness; a woman who lived near Brenda. I went to see her.'

'Is that what this is about? Yes, I was there. I was investigating Operation Elena then. We knew Glazer was bent and we thought she might have evidence against him, so, when I heard she'd been killed, I went there and looked for it. Nothing to get wound up about.'

It was a good story. I almost believed it.

'What did you find?' I said.

'Nothing,' Bradley said, flicking his ash onto the floor. 'Waste of time.'

'Did you find any photos?'

'Photos?' Bradley said.

'Yeah. Things that come out of cameras.'

Hayward wasn't saying a word. I think this was the first time he'd heard any of this. He must've been wondering why that was.

'No, we didn't find any photos, Joe,' Compton said. 'Why do you ask?'

'You were looking for drugs.'

'Who told you that?'

'Brenda's neighbour. She said you told her you were looking for drugs.'

298

I could see dots of sweat on Compton's brow. I knew way more than I should. What else did I know?

'That's what we told her,' he said. 'It seemed best. We wanted to keep a low profile. Drugs round there were a common problem.'

'You're lying, Compton.'

'What do you mean?'

'I mean fuck you. You weren't investigating Operation Elena back then. Glazer was still running it, which he wouldn't have been if anyone was suspicious of it. The investigation into Glazer came after.'

'Okay. Look, there's stuff I can't tell you, that's all. You just have to trust me.'

'Why should I trust you? You've lied to me from the start.'

'Not from the start, Joe,' Compton said, smiling.

He looked at Bradley and Hayward. It was all funny. Bradley made an effort to smile, but his eyes gave him away. Hayward didn't bother at all.

'Joe,' Compton said, all friendly now. 'Joe, you've got things all wrong. We're the ones who were out to get Glazer. Remember?'

'Yes,' I said. 'You wanted him alright. You wanted him dead.'

'Bollocks,' Bradley said.

'Who do you work for, Compton?'

'You know who.'

There was a surge of pain in my side that made my head swim for a second. Then the sweat came. I don't think they saw it. I said, 'I know who pays your bills. I know you

299

wear a uniform. But I don't know who pulls your strings. One thing I do know, you don't care about any anti-corruption shit.'

'You don't know what you're talking about, Joe, old son. You've gone paranoid.'

'All them blows to the head, probably,' Bradley said, waiting for a laugh from the others. He didn't get one.

'We're investigating Glazer because he's corrupt,' Compton was saying. 'That's all. Simple. No conspiracy. You know he was bent, Joe. You know better than anyone; he grassed your woman up to Marriot, didn't he? And Marriot got Paget to kill her. Right?'

'That's why you killed Marriot and Paget isn't it?' Bradley said.

'I know about you, Bradley,' I said. 'You were Special Branch, weren't you?'

Hayward was looking from one to the other. Bradley stared at me, his mouth open.

'I saw a copper called Rose,' I said. 'Remember him?'

'No,' Compton said.

'He was a DS, ran a few informants. One of them was a woman called Margaret Sanford. She was Brenda's neighbour. You took over running her from Rose. You used her to keep an eye on Brenda. This was before the film was even made, which means you had foreknowledge of the film, of Brenda's part in it, of her plan to get a copy to send to Glazer.'

Compton looked at me for a long time and I saw him as he really was, without pity or conscience, cold and deadly. Then, he half smiled and spread his hands. He didn't

300

care. People like him never do. People like him and me. I could've killed them then and there, and wouldn't have felt anything about it. But I wanted to end this, get things straight, finally. For that, I had to wait a while.

It was the photo in Tina's album that did it, told me what was happening – the photo of Tina on the beach; the pale skin, black hair. I'd seen her years back, in the Fox and Globe, when I'd gone there with Brenda. Well, it was the photo and her knifing me. She'd done it out of fear; fear that I knew what she'd done.

By itself, it wasn't much. But when I added it to everything else I knew...

Meanwhile, my blood was seeping out, my head was getting lighter, fuzzier. The room moved. I stumbled forward a half step. None of them saw it. They were all too worried, each in their own way.

'John,' Hayward was saying. 'What does this mean? What's he talking about?'

There was panic in Hayward's voice. I think he'd seen the same thing in Compton I had and that, I think, more than anything, frightened him. Everything he thought he knew was crumbling, and the cause he'd been devoted to – fighting corruption and murder – and Compton – the man who'd embodied that cause – all that was becoming dust in front of him.

'He doesn't know what he's talking about,' Compton said.

'Beyond his understanding,' Bradley said. I think he wanted to say something just to remind everyone he was there. 'He knows fuck all.'

301

But I did know. Finally.

I said, 'You're MI5, aren't you, Compton? You must be if Bradley was from the Branch. My guess is you had this bloke in the film under surveillance. You would've known he had a thing for kids. So, when he made contact with Marriot, it would've been easy to figure out what he wanted. There was your chance to get him, to blackmail him, control him. But you couldn't trust Marriot, so you investigated people working for Marriot, and found a woman you could put the frighteners on. Her name was Tina.'

'John,' Hayward said. 'Sir? What's he on about?'

'Shut up, Del,' Bradley said.

He was still smoking his cigarette. I had the feeling that when he stopped, people would die.

'What the fuck is he on about?'

I turned to Hayward.

'They used you, Hayward. They needed a real copper to get onto Glazer's vice unit. They fed you the same spiel they've been feeding me, that they were investigating Glazer's connection to Marriot.'

His face was grim. He was standing now with his feet a little apart and his arms by his side. He looked like he was getting ready for a fight, but hadn't decided who it was going to be with.

'Why was this so important?' I said to Compton 'Who is he? A terrorist? Arms dealer? Politician?'

'Something like that. He's foreign. He's powerful. And if we get him under our thumb, we'd have that power. You were a soldier once, right? You fought for God, for Queen and country. You must understand loyalty.'

302

'Fuck Queen and country. Fuck God, too. None of them ever did anything for me. And fuck you lot.'

'Look, son, I know what this means to you. The man in that DVD is a vile human. He used people, abused them, your woman included. But he means a whole lot more to us. We'll make him pay, don't worry about that. Leave it to us.'

I didn't say anything to that. It was interesting, in a way, watching Compton work, watching the absolute certainty of his authority override his fears.

'You want him?' Compton said. 'What are you gonna do? You'll never find him. You'll never get close. Look in a mirror, son. You haven't got what it takes. We're out of your league.'

'That's what Eddie Lane told me.'

'He was right.'

'I know.'

'Joe, you may hate us, that's fine, but we didn't do anything to hurt anyone. We didn't kill your woman.'

'Yeah,' I said. 'Paget and Marriot did that. And now they're dead.'

'You should know,' Bradley said.

'You're right, I killed them. I keep killing people. It's a bad habit.'

Bradley glared at me. I turned back to Compton.

'Paget had a copy of the DVD. He probably had copies of all the films that Marriot made, and they're probably sitting in some bank safety box. But I don't think he knew who was on the DVD, otherwise he and Marriot would've used it before. Marriot would've used it to keep out of the nick.'

303

'So?' Compton said.

'So then Marriot gets out of prison, and he and Paget try to take over Cole's turf and use me as a scapegoat. It goes wrong and I kill Marriot. Now Paget is running for his life, me and Cole both after him. And he goes to Dunham for protection and offers a copy of the DVD as a fee.'

'What's the point of all this?' Bradley said.

I turned my gaze back to him. I watched his eyes as he began to understand what I was doing.

'The point is: how did Paget suddenly know the DVD was valuable?'

Compton didn't say anything for a moment. I think it wasn't a question he'd ever asked himself. He looked away, towards the bodies on the ground.

'How?' he said finally.

I kept my eyes on Bradley's. He knew what was coming. His jaw clenched.

'There's only one way it works out: one of you told Paget what the DVD was worth.'

'What?' Compton said.

'Bollocks,' Bradley said.

'Why would one of them do that?' Hayward said.

'Because one of them is working for the British Security Service, and the other is working for the man in the DVD. That one tried to make a deal with Paget, maybe tried to buy the film back. Paget wasn't interested, though. Instead, when he knew Cole was after him, he went to Dunham; the only one he thought could give him protection. And he told Dunham what the DVD was worth, and why.'

Bradley tossed his smoke. I think he knew he was walking into death.

They stood still, as if they were in a play, each in a role, each waiting for his cue. The air got staler, colder, deader.

Compton was looking at the ground, his brow creased, his mouth shut tightly.

Hayward watched him, then Bradley. He didn't know what was happening.

So we all stood there, waiting for something to happen.

Then Bradley twitched. I went for my gun, but Hayward was quicker.

'Careful,' he said, holding the .32 semi at hip height. He had the gun pointed at me. I had to hand it to him; he'd unbuttoned his jacket and got the gun out without me noticing.

I let it go, pulled my hand slowly from my jacket pocket, let it drop by my side. The wound was cold now. Blood had soaked through everything and saturated it.

They were all watching me. Compton saw my blood dripping onto the floor. His face cleared a bit, like he knew I didn't have enough strength left to do anything.

Bradley had his head tilted a bit forward so that he was looking up at me with narrow eyes. He had his tongue in his cheek and moved it, as if he was weighing up whether to kill me. That's probably what he was thinking. He'd always wanted to kill me. I knew that now.

Compton's gaze was more sure of itself. I was just a lump to him. I was muscle, but not much else – no brain, anyway.

But then his eyes narrowed and he was thinking about what I'd said and maybe thinking I wasn't so fucking dumb after all.

Hayward's look was hard, sure, but it was serious, professional. To him, I was a threat. I was the enemy, and dangerous too. He gave me credit, which was why he was first to his gun. But there was no hatred, no personal feelings at all. I might have been a rabid dog that had to be shot. That was fine.

Bradley took his gun out slowly. There was murder in his face.

Then Compton turned to him. He said, 'He's right. Someone told Paget, and it wasn't me.'

Bradley didn't move for a moment. He smiled, shook his head. Then he swung round, his gun aimed at Compton. Hayward saw it, swung round too, bringing his gun up so that it was pointing at Bradley's chest.

'Don't,' Hayward said.

Compton stared at Bradley.

'Cunt,' Compton said.

'What the fuck?' Hayward said.

Everyone was his enemy.

'Take it easy, Del,' Bradley said to him.

'Take it easy? Fuck off,' Hayward said. 'Ten minutes ago I had two colleagues, two friends. I had a job and a boss. I was a fucking copper. What the fuck have you done?'

While Hayward was losing his bottle, Bradley was working out what to do, who to kill first. I could see it, and so could Compton. Hayward wiped sweat from his forehead.

Everything stopped again, everyone waiting for everyone else.

Then Bradley glanced at me. He'd made his decision and I knew he was going to kill me. Hayward locked his hammer back, Compton reached for his own piece. There would be blood, we all knew that. I steadied myself, tried to figure out what I could do. I couldn't think of anything.

Then the door burst open. We swung round as one. Eddie walked in, flanked by three men, all armed. The men fanned out, guns up, pointed at all of us.

Eddie stood in the middle of them, his hands empty. He would be armed too – he was always armed – but for now he kept his gun in his shoulder holster. For now he was playing it cool, but I knew he was worried, maybe even scared. He would've clocked the bodies on the floor, but he made a point of ignoring them. That's how worried he was.

Bradley's gun wavered, Hayward's piece was pointed at Eddie who glanced at it, then at Compton, then at me.

'Joe?' Eddie said. 'What's going on?'

'You took your time.'

'That sounds like you were expecting me.'

'I was.'

That amused glint came into his eyes. He nodded. He smiled, but it was an effort. I liked that, and he could see that I did. He was so fucking clever, and I'd used his cleverness against him. He must've hated me then more than he'd ever hated anything.

'Browne's phone,' he said. 'You found out it was bugged. You knew if you called him, we'd hear.'

I said, 'Yeah. That was a neat thing with Buck.'

'I thought so.'

He wandered over to the bodies, glanced at them. Compton had moved back.

'So you got him,' Eddie said to me. 'Buck. You got him. I kinda thought you might.'

'Yeah. I got him.'

I nodded towards Compton and Bradley and Hayward.

'I think you know this lot,' I said to Eddie.

'What makes you say that?'

'I'll come to that,' I said.

'Okay, Joe,' Eddie said, still looking like it was all fun for everyone, even if he was too fucking cool to join in with it.

I turned to Compton.

'See, Dunham wants the DVD too. He and Eddie here thought they'd get it from Glazer.'

'Glazer?' Eddie said.

'Yeah, Eddie. He's the copper your men kidnapped,' I said. 'Remember? The one you set Buck on. But you've all been chasing Glazer for nothing.'

'What are you talking about?' Compton said.

'You thought the same as me, Compton. We thought that Brenda must've sent him a copy of the film as evidence, and that Glazer had then grassed her up to Marriot.'

I turned to Eddie.

'And you and Dunham thought the same thing, but only because I told you. So, we all went after Glazer. I wanted him because he'd got Brenda killed. The rest of you because you thought he had a copy of the DVD. But he didn't have one. He never did.'

'What makes you think that?' Eddie said.

'Because he told me.'

'And you believed him?'

'He told me he'd grassed Brenda up to Marriot. If he admitted that, why wouldn't he admit to having the DVD? Besides, Buck had been working on him long enough, so, if he'd had the DVD, he would've said so.'

'So what does that mean, Joe?'

'It means, as far as you lot knew, there were three copies: Paget's, Glazer's and mine.'

'Yours?' Compton said.

'Yeah. I had a copy that Brenda left to me. I only found it a couple of weeks ago.'

'Why the fuck didn't you tell us?'

'I'm telling you now, Compton.'

'He wants to deal,' Bradley said.

'No he doesn't,' Eddie said, looking at me.

'He's right,' I said. 'I don't want to deal. I want to kill you all.'

'You're an idiot,' Compton said. 'You give us that DVD, you can name your price – immunity, money, even.'

He said some more, but I wasn't listening. I was looking at Eddie, who was looking at me. I think he knew he'd fucked up. I think part of him was glad. He'd hated what Dunham was doing, and he'd hated that Dunham's wife hated him for doing it.

'You said to me I wasn't big enough to get him,' I said to Eddie, 'the man on the DVD. Remember?'

'I remember. I was right. You're not.'

'Yeah,' I said. 'You were right. I'm not big enough.'

Compton's lips curled upward. He seemed happy that I'd seen reason. But Eddie – well, the glint had long gone from his eyes.

'What the fuck have you done, Joe?'

'I gave the DVD to someone who is big enough. I gave it to Cole.'

Compton's face had gone as grey as the rest of him.

'You dumb cunt.'

His voice was cold and clean, but there was fear in there. I didn't care about him, though – not right then. I was watching Eddie.

'What do you think Cole will do?' I said. 'I've burned you, Eddie. I've burned the whole fucking lot of you.'

Eddie nodded.

'Yes, you have. Well done.'

Then I turned to Compton. His gun was in his hand, by his side. He was waiting to use it, but he was keeping his options open. Bradley, me... so much choice.

'There's something else, Compton,' I said. 'I told Browne I was meeting you. Eddie heard that because he had Browne's place wired. Why do you think he's come with three men?'

Compton looked from me to Eddie, then back to me. He said, 'I... uh...'

'He's here to kill you, Compton. Eddie's here to kill you.'

Hayward's gun had been back on Bradley, now it moved again to Eddie.

Eddie smiled.

'Why would I do that, Joe?'

'Because that DVD was valuable, and you had to get rid

310

of the opposition, anyone who might want it or have it or even know about it.'

I watched as the men in that room glanced at each other, and at me. Most of them wanted me dead, I knew that. And I knew too that, soon, I probably would be, and I didn't much care. But, whatever they felt about me, I was no longer the great danger. Now, each of them was more scared of the others, of each other.

And that's what I'd been counting on. That was what I wanted. Hell was let loose; I'd let it loose, and it didn't matter a fucking thing to me. Let them destroy each other, let them tear each other apart, let them bleed.

I thought Hayward would be the first to lose it. He was panicking so much he didn't even keep his aim steady. Instead, his gun went from one person to another. Then, Bradley knew he was fucked unless he killed Compton and Hayward and me, so it might've been him. But Eddie's men were starting to get the wild look in their eyes. They probably knew less than Hayward, but they couldn't have reckoned on a head to head with the law so they were scared, wondering what their boss had got them into, wondering how they could get out alive.

Eddie seemed cool about it all, but his eyes were narrow, looking from one man to the next. His hand flexed.

I had them all, all the ones who'd hurt Brenda or profited from her death. With the DVD in Cole's hands, with his promise of revenge on the man, whoever he was, I finally had them all.

Eddie looked at me. That glint came back into his eyes. He said, 'Fuck, Joe.'

He went for his gun.

'Don't,' Compton said quietly.

I didn't know who he was talking to. Anyway, it was too late.

I don't know who fired first. Maybe it was Bradley; he'd been itching to kill everyone. Maybe he decided to try that. Or maybe it was Hayward; the only real copper there, but now useless, not knowing what he was doing. Maybe it was one of Eddie's boys who were all trigger happy. Maybe it was me.

I saw Bradley swing his gun towards me. And then he took a half dozen rounds, mostly in his face. I think Compton was one of the ones who shot him. Hayward was firing wild. He even shot Buck, who'd been dead an hour. Buck's head blew apart.

I tried my best to kill them, but I could only manage to lift my gun and empty the magazine at the shimmering shadows before me. I might've hit something.

The large room had become small, none of us could hide from the onslaught, from the furious firestorm. The sound was deafening and the shouts and screams were dulled out by the thunder. There were ricochets, concrete chipping, plaster bursting. A couple of rounds punched into the floor at my feet and bounced off somewhere. Someone took a light out, but I think that was a dying shot, the man firing on his way down.

I felt the air move with rounds coming at me. I heard the buzzing and found myself back on that mount, ducking away from Argentinean fire.

Two of Eddie's men got hit. I don't know who shot them.

They died, there and then. Eddie was hit and fell, but he managed to stand again and lift his gun and fire at Compton who fired back, and at me.

Then it was all over, and the sound echoed away and left roaring silence and smoke. I felt blood trickle from the cut.

Hayward stared at me, his dark face almost white. He dropped his gun and turned and walked out, his shoulders tight, his arms straight by his sides.

Eddie managed to stagger, doubled over, to the door with his other man helping him.

Compton was still standing, but his face had gone white and he was clutching his stomach. The room span around me, the noise still bashing my ears. I fell to one knee. Compton fell to both knees.

'Madness,' he said, when he was able to speak. 'This was madness. Why? Why did you do it?'

I saw him swirl. I saw him try to lift his gun. I heard the words. I saw the room swim around me.

'Because you killed her,' I said.

'No. No.'

'All of you killed her.'

'No. Not me.'

'You knew she was trying to get evidence against Marriot. You knew she'd pay for that and you didn't give a fuck. You could've helped her, but you didn't, and she died.'

He looked at me and then at the blood in his hand.

I got up, moved one foot in front of the other. I stepped in the blood of a half-dozen men and left five bodies behind me, and Compton, bleeding from the gut.

FORTY-ONE

There was this time, in that summer, a day when we didn't say much. I'd gone round because she'd called me up the previous night and told me to get there for lunch, told me not to eat anything.

She'd made us a picnic. It was a big thing for her, I could see that. She'd made sandwiches and a cake. She'd bought those small pork pies and sausage rolls. She had a couple of bottles of wine. And she'd put the whole lot in a cardboard box with some napkins and plates and cutlery.

It was a warm day, and bright. There wasn't a cloud out there. And it was midweek, so the people were at work.

She smiled at me when she opened the door. Then she put her arms around my neck, standing on tiptoes. She kissed me. She hadn't spoken. She hadn't needed to.

We went to a small park. I can't remember where. It doesn't matter.

We sat on the grass and ate the lunch and drank the wine. Then, we lay beneath the blue, blue sky. That's all we did, just lay there and stared up at forever. I lay on my back and Brenda lay sideways, her head on my chest, her hand on my stomach.

That's how I think I'll remember her, if I can.

Just that. Both of us on a warm day in London with the endless blue sky above. Just that, and nothing more.

FORTY-TWO

She opened the door and looked up at me like I was death itself. Maybe I was.

She moved back a step. She had no life in her. She was limp, pale, worn out. Her hands were by her sides, as if she wanted me to see she didn't have a knife this time. She stood like a ghost and watched me move towards her, watched me in the way you'd watch an oncoming storm when you're exposed and alone and far away from home.

As I got near, her hand went up to my chest, but there was no strength in it. I don't think she was trying to stop me. Maybe she just wanted to see if I was real, if I was warm and alive, if a heart beat inside me. Anyway, her hand fell away and she turned her face up to me.

'I'm sorry,' she said.

'Yeah.'

I closed the door behind me. She didn't try to run, didn't scream for help, even though she must've known what I wanted to do to her.

It had been a few weeks since she'd stabbed me, but she hadn't run. Instead, she must've been waiting every day for me to come back.

'I had to,' she said.

316

'Yeah.'

'You know why?'

'Yeah.'

'Is that all you're going to say?'

She put both her hands on my chest this time, and pushed and then, as she started to sob, she beat at me.

I said, 'Yeah.'

Her fists pounded into my chest. They bounced off me like hail stones bouncing off a concrete road.

'For God's sake, Joe,' she cried, as her hands grasped my shirt, holding it to keep her from falling down. 'Hit me, cut me, kill me. Do something.'

'Is that what you were expecting me to do when I came here before? That time when you opened the door and saw me and fainted.'

She nodded.

'I thought you were here to kill me,' she said, 'I'd been waiting for you. I thought, Now he knows.'

'And all that stuff you said, about us starting again somewhere, about me stopping, all that was...'

'Yes.'

I caught her by the wrists and held her, pulled her towards me. She gasped and her eyes widened in shock.

'I know what you did,' I said. 'I know you betrayed her.'

'I loved her.'

'I know.'

'Kill me, then. That's what you want, isn't it? It's what I've been waiting for. I thought about running, but I knew you'd find me and if you didn't, I'd find myself. And I didn't want that. So, do it. Kill me.'

I let go of her wrists.

'Why didn't you finish me when you had the chance?' I said. 'You knew I'd come back for you if I could.'

She nodded.

'Yes,' she said. 'I knew that.'

'You had me. You had that knife in me and all you had to do was push.'

'Yes,' she said again. 'I knew that.' She took a step back, seemed to shrink into herself. 'I couldn't do it.'

'Why not?'

'I had to. I mean...'

'They forced you? Compton and that?'

'Yes. No. I... he told me I had to call him if you came back, if you were getting close to knowing what had happened. Compton's scared of you, you know. Really scared.'

'And you were scared of him?'

'Yes,' she said in a small voice.

'So it was his idea, to stab me?'

'No, Joe.'

I nodded.

'Go through,' I said, nodding down the hallway. She backed away from me a few feet, then turned and walked softly into the lounge.

There was music on, an old soul track.

'Turn it off,' I said.

Tina walked over to her stereo unit, pushed the button, made everything quiet. She turned, walked towards me, stopped.

Neither of us talked for a while.

Finally, I said, 'I've seen Compton. I think I understand it all now.'

She nodded.

'He came to you first?' I said.

She nodded again. Her lips were pale. I thought she might faint again. Her hands were holding each other. She said, 'He had evidence against me, told me that he could put me away for a long time. I... I used to do drugs, and sell them. I couldn't go to prison, Joe. I couldn't.'

I didn't say anything. I felt cold. She looked up at me and, seeing something in my face, looked back at the hands she was wringing together.

'So,' she said, 'I was his. He told me there was a man. I don't know who he was. But Compton knew him, knew all about him. He knew he'd been to see Marriot. And he knew he liked children. I don't know how he knew that.'

'Compton was MI5,' I said. 'He had the man under surveillance. Probably for months.'

She nodded, but I don't think she was listening.

'Compton knew I worked for Marriot,' she said. 'He knew all about me. He knew everything. It was frightening.'

'Go on.'

'He asked me about Marriot, and about what he did with these sorts of men. I told him, and I told him that Marriot made films, to use as blackmail.'

'What else did you tell him?'

When she looked up at me again, there was a blank expression in her eyes.

'What else?' I said.

'I was scared, Joe. You don't know what it's like to live

319

your life scared of men, all men. Paget would've cut me up if he'd known I was talking to Compton. Compton would've sent me to prison for ten years if I'd held out on him. These men, Joe. All men…'

'I know,' I said. 'What else did you tell him?'

'I told him what Brenda had told me, that she'd contacted a policeman who was working vice. She'd read about him or seen him on TV or something. Some operation – Elena, or some name like that. I told you that, didn't I?'

'Yeah. You told me.'

'Anyway, Brenda said she'd contacted the man in charge of the operation. But she didn't have any evidence to give him.'

I felt the muscles tighten in my shoulders. She saw it, but didn't move away.

'I know why you wanted to kill me,' I said. 'I understand. I'm just like them. I'm a man and you're as scared of me as you were of Marriot and Paget and Compton.'

'Yes,' she said softly.

'You told Compton. About Brenda, what she was doing.'

'Yes. He thought about it, then told me he had an idea, a way of keeping me and him out of it. Let Brenda do it, he said. Let her steal a copy of the film, then take it from her. And all I had to do… all I had to do—'

She collapsed then, doubled up, with her hands to her face, sobbing. She crumpled into a ball and fell to my feet.

I was sick of myself, of terrifying women, threatening them with violence, with death. In my mind, I was doing it for Brenda. But I also knew I was betraying Brenda by doing it. I was just another in a long line of men who hurt

320

women. Tina had suffered at the hands of men most of her life. I couldn't let myself be another one.

So, I waited. Finally, she rolled over onto her side. Her crying stopped. She wiped her nose, her eyes.

'We met in a pub one night. She asked me if I could get a copy. I told her I was scared. She told me she was safe, we were safe. She had a protector, she said. A man. A hard man. He fights death, she said. He doesn't lose, she said.'

She moved her hand out, touched the tip of my shoe. I crouched down. She flinched. I put my hands under her, lifted her, took her to the sofa.

She wiped her face again. She wouldn't look at me. She curled into a ball, her knees up against her chest, her hands around her legs.

'I persuaded her to do the film, Joe,' she said quietly. 'I told her I was too scared to make the copy.'

I sat down in the chair opposite her.

'I thought it must've been something like that.'

'Compton gave me a laptop. I gave it to Brenda, explained how to do it. We made the film. Then, when Marriot was showing the bloke out, Brenda got a small laptop from her handbag. It was called a notebook. She used some cable to plug it into the camera and made a copy.'

She looked up at me.

'Can I have a drink?'

I stood, went to a cabinet and got her a half bottle of vodka and a glass. I handed them to her. She cracked the lid open, poured half a glass, drank it all.

I sat on the sofa next to her. She looked at me over the

rim of the glass. When she'd finished drinking, she wiped a hand across her mouth.

'I knew she was scared,' she said. 'I think she was more scared of making the film than of betraying Marriot and Paget.'

'And then?'

'Then... then she died.'

'Yeah,' I said. I knew that part.

'And then all hell broke loose. Compton came to see me, said it's gone wrong, said Brenda's dead. He was panicking. He didn't have the DVD yet. He said we've got to cover our tracks. He asked me if there was anything connecting me to Brenda. I told him she had some photos of us. There was one that I knew she had. We were on a beach—'

'I saw that,' I said 'I saw a photo, Brenda showed it to me. She was on a beach, smiling.'

'Yes. We had a holiday once, me and Bren. We went to Norfolk, to the seaside.'

'You told Compton about the photo.'

She nodded.

'There was that one and a couple of others.'

'That's why he took them all from Brenda's place, because he didn't want anyone to connect you and her as friends, in case they got the idea you might know something about her death. He had to take all the photos, though, otherwise someone close to her, like me, might realize which ones were missing.'

'Yes. We had to cut all ties. I did.'

'And the DVD? The copy Brenda made?'

'I asked Compton how Brenda had died. He said he

322

didn't know. Said she'd been found cut up in an alley. Then I knew. Marriot had found out she was grassing him up. Paget would've used a knife. It was his thing. Day after she died, I got a copy of the DVD in the post. I was supposed to give it to Compton.'

'But you didn't.'

'How do you know?'

'Because Compton wouldn't have wanted Glazer if he already had a copy. He would've used the copy he had, years ago. So, you didn't give it to him.'

'No. Brenda sent it to me to hide. Compton told me I was to give it to him if Brenda gave it to me. Then... then Brenda died and...'

She took a deep breath.

'I destroyed it. I didn't know what else to do. I was scared. I couldn't trust the police. Paget and Marriot would've killed me if they'd known I had it. If I'd sent it to the papers, Paget and Marriot would've worked out it came from me. Anyway, Compton would've known, and would've known I betrayed him. So... I burned it.'

'You had black hair,' I said. 'In the photo.'

She nodded.

'The pub you went to that time, to meet Brenda, it was a place called the Fox and Globe.'

She nodded again.

That was the night, in the Fox and Globe. That's why we'd gone there, why Brenda had wanted me there with her. She'd met Tina, told her about me, showed her who I was, to tell her they had protection. 'He fights death,' Brenda had told Tina. 'He doesn't lose.'

323

The girl with the dark hair and the pale skin: Tina. She'd dyed her hair, of course. That's why her skin had seemed too white to me.

I remembered how Brenda had been, after she'd come back from the bar, how she'd stood there, at the table, and looked at me with a smile on her face, and pain in her eyes, and asked me to dance with her.

'She said she had protection,' Tina was saying. 'I didn't know what that meant until I saw you. I understood what she was doing then, that she knew she was risking her life but with someone like you, she thought they might not do anything to her. Anyway, that's what she told herself.'

I listened to what she said. I didn't know words could hurt so much. Was I, then, just protection, after all? Part of me believed it, had always believed it. Part of me knew, or thought it knew otherwise.

'But you knew better,' I said. 'You knew she wasn't safe, even with me.'

'I told her. I tried to. She wouldn't listen.'

Did it really matter? If she hadn't loved me, wouldn't I still want to help her, avenge her?

'She loved you,' Tina said, perhaps knowing what I was thinking.

I found that my hand had moved up to Tina's throat. She kept her hands in front of her, and looked up at me with huge eyes.

'Do it,' she said.

I felt her blood pumping through her carotid artery. I didn't need to put much pressure on there. Just a little. Just a little.

Maybe I was all killed out, the need for death all used up. I think, though, I was so sick of it all, the endless blood-letting, that I just couldn't face it any more.

I stood and turned away from her and started to leave. But then I stopped, turned back.

'There's one thing I want,' I said.

'Anything, Joe.'

'I want a picture of Brenda. As a girl. On her first day of school. Anything. I don't have one. I want something, a memory, her memory.'

She walked slowly to a tall, narrow chest of drawers, opened the top drawer.

She handed me a photo. I looked at it, saw Brenda on the beach. She was smiling.

So there it was. I'd finished, closed the circle. Everything at the end had started at the beginning, and I'd had to crawl my way back there, back through mud and blood and fog and madness, back through death and fury and memories of death and fury, back through pain and betrayal and the dullness and greed of powerful men, back through the fear and agony of women and children. Back. Back.

But I'd made it, back to the start, and I'd closed the circle.

Everyone had now paid for Brenda's death. Paget and Marriot had died at my hand. Glazer at the hands of Buck, who'd died at mine. Bradley had paid for it, and Compton too. Even Eddie and Dunham; they'd had nothing to do with Brenda's death, but they'd tried to profit from it. Even they would pay, Cole would make them.

And the man in the DVD. Cole would use him first to get back at Dunham, or get peace, at least. Then Cole would make the man suffer, somehow. I trusted him to do that and if he didn't... well, I'd make Cole pay too.

And Tina. She'd paid, perhaps more than anyone because she'd loved Brenda and had betrayed her. She'd paid every day since, and would pay every day now, forever.

But how did I feel about it?

In truth, I felt nothing. I was hollow, bloodless, finally. I kept thinking that I'd failed in the one thing I was on this earth for: Brenda had died, and I'd not stopped it, and for that I hadn't paid.

FORTY-THREE

When I got back to Browne's, he was up, and sober. I trudged in, shrugged out of my wet coat, pulled my boots off.

'Well?' he said.

'Well,' I said.

'Cuppa?'

I nodded.

He disappeared and came back with two mugs of tea. He handed me one. It was hot and strong.

His place was boarded up at the front. We'd taken the boards from the back and nailed them over the door and front window. He preferred it like that, he said. It meant he didn't have to look at the groups of people who gathered to stare at a crime scene.

The law had come round. I'd made myself scarce. Browne swore blind that it had been a burglary. They laughed at that, but we hadn't heard anything more from them. I reckoned the word had come down from up high. Compton's bosses must've shat themselves over the whole thing and now all they wanted was for it to disappear.

So, we settled into some kind of routine. He'd prod and poke me now and then, stare into my eyes, ask me questions. Who was I? Where was I?

327

I'd ask myself the same questions. Neither of us got a good answer.

When I told him I hadn't killed Glazer, he nodded. When I told him I hadn't killed Tina, he smiled.

He started gardening. He liked it, read up on it. He dug up the violet he'd found in the garden, put it in a pot, brought it indoors.

He got some colour to his face, seemed fitter, brighter. All that outdoor work, he told me. I didn't buy that.

He still got pissed, of course, but not as much and not as often.

'What are you going to do now?' he asked me one evening as we sat and watched a Bogart film.

It was a good question.

'Grow old,' I said.

He smiled at that. Well, I think it was a smile.

'Hate to dampen the party mood, but I don't think you'll get there.'

'Probably not. But I'll try.'

'Yes,' he said. 'Fight the dying of the light. Knowing you, you might actually make it.'

Fight, I thought. Yes, I'll fight.

'Growing old's not such a bad thing,' he said. 'It's what Brenda would've wanted.'

Maybe he was right. Maybe I had paid after all, simply by not dying. Maybe I was still paying.

Later, as we sat in front of the TV and watched a programme about people sitting in front of the TV, I tried to think what life might've been like, if Brenda had lived.

It didn't work. I couldn't make it into a picture.

But I had that photo, at least. Photos are the cycle completed, the past now.

Yes, I'll fight. What else could I do?

HOW TO GET YOUR FREE EBOOK

THE KILLING MACHINE

FREE
EBOOK

TO CLAIM YOUR FREE EBOOK OF *TO DIE FOR*

1. FIND THE CODE

   This is the last word on page 283 of this book, preceded by
   HOZ-, for example HOZ-code

2. GO TO HEADOFZEUS.COM/FREEBOOK

   Enter your code when prompted

3. FOLLOW THE INSTRUCTIONS

   Enjoy your free eBook of *TO DIE FOR*